W9-BXY-888

ACCOMPLISHED

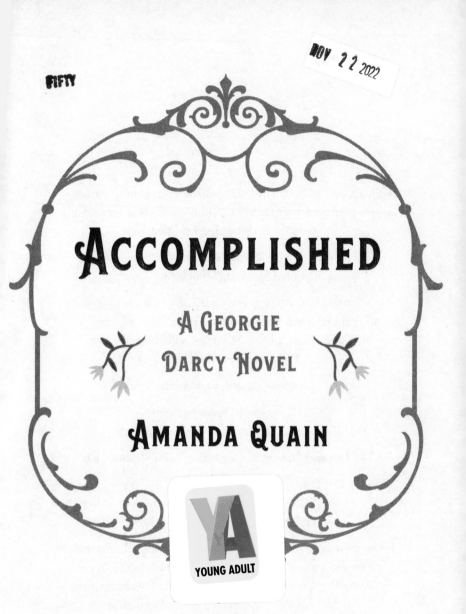

ACCOMPLISHED

A GEORGIE DARCY NOVEL

AMANDA QUAIN

W

WEDNESDAY BOOKS
NEW YORK

First published in the United States by Wednesday Books, an imprint of St. Martin's Publishing Group

ACCOMPLISHED. Copyright © 2022 by Amanda Quain. All rights reserved. Printed in the United States of America. For information, address St. Martin's Publishing Group, 120 Broadway, New York, NY 10271.

www.wednesdaybooks.com

Designed by Devan Norman
Case stamp illustration © Shutterstock.com

The Library of Congress Cataloging-in-Publication Data is available upon request.

ISBN 978-1-250-81781-5 (hardcover)
ISBN 978-1-250-81782-2 (ebook)

Our books may be purchased in bulk for promotional, educational, or business use. Please contact your local bookseller or the Macmillan Corporate and Premium Sales Department at 1-800-221-7945, extension 5442, or by email at MacmillanSpecialMarkets@macmillan.com.

First Edition: 2022

10 9 8 7 6 5 4 3 2 1

To Dustin, for giving me the world,
and to the Big Red Marching Band, for giving me Dustin.

"What sort of a girl is Miss Darcy?" He shook his head. "I wish I could call her amiable. It gives me pain to speak ill of a Darcy. But she is too much like her brother—very, very proud. She is a handsome girl, about fifteen or sixteen, and I understand, highly accomplished."

—GEORGE WICKHAM
JANE AUSTEN, *PRIDE AND PREJUDICE*

CHAPTER ONE

My big brother, Fitzwilliam Darcy, could suck it.

I mean, seriously. He'd already spent the last four months being whatever the brother-equivalent of a helicopter parent was, but this truly took things to a whole new level. He didn't even pretend this little Saturday visit was because he missed me, his one and only sister. It was explicitly to check in on me, to make sure I had plans to do my homework and go to class and not illegally deal Adderall to my fellow high schoolers.

Which, sure, is what happened last year. But I wasn't about to do it again.

As I stepped out of my dorm at Pemberley Academy and into the bracing central New York air, I shivered and pulled my peacoat closer to my chest. September was such a crapshoot up here—it could be seventy-five degrees and perfect, or it could be down in the thirties, just to mess with all the new kids whose parents shipped them up from Florida for the best education on the East Coast. I'd grown up out here, knew how to deal with cold, but freezing September days still always felt like a betrayal.

At least I wouldn't be exposed to the elements for long. Fitz's car was parked directly in front of the dorm—if he were any closer, he'd already be in the wood-paneled lobby. He'd finally bought something new in the couple of days since he'd dropped me off at school, so I didn't recognize the exact model, but Fitz always got the same kind of car. Classy, not at all flashy, but expensive enough for people who knew cars to stop and take notice. I was not one of those people, so as I climbed into the passenger seat, I only mentioned—

"This car has fewer cup holders than the last one."

"Hello to you, too." Fitz's car may have changed, but he never did. Tall and dark-haired, people usually managed to guess that we were siblings at first glance, with our shared sharp features and hazel eyes. The main difference was the constant look of disappointment glued to my big brother's face whenever he was around me. "It's good to see you."

"Same. Why did they take away some of the cup holders?" I drummed my fingers on the armrest, which was definitely heated. A nice touch, a classy consolation now that he'd moved back to freezing upstate New York to babysit me. "Where are you supposed to put your drinks?"

"There are still two cup holders in the front seat, which only holds two passengers." Fitz sighed as he pulled out of the driveway of my dorm, turning to head off campus. I was allowed to have guests in the dining hall, and the entire staff at Pemberley would fall to their knees in praise if Fitz showed up for breakfast. Ever since he'd graduated the year before last, it was all I'd ever heard from everyone. *How's Fitz? Where's Fitz? Such a shame, I heard he had to transfer, he must be happy to be closer to you.* Which was exactly why I'd never let him join me there. "Why would you need more than two cup holders?"

"You're telling me you don't foresee a single circumstance in which a person might want more than one drink?" As we passed through the gates of Pemberley, I let myself exhale. Those gates, with their cast-iron finishes and literal spikes on top, felt like my personal iron maiden these days. Ever since The Incident, but, if I was being honest, before that, too. "Picture it with me, big brother. You're driving cross-country. Epic road trip. Grand Canyon, probably."

"It would be a better use of both time and money to fly."

"Okay, but you didn't." It was as good a distraction as any, to banter the way we used to, to pretend for a few minutes that The Incident hadn't irreversibly ruined us. That the last six months of our lives hadn't been garbage. I flicked at the lock on my door, up and down, until Fitz activated the child locks and I was forced to stop. "You're driving. It's late. You need some caffeine, but it's also about a million degrees, because you're in the desert, and our pale Yankee bodies aren't suited for those kinds of conditions."

"And?"

"And . . ." I paused for dramatic effect. Tall trees, some of their leaves already changing, whipped past my window. "And you want coffee, but you also need a cold drink! Boom. That's two cup holders, right there, and now you've deprived your passenger of their beverage options. That is terrible hospitality."

"Well, when you take up interior car design, that can be the first thing you correct." If you didn't know Fitz, you'd never hear the edge of a joke in his voice, but I'd learned to recognize it. This was what his sense of humor had whittled down to over the last few years. Brief glimpses of what my brother used to be.

We pulled into the parking lot of Townshend's, a diner that Fitz (of course) had discovered when he was at Pemberley. We'd driven here together at least once a month my freshman year, his senior, when he'd pull himself away from the demands of applying to all the world's top colleges and leading the debate team to victory to hang out with little old me. We'd order bottomless pancakes, even though the diner had threatened to take them off the menu after one specifically epic eating extravaganza the day before spring break. For an extra couple of bucks, they'd put whipped cream and M&M's on them, too. Fitz's laugh would be more than an edge to an admonishment and I'd be glad to hang out with my brother, the only family I had left.

It wasn't the sort of place our parents had taught us to visit, with its absence of cloth napkins and a sommelier, but since my dad passed away four years ago, when I was twelve, and my mom had taken the opportunity to abandon me and my brother to the staff and to each other, it wasn't like there was anyone to stop us.

Now I just had Fitz to stop me.

"No. No way." The squeals of the hostess echoed through the relatively empty diner as we pushed through the door, the warmth of the overactive heater inside a welcome reprieve from the biting cold. "Tell me that's not Fitz Darcy."

"Jenn." Fitz raised up his mouth in what might be called a smile, had his eyes gotten involved. Squeals were basically standard when grown-ups around Pemberley saw Fitz. If the teachers, support staff, and local townspeople could have voted for homecoming king, it would have been him, every time.

I mean, it wasn't, because the homecoming court was a teenage popularity contest and actual human popularity among our peers was not something that either of us had ever excelled at. Fitz was more the valedictorian type, while I was . . . neither of those things. But still.

"What are you even doing here?" Jenn led us to our table way more slowly than I would have liked, my stomach already growling. "Hasn't the semester started for Caltech? Or do you geniuses out there need less time in class than everyone else?"

"I'm at SUNY Meryton this year, actually." The remnants of Fitz's smile disappeared as we settled into the torn vinyl booth at the back of the diner, where the smell of griddled foods threatened to overwhelm me. "I transferred to be closer to home."

"Why would you—oh." Jenn's face flashed with a recognition I needed to get used to as she looked over at me, and I wanted to melt into the vinyl, become one with the vinyl, since I was pretty sure vinyl booths never had to feel guilty about a single mistake they had made over and over again for the rest of their lives. Plus, they got to live next to the pancakes, and kids dropped food into the cracks of the seating all the time. It would be a less humiliating life than the one I currently led. "Right."

The Pemberley Academy gossip mill churned hard and fast. It had been all over school within hours when Brian Churlford's dad, a state senator, had gotten caught taking his mistress on a Canadian joyride. The GroupMes had lit up when Andrea Smithing paid one of the townies to take the SAT for her, and she'd gotten kicked out.

So when I, Georgiana Darcy, heiress to the Darcy empire, little sister of school Golden Boy Fitz Darcy, got caught up in a drug scandal at the end of sophomore year, yet managed to avoid expulsion simply on the basis of my family name? People found out pretty quickly.

My fingers twitched and I willed myself not to curl them into fists. Darcys didn't show when they were upset.

"Our usual order, Jenn, thanks." Fitz's hands gripped onto the plastic menu, white around the knuckles. "And add an orange juice, for my sister."

"I just brushed my teeth," I said, as Jenn took the menus and fled the scene as fast as she could, obviously grateful to avoid Darcy Drama. "You don't need to order for me."

"I know the way you eat when I'm not around, Georgie." He pulled out his phone to fire off a quick text, then turned his undivided attention back to me. "The vitamins in that juice might be the only ones you get all week."

"Funny." I rolled my eyes. Fitz was just three years older than me. Not old enough to act like my dad, and yet. I squirmed under his gaze, intimately aware of the oncoming conversation that I had no way of avoiding.

Sure enough, Fitz leaned forward on his forearms across the table, fingers intertwined. No elbows involved, naturally. My brother might be in a trash diner eating trash pancakes, but he was still a Darcy, and he never forgot it. Never let me forget it.

"Have you heard from him?"

Actually, no, I hadn't expected the conversation to go to *him* that quickly, this early in the morning. My stomach churned unpleasantly. "Obviously not." Jenn returned with our drinks, a huge mug of coffee for Fitz and a Diet Coke for me. The small glass of orange juice she set down next to it was accompanied by an apologetic smile as she backed away. "He doesn't have my number anymore." Fitz had gotten me a new phone number in the weeks following The Incident, once he'd pulled me out of school. It was a real boon to my already nonexistent social life.

"He hasn't tried to email you?" Fitz continued to press as I blew bubbles in my Diet Coke, which I knew would annoy him. The soda annoyed him enough. "Or . . . slide into your DMs or something?"

I grimaced. "No, Fitz, Wickham hasn't tried to 'slide into my DMs.'" It was barely a lie. Just a . . . rearranging of the truth. And I hadn't even read his emails, which had all poured into my phone when Fitz briefly reinstated my internet privileges over the summer.

Hadn't read them that much, anyway.

More than once.

Fine, twice.

"Beanpole."

"Don't call me that." He'd taken the nickname up after Dad died, in some sort of weird-for-a-then-sixteen-year-old paternal instinct. "What did you want this to be, Fitz? A super-fun breakfast where I tell you that hey, it doesn't matter that I got pulled out of school two weeks before the semester ended last year? That I had no way to contact anyone the entire summer, so I couldn't even try to explain my side of the story, and now the entire student body hates me?"

"If you hadn't gotten mixed up with a drug dealer—"

"I *didn't know* he was a drug dealer!"

"Pancakes!" Jenn's voice, a trilled out singsong, cut through a fight that was quickly turning vicious. Before I got to add, *and you're the one who wanted us to be friends.* Fitz and I both leaned back, my brother straightening the collar of his button-down. I didn't bother to try and adjust the wrinkles out of my tie-dyed Camp Sanditon T-shirt. "You two know the drill. No new plates until this one is finished. Are we trying to break any records today?"

"The world is wide and full of possibilities, Jenn." I kept my gaze on my brother as I spoke, his eyes smoking with anger. "Let's not rule anything out."

The two of us spent the next ten minutes in relative silence, punctuated only by my aggressive chewing and the whoosh of the whipped cream can. Jenn brought plate two out to me the moment I finished my first, which left me with a lot more goodwill toward her than I'd started with. Fitz, meanwhile, had only moved a few of his pancakes around, clinging to his coffee cup like it was a lifeline as he watched me.

"You're going to choke."

"And you're going to lose our pancake battle." I nodded toward his plate, where the glob of butter on the top of his stack had melted into a mess of grease that dropped all down the sides of his food. "Catch up."

"I'm not that hungry."

"Right," I said. Fitz's appetite had declined when our dad died and disappeared entirely after he'd found me with Wickham. His coffee consumption, on the other hand . . . Jenn filled up his cup without a word as she passed by, and he winced as he took a long draw. "That stuff's going to give you an ulcer."

"Trust me, coffee isn't going to be the thing that gives me an ulcer." He looked away from me, down into the inky blackness of his cup. This time, I was the one who winced. No one delivered an underhanded jab like a Darcy. Fitz had learned *that* skill from our mother. "No friends left at all?"

"Not a one," I said, around a mouthful of pancake. Not that I had many to begin with. I'd never quite managed to find my rhythm at Pemberley, and once Fitz had graduated, things obviously went from bad to worse. The few friendships I had made in band were quickly destroyed in the wake of Wickham. "Well, someone held the elevator door for me, last night, when I went down to the stacks in the library. But then they saw my face and they pressed the door closed button right before I got there. Except those don't work and so I got in the elevator anyway, and we were stuck together for four floors." The memory stung, while Fitz looked . . . well. Unaffected.

My brother used to take my side no matter what. But even before The Incident, if I was being honest, things had shifted between us. It didn't change all of a sudden, after Dad died. Or even after Mom left. It happened gradually enough that I never noticed, like how you don't feel yourself growing taller but suddenly none of your pants fit.

I didn't notice that Fitz and I were growing apart until suddenly, we didn't fit. When Fitz told me that he was going to California for school, at first I'd thought, *How could he?*, but months of unreturned calls and unanswered texts became *Of course he did.*

And then I'd let Wickham destroy our relationship the rest of the way.

"I remember how slow those elevators are." Fitz sighed, then cut off the world's smallest piece of pancake and popped it into his mouth, making sure he had chewed and swallowed it completely before he spoke again. "I'm not trying to ruin your life here, Beanpole. Can you maybe try to understand that?"

Yeah, I didn't need to hear him repeat it. I knew what Fitz thought—that the only person who had ruined my life was me.

So, I returned to my bubble-blowing. Trying to talk to my brother about this was pointless—always had been, and always would be. He didn't want to hear about the reasons I'd messed everything up. He wanted me to move on, with his direct supervision to make sure nothing like this ever happened again. To just pretend it had always been like this between us. Like he hadn't been my best friend before, and not just a weird quasi–father figure.

And I had a plan. I did. But telling Fitz would only lead to admonishment, and for once I was going to take care of things myself.

"You'll have to talk to me eventually," Fitz finally said, draining his coffee. "We're going to have these 'hangs' every weekend until you're back on your feet."

"Add 'hangs' to the list of words you shouldn't say." Just watching Fitz drink that much coffee made my own heart speed up. "Do you want me to bring my homework with me? Let you initial it before I bring it back to my teachers?"

Fitz dropped his fork onto his plate and opened his mouth, but he didn't speak. I could *feel* the unsaid words between us. Feel his disappointment, the truth at the base of all of our conversations now. *I left California for you, so you better not screw this up any more than you already have.*

He'd never say it. That would involve discussing our feelings way more than any self-respecting Darcy ever did.

But it was always there. Every time he texted or called me to check up. Every time, over the summer, when he'd cut off my internet privileges or made me read in the living room, where he could watch me. When he'd searched my room, the day he'd taken me back home at the end of the spring, to make sure I didn't have anything illicit there.

I could still remember what it was like last time, when he'd dropped me off at Pemberley at the start of my sophomore year. He'd hugged me tighter than he ever had before.

"*You'll be okay, Georgie. Pemberley is yours for the taking, right?*"

"*I'm going to miss you.*" *My voice was embarrassingly thick with tears, as it had been all morning. Luckily, there was no one else around. Fitz and I were at Pemberley a week before any of the other students arrived, so he could settle me in before he headed to California. Darcy privileges.*

"*Not as much as I'm going to miss you, Beanpole.*" *He pulled back from our hug, where I'd left a trail of snot on his Oxford shirt. So mature. "But you'll be fine. I promise."*

"How do you know?" I didn't feel okay. I'd spent my whole freshman year glued to my big brother's side, and now what? I was just supposed to exist here without him? No one knew me like Fitz did. "What if I spontaneously self-combust?"

"Darcys don't self-combust." Fitz's eyes crinkled with the hint of laughter, something I would soon see only over FaceTime. "But I do have something that'll cheer you up."

"Caltech is opening a satellite campus in the middle-of-nowhere New York?"

"Almost." Fitz leaned past me, out of my dorm room—a single again, thank God—and into the hallway. "Wickham? Want to come out?"

I whipped around, faster than I would have assumed humanly possible. No way. No way.

But there he was. Wickham Foster, our former childhood neighbor and, oh yeah, the person I'd had a gigantic crush on for literally forever, here, at Pemberley Academy, in the (extremely well-toned, by the way) flesh.

"Wickham?" I managed to keep the squeal out of my voice—oh, the restraint—as he sauntered over, grinning. Wickham never hurried. "What are you doing here?"

"I transferred, kid." He shook Fitz's hand, then reached out and pulled me into a hug that made my whole body zip from the contact. It had been a couple of years since I'd seen Wickham—the funeral, I realized with a start, was the last time—and although he'd always been aggressively good-looking, it was like all of his already hard edges had sharpened into focus.

"You'll show Wickham around, right, Georgie?" As Fitz turned to me, I reminded myself that he had no idea how I'd felt about

Wickham, growing up. Or possibly now. "He'll be in band with you. You can help him get adjusted."

"Of course." *I stood up tall, put on my best smile, and did my best to look like a bona fide sophomore in high school. Wickham glanced over toward me again, and this look was slower than before. Like it meant something.* "It would be my pleasure."

"Mine, too," *he said, and it was a good thing Fitz stepped away to check something on his phone just then, because he wouldn't have liked the way Wickham looked at me.*

Maybe it would have been better if he'd seen. Maybe he could have stopped it. Or maybe I'd already stepped onto the path toward my inevitable destruction, and there was nothing my brother could have done.

Now, back in our booth, which felt more claustrophobic with every passing second, Fitz pushed back his plate of barely touched pancakes. Instead of saying anything, he waved Jenn down once again.

"Check, please."

Just like that, he was finished with me. Just like everyone else.

CHAPTER TWO

Lying on my back in my dorm room bed the next afternoon, the velvety-plush comforter I'd taken from the Darcy estate in Rochester beneath me, I stared up at the *Sage Hall* poster I'd taped to my ceiling and tried to will myself to disappear into it.

When I'd first put it up last Thursday, my new roommate, Sydney—in the first words she'd spoken since we'd both arrived— had wrinkled her nose and asked, "Did you put that up there because it's like, a sex thing?"

It didn't seem worth pointing out that she'd already decorated all four walls of our tiny double with framed photos of flowers that looked like they'd been discarded from the dressing room decorations of a Forever 21, leaving the ceiling as the only space for my poster.

I'd just looked her straight in the eyes, whispered, "Only one way to find out," and continued my unpacking until she eventually fled the room to hang out with the other girls in the color guard and undoubtedly spend the whole time crying about how she couldn't *believe* she'd ended up with a roommate like me.

The feeling was mutual.

No matter how much I stared at the cast of my favorite BBC show posed in a family portrait with their huge manor house behind them, crowd-favorite servants lurking in the background, I didn't get sucked into the rabbit hole. I sighed and sat up, pulling my laptop toward me. If I couldn't put myself in the show IRL, I could at least spend the rest of my day reading about it.

I'd gotten into *Sage Hall* back in middle school, right after my family fell apart. Fitz was up here at Pemberley, I was being cared for by a rotating cast of staff, and Mom had finally admitted she wasn't coming back from whatever Eat-Pray-Love bullshit she had embarked on that month, signing her rights of guardianship over to Fitz, who got emancipated minor status at sixteen to make decisions for both of us. Things at home weren't, like . . . fun, so I spent most of my days scrolling through Tumblr. A few dozen *Sage Hall* GIF sets in, and I was intrigued. Ten minutes into the first episode, and I was hooked.

I wrote my first fan fiction a month later, which was absolute garbage that I'd since deleted from the bowels of the internet. But I kept writing, kept working, and got kind of good, I guess. And I found people like me, who didn't know what my last name meant to the world. Who just thought I was cool, that my fics were worth reading.

Not that I'd put up anything lately. I hadn't written since Wickham.

Anyone else would have been expelled. I should have been expelled when Fitz showed up last year and discovered Wickham dealing Adderall out of my dorm room. Even though Fitz scared him off without involving the cops, the dean found out, and it took everything in Fitz's power—the power of my family name—to keep me from expulsion. Since there was no evidence tying me to a crime, or even a violation of school rules, I'd told them the truth: that I'd had no idea what Wickham was doing. And since no one testified to the board that they'd ever seen me involved with the drugs . . . they'd let me stay, a testament to my privilege as a rich white girl but, more specifically, a Darcy.

Wickham hadn't been so lucky.

It seemed, afterward, like everyone *except* me had known Wickham was taking advantage of my single room as his distribution headquarters whenever I wasn't around. All my fellow rich kids hated me for cutting off their supply, and everyone else thought that I'd reported the considerably more popular Wickham because I couldn't keep my nose in my own business. I was an irredeemable narc in the court of Pemberley Academy.

I, naturally, had fallen for the biggest lie of all, because I'd thought that Wickham loved me. I'd sure thought I loved him.

So now I was here, stuck at Pemberley surrounded by the results of my mistake, the naivete of a sixteen-year-old-girl with a crush on her childhood neighbor who thought he might actually care about her when no one else seemed to.

But, of course, it turned out Wickham was just using me. Using my room and my ignorance with plans to use a lot more.

His emails still taunted me from my in-box, even though I'd managed not to read any of the ones that had come in during the last few days. They all had tantalizing subject lines like "Hey" and "Sup, kid?" which would be enough to make me auto-delete an email from anybody else.

And I knew what they said, too, because they were certainly just echoes of the ones from earlier in the summer, containing nothing but manipulations designed to get me to let him back into my life. To let him twist his way in until, once again, my life was nothing but Wickham. And I couldn't do that again. I wouldn't.

I really needed to delete them.

But God, every time someone in the hall glared at me, every time I got that ache inside that I'd never be good enough . . . it made me want him.

I took a deep breath, tried to clear my head. Fitz would want me to tell him that Wickham was still contacting me, obviously, but there was no way I would admit that to him.

The day he'd found us in my room was still seared into my brain.

Wickham in the doorway, trying to block Fitz from entering, Fitz shoving past him, shouting like I'd never heard my brother shout before—

No. No way. The way he'd looked at Wickham had been horrifying enough, but the way he'd looked at me? Shut it all the way down. I wasn't going to dredge that memory up any further. I tore my eyes away from the doorway, toggled over to a Word doc I had been working on. I wouldn't, I told myself sternly, break my brother like that again.

At the top of the document, the title read, *Georgie Darcy's Guide to Rebuilding Her Extremely Broken Reputation, Making Actual Friends, and Proving Once and for All that She Deserves to Carry on the Darcy Name, No Matter What Aunt Catherine Said in the Family Newsletter.*

A little long in the tooth, maybe, but brevity had never been my strong suit. This blinking page of double-spaced Times New Roman was going to save me.

I'd made it last week in the midst of packing for school, a whirl of Fitz checklists and Google Calendar invites to events such as "Go Over Class Schedule: Kitchen, 3:30 p.m." and "Evaluate Wardrobe for Updated Needs: Bedroom, 10 a.m." My brother loved a Google Calendar invite.

Did I mention that we were like, a really fun family?

Anyway, the checklists that accompanied each event and appeared outside my room each morning like an itinerary for the world's worst cruise had given me an idea. The Darcy love of organization may not have been passed on to me fully, but even I had to admit that everything in life was easier when you broke it down into manageable steps. And the Herculean task of rebuilding my reputation? Definitely needed to be broken down.

The problem was, except for my awesome title, the document was completely empty.

It wasn't like I hadn't tried. I'd opened it once a day at least, stared at the blinking cursor as it mocked me and my apparent inability to manage even the simplest of plans. It was just that I'd never had to *do* anything like this before. Being a Darcy came with certain perks, the most relevant one being that my place was established at Pemberley. I was Fitz's sister. I didn't need to be anything else.

But I'd blown that up last year. Now I needed to . . . un-blow it up.

A notification popped up on the bottom of my screen, and I toggled over without thinking much about it. It was from the fanfic site I wrote for—a new comment on one of my stories.

Ah, yes. There it was, the closest I'd ever come to success in anything.

I guess I'd been kind of big. There weren't that many people writing my favorite ship, Jocelyn and Andrew, aka JocAndrew, when I got into it—she, the rich twentysomething who wandered Sage Hall looking for love in all the wrong Regency places, and he, the dashing rogue stable hand who seemed like he was destined for far more excitement than Jocelyn could offer. But I'd known that Jocelyn could be a hell of a lot more than the show had given her credit for, and when I didn't find fic that showed her that way, I wrote it myself.

People liked it. *Really* liked it. I'd even started to work on my magnum opus, as it were, a full novel-length fic about my favorite pairing.

It had, maybe, gotten a little self-inserty near the end. When things got intense with Wickham, my own dashing rogue.

I'd stopped updating it when I started skipping class to hang out with Wickham in my room, not knowing at the time that I was interrupting his selling windows. And then, afterward . . . I don't know. Forbidden love had a lot less appeal than it used to.

The comment on my fic looked nice enough, but I cleared out the notification without more than a cursory glance. I didn't want to hear from another person begging for an updated chapter I couldn't produce.

I clicked over to my in-box, where his emails sat collecting metaphorical dust. I just wanted to get over him. Move on, start over, and again, definitely *not* reply to one of the emails I hovered my mouse over, considered clicking on.

And speaking of moving past it. My stomach flipped as a calendar notification popped up on my computer. I had marching band on Monday, my first practice of the year. I'd had to miss band camp because of my Fitz-imposed exile, something else I wouldn't have gotten away with without my family name.

There would be people I had to face when I got there, people I hadn't seen since last year. People who I had hurt.

Fun.

But it was fine. It had to be fine, right? The marching band was full of other weirdos and misfits like me. Other people who had made mistakes, even if those mistakes hadn't gotten our best trumpet player expelled. And once I figured out how, exactly, to convince them that I wasn't the worst person ever to exist, they'd forgive me. They had to.

Next to me, my phone buzzed, and I jumped. It was an incoming call from Fitz, who presumably wanted to make sure I hadn't gotten caught up in any criminal activity in the day since I'd last seen him. You never knew, with me.

I considered letting it go to voice mail, but then he'd just drive down here again and it would be a whole thing, so I picked up.

"What's up, brother?"

"Hey, Georgie." I heard Fitz sigh into the phone. "Just checking in."

"Good call. I got arrested since you talked to me last. Also, I burned down a bridge. Glad you stopped me before I went full steam ahead with the school arson." I put the call on speaker as I rolled over onto my back. Sydney wasn't going to be back in the room until late, in case whatever social-pariah disease I had was catching, so it wasn't like I was disturbing anyone. Even if it was Fitz, it was nice to have someone else's voice fill the empty room. "Do you want me to have the bills from the city sent to you directly?"

"It's a good thing I already wired over your allowance." Fitz's voice was dry, and I could just picture him, with his stick-straight posture, allowing his head to drop for just a second. "You can pay for it yourself."

"It is important for me to learn independence." I sighed and stared at the back of my door. I would have left it undecorated, because it was a door, but Sydney had put up one of those motivational kitten posters that I thought were a prop designed for sitcoms. "Shouldn't you be out partying or something? That's what all the movies say you should do in college." HANG IN THERE! the poster implored me.

"Charlie made me go to one last night." Fitz had met Charlie Bingley at their transfer student orientation over the summer, and even though he wasn't the type of guy my brother was usually friends with—aka, he was fun—it seemed like he'd be good for him. I didn't think Fitz had attended a single party during his freshman year at Caltech. "He joined a frat already. It was about as bad as I'd expected."

"You didn't get drunk and dance the night away?"

"You know I don't dance." He didn't drink, either, but that went unsaid. After Wickham, both of us stayed away from any sort of controlled substances. "And I don't know who I would've danced with. Charlie abandoned me the second we got there for this girl he spotted across the room. Jane something."

"No Love at First Sight moment of your own?"

"Please," Fitz scoffed. "Charlie kept trying to pawn me off on the girl's sister, but even she wasn't pretty enough to tempt me."

"Fitz." He was joking, probably, the sort of deeply sarcastic joke that Fitz found funny but he forgot to tell anyone else. That didn't make it right. "Don't be gross." Careful to make sure the sound on my computer was turned off, I pulled up Tumblr and began to scroll through the *Sage Hall* tag. Just in case this conversation was going to turn toward some sort of discipline toward me, I wanted to be prepared with a distraction.

"Sorry." He sighed again. "She was just one of those . . . she just had something clever to say about everything."

"You talked to her." Noise from the hallway, but no one stopped at my door, so I didn't need to take Fitz off speaker just yet. "And here I thought you just stared at her from across the room like a serial killer."

"Charlie was very insistent." I'd met Charlie over FaceTime a few weeks ago, and this didn't surprise me. "But I'll do my best to stay as far away from Lizzie Bennet as I can."

"You got her name?" Images of Jocelyn and Andrew danced across my screen, pics of them staring at each other from across the room I'd spent weeks analyzing. Now they made me feel slightly ill. "How interactive of you."

"Again, Charlie, insistent." He kept going, muttering something about parties and how he didn't even like them when they were civilized, which this one *certainly* wasn't. I scrolled away, tuning him out.

I missed writing about them, I thought as Fitz droned on, probably talking about how terrible the music kids these days listened to was or something. Missed the way my fingers flew across the keyboard, only looking up from my screen to glance at the corkboard I'd hung over my desk and decorated with the best pictures I could find of my OTP. Everything fell away from me when I wrote, encompassed me in the world of *Sage Hall*, where a parent's death was nothing more than a soon-forgotten plot point and the older brothers who went away for school came back to visit every other episode.

I let my mouse drift over to my mail icon, like it had a mind of its own.

"Did I mention she has four sisters? Honestly, Georgie, who has that many children anymore? In this economy?"

"Are you still talking about Lizzie Bennet?" I glanced down at the time on my computer. He'd been droning on about this girl he apparently hated for five minutes now. Fitz wasn't even a rambler by nature. Words were something other people did.

"She's just . . . never mind." Fitz harrumphed, because he liked to be no farther than three degrees of separation from his own future nursing home at any given point. "I just don't understand how someone like that can be so assured of her own amusement."

"Confidence?" Back to Tumblr and ooh, this was one of my favorite GIFs. Jocelyn and Andrew in a crowded room again—there were a lot of crowded rooms in *Sage Hall*, the better to stare at people lovingly across, my dear—in Season 2, where the fandom was just starting to realize they might be *something*. He gives her a brazen smile, refuses to look away, and she just keeps watching him. I used it to inspire, like, twenty of my own one-shots. I could always try it again. Try to ignore how Andrew's smirk looked just like Wickham's.

But if I started writing, I'd just end up crying, and I'd *definitely* respond to his email.

"Hey, Fitz?" I interrupted my brother, who had gone off on some sort of other tangent, the only words of which I caught sounded like "unbelievable" and "brought her cat with her." "Do you mind if I run? I have . . . my period."

That was the worst excuse I'd ever come up with, but the good thing about being a girl trying to get out of a conversation with her brother was that a single mention of menstruation would hopefully do the trick.

"Kind of early, isn't it?" Of course, when said brother was Fitz, whose response to my getting my period for the first time right after Mom left was to buy us each a copy of *The Care and Keeping of You* to read together, he was harder to push off the phone. "Don't your cycles usually run closer to four weeks than this?"

"Goodbye, Fitz!" I basically shouted before I hung up. Just because my brother was super evolved about menstruation didn't mean I *wanted* to talk to him about it. I tossed my phone to the side and let out a long sigh. From out in the hall, I heard a gaggle of girls laughing together. Intellectually, I knew they likely weren't even talking about me, but ever since The Incident, I jumped whenever I heard anyone laugh. Unable to relax—what else was new—I ignored my better judgment and opened one of the old emails from Wickham, fast, like if I pretended it was subconscious it wouldn't be my fault.

Hey kid,

I miss you. Did I mention that? Yeah, he did, he always mentioned that. *I wish I could see you.* That made him the only one. *I know exactly what I'd do with you.*

Toggle away. Toggle, toggle, toggle, try to burn the memory of him out of my mind, remove the memory of some of the things we'd done—plus some of the other things I'd imagined we'd do, in the ridiculous fairy tale I'd built up for us—and how they'd felt. How he'd made me feel like a person, not Fitz Darcy's baby sister.

Except that wasn't how he'd seen me, I reminded myself. No, I definitely wasn't a baby to him, but I *was* a means to an end. His roommate last year had literally been the son of the attorney general, so using his room for his transactions was way too risky. I was anything but a risk.

Leave it, Georgie. Fitz's voice came into my mind, unbidden as always. *Just forget about him.*

God, though, I still wanted to respond.

Maybe that *was* what I needed to do. Maybe I needed to—just ignoring him hadn't made him go away. I'd been stuck, stuck in the same rut since Fitz pulled me out of school, a rut of guilt and shame and self-doubt. There had to be a reason I didn't have a plan for fixing my life. Maybe I needed to get a better look at what I was moving past.

Maybe I missed his eyes.

Another old email. From the beginning of the summer.

Still missing you. I hope you're still missing me. I know you have to listen to big brother, but you won't have to forever. That one stung, even as I closed it, remembering how Fitz had looked at me in the diner. If he had his way, he'd control all my actions from now on. That had, after all, been our entire summer.

And I was tired of it. I was tired of being controlled, of Fitz knowing what was best for me, of hiding away while the world laughed at me from the outside and whispered about things I didn't even do.

How big of a deal was an email, anyway? I could write him back and it didn't mean we were getting back together. Wickham was a thousand miles away, last I'd heard. I could respond, and I could figure out where everything went wrong. Then I really could start over, be the Darcy that Fitz wanted me to be.

There was another new message from Wickham, from earlier today. I shouldn't have read it.

I did, obviously.

Hey, kid,

Guess who's coming back to town?

Oh.

Oh.

Well. Fuck.

CHAPTER THREE

If Fitz knew what I was doing . . .

Honestly, there were a million different reasons he'd be furious with me. Breaking curfew. Responding to Wickham. Not dressing warmly enough. I needed to get him a planner for Christmas, somewhere he could bullet journal lists of all the ways I disappointed him.

The Wickham thing would be the biggest, though.

Just beating out not wearing my coat.

I'd replied to Wickham's email as soon as I'd seen it, before I could think better of it. Typed out my response with shaking hands.

Wickham—
Meet me at 10 p.m. by the old spot.
Georgie

I'd barely been able to stay away from him when he was just an email in my in-box. If he really was back in town, I needed to see for myself.

So here I was. Breaking the rules of both Pemberley Academy and Fitz Darcy by sneaking out of my dorm after hours to see Wickham. Had it been twenty degrees warmer, it might have been last spring again.

But this was different. This wasn't because I *wanted* to see Wickham. I just . . . I had to see him.

The distinction was murky, but I'd figure it out.

I shivered in the autumn air, because there was no one around (yet) that I had to hide my vulnerability from. Wickham was, predictably, late. I paced back and forth beneath the oak tree that stood guard by this side of the campus's gate, hiding a few loose poles that Wickham and I had used last year to sneak in and out of campus after hours. I'd half expected it to be fixed when I got here, but apparently that was the one secret we'd managed to keep.

God, I hated that I carried some weird, twisted pride that Wickham and I still had secrets. But there it was. If I couldn't be honest with myself here, in the freezing darkness at the end of campus as I waited for the fruition of a bad idea, when could I be?

And when I heard the scrape of metal on metal that meant someone was coming through the gate, I felt . . . well.

No one had ever claimed to want me as badly as Wickham did.

He unfolded himself to his full height, six foot whatever it was, brown hair longer than I remembered and pulled back into a low ponytail. Even in the dark, I saw the gleam in his eyes, the look that said *I have a secret*, that made you want to do anything to find out what it was. He smirked when he saw me, because he'd gotten jammed on smirk mode sometime around puberty, and shoved his hands down into the pockets of his ripped jeans.

"Hi, Georgie." His voice sounded just like I remembered.

"You're back." I nodded toward him, but unable to maintain eye contact, my gaze dropped down to the ground. "You're supposed to be in Florida. Wasn't there like, a single school down there that didn't know better than to admit you?"

"Aww, you remembered." Wickham's teasing had a sharper tone than anyone else's I'd ever met. "And here I thought I wasn't worth the memory space."

"Did they already kick you out?" I'd just stare at his shoes. Scuffed and impractical for the weather, but Wickham never seemed to get cold.

"I had some unfinished business up here, it turns out."

And then he kissed me.

He closed the distance between us in a single step, lips crashing over mine, kissing me like nothing had changed, like we were back in my dorm room in the early spring, pollen drifting in through an open window, as he told me all the ways he wanted me when nobody else did. The scent of him was a vicious reminder of everything we'd had, a cruel feeling in the back of my throat of how easy it would be to fall right back into last May. I melted into him, his chest crushed against mine as he held me.

His hands went into my hair, pulled curls loose from my ponytail, and my hands shifted to his waist for a moment longer than they should have before I remembered I didn't do this anymore. I didn't do *Wickham* anymore.

Shit.

I stumbled back, away from Wickham and his warmth, and to his (miniscule) credit, he didn't follow me, didn't try to grab me again. Wickham sucked, but he wasn't that kind of terrible. He just watched me, smirked as I tried to collect myself, to straighten out my jacket and smooth my hair back behind my ears like I hadn't felt that kiss in every nerve ending. I opened my mouth to speak, but closed it again, crossed my arms over my chest like that would keep us fully apart. I was here for information. Nothing more.

"You shouldn't have come back." I was amazed that I got the words out, with the way my chest had seized up. I shook my head, my ponytail smacking my cheeks, and I hated how young it made me feel. "Whatever you think you have here . . . you don't. You should go."

"Or what?" His smirk only deepened. "It's a free country, kid. And I always liked this town. Thought I'd give you someone to hang out with."

"That's not going to happen." I'd lost control entirely, it seemed, the conversation veering away from my grasp. All I needed to do was find out why he was back and then ensure he got lost forever, but the plan that had seemed so simple in my dorm room was a thousand times more complicated in the moonlight.

"Yeah?" God, that stupid smile, which had made my heart skip a million beats last year. "I know you're not hanging out with anyone else. I've still got friends at Pemberley. More than you, I'd guess."

Nothing Wickham said should hurt anymore.

The first time I'd seen Wickham, I was eight years old, and I was in a *Princess Bride* phase. One of my nannies must have put it on, because it wasn't the sort of thing either of my parents would have been into. But I got into it, way into it, and I'd run around the grounds of the Darcy estate, pretending to be Princess Buttercup in a long red dress my dad had ordered for me.

I was in that dress the day I saw Wickham, and even though he hadn't gone full dashing rogue yet, I knew a Westley when I saw one: a bandit farm boy hiding under the disguise of a pirate who would treat me like the princess my dad always insisted I was.

He'd come over with his mother to introduce themselves, said that they'd moved in down the road. Fitz and Wickham hit it off right away, and when they ran into me out on the grounds . . .

Nice dress, Wickham had said, all of ten but not mean to me like some of the other boys Fitz was occasionally forced to socialize with. *From* The Princess Bride, *right?*

I'd nodded, dumbstruck, and already in love, whatever love was when you were eight, and then nine, ten, eleven, and on and on and on.

Maybe I was here, talking to him under a tree, because I was still looking for the good kid who had turned into a bad guy. Wanted to turn him back into the boy who had noticed me.

Nice dress.

It started with a dress and it ended with my brother screaming in my room, and the way I'd felt about Wickham in the middle made the end ache even more.

He was still talking.

"I never wanted to get you mixed up in all this. If Fitz hadn't gotten involved . . ." Wickham shrugged, ran his hand over his hair. His words hit in my gut, the whiplash between his gentle coddling and his manipulations. He always knew how to work me, to twist me around until I just gave in to whatever he wanted. "He has a real knack for getting in the way, doesn't he?"

The problem with Wickham was that he was very rarely wrong.

"Why do you even want to see me, Wickham?" The question escaped me before I could stop it, as I pulled my coat closer around my body, but he didn't come all this way just to . . . to kiss me and reminisce. Sometime in the last five minutes, I'd lost all of the blustery determination I'd had when I'd marched down here. Wickham was like an infection. Of course he wouldn't go away on his own.

"I missed you." He stepped in, not so close that I needed to back away, but closer than two strangers should stand. Though we weren't, were we? Strangers. I'd known Wickham longer than I'd known most people. Hell, I knew him better than I knew most people: knew the sharp angle of his jawline, the way his hair curled down around his ears, how he looked when he ignored everything else around him that wanted his attention and turned it all, full-force, on me.

Undivided attention was rare for the younger sister of Fitz Darcy, and even though I knew, deep down, that Wickham's attention was hollow, I craved him.

"We had fun together, didn't we?" He reached out a hand, ran it over my hair. "I miss hanging out with you."

I miss you, too. I was strong enough not to say it out loud, but it wasn't like Wickham didn't know. Besides, I could have stepped back, taken back the distance between us. I didn't.

Touching Wickham was like being hooked up to a hard drive. I was downloading old memories I'd done my best to delete.

Like last winter, when we'd hid together behind the faculty lounge, snorting into jackets pulled up around our faces to hide our laughter, Wickham whispering a running snide commentary about the teachers into my ear as they crossed to the parking lot. It was the first time I'd felt his breath on the side of my neck, and I'd never felt anything like it.

Snap back, Georgie. Focus.

"What do you say?" His other hand came up to cup the side of my face, and I leaned in, let something feel good for a minute. Like when he'd pulled me against him in the unseasonal rain during the end of December last year and I cried as I showed him the text, that Fitz wasn't coming home for Christmas, when he hadn't answered my calls in weeks and I just needed someone to think I was important. *"You have me, don't you?"* Wickham had held me against him and let me cry. *"You don't need anyone else."*

More like I didn't have anyone else.

His thumb brushed against my cheek. "I can make things right. I've got some new ideas up my sleeve. Easier stuff, safer stuff, where we work together this time. And I can protect you, right? There's no way we'll get busted." He was going to kiss me again. Maybe I'd let him. "You'd be perfect for this, kid. Absolutely perfect." It took me a second before I fully heard him, before I processed the words he was saying.

That . . .

The wind whipped even harder, blowing back my curls.

That just about figured, didn't it?

"Are you kidding me, Wickham?" I stepped back, pulled my face from his hand so fast it was almost violent. I was shaking, I realized, and although it may have started from the cold it was tinged with my anger. "That's why you're here? You've got some sort of . . . new scam you're trying to pull?" Anger with Wickham, and anger with myself for almost falling back in.

"Didn't realize your junior year was so full of other plans." The edge in his voice was sharp as a razor. There was the other side of soft words and cupped faces. He was a Taylor Swift lyric wrapped around a knife. "Which is taking up more of your time, being elected to homecoming court or having long, meaningful chats with your big brother?"

"Shut up."

"You wouldn't have met me tonight if you didn't need me, Georgie." As he shook his head, his ponytail brushed against his shoulders. "We need each other, just like we always have." His terrible grin. "After all, if you don't want to help, I can always tell your brother about this little chat."

"You wouldn't." Any blood left in my face quickly drained away. "Wickham. You wouldn't."

"Wouldn't I?" He cocked his head to one side, looked at me hard. "You think my parents liked it when Pemberley decided they didn't want anything to do with me, either? Funds are tight. And all it would take is one email to Fitz for him to pull you out of Pemberley before you could say, 'Don't.' Not as good as having you in my corner but hey," he shrugged, "then there wouldn't be anyone here to get in my way."

"I can't do anything about your parents." Wickham wasn't some down-on-his-luck kid trying to make a living any way he could, I reminded himself. His dad wasn't Darcy rich, but he'd supported Wickham his whole life with plenty of disposable income to spare. Wickham dealt because he liked the rush and the power, nothing more.

It was probably, the sane part of my brain reasoned, why he'd come back after me.

"So work with me." His voice was low and soft, the melody to a kinder song than the one in his eyes. "Work with me, and I'll make sure your brother doesn't find out. What's your alternative? You'd really rather sit around alone and miserable to prove some kind of point than admit you still like spending time with me? Because if so, fuck, you're more like your brother than I thought."

A dig designed to hit home. This was the problem with people who knew you well.

"I'm not just sitting around miserable." A plan, I needed my plan, I needed something I could throw back in Wickham's face so that his stupid smirk would fall away, even for a second. Something that would send him away without sending him straight to Fitz. Unfortunately, "I'm over you, so get out" held less merit as a statement when your face had just been cupped in someone's hand.

He didn't let up.

"No, of course not." His smirk twisted into something darker. "You're the perfect Darcy, aren't you? Isolated in your room, no friends, no prospects . . . yeah, your brother must be real proud."

The perfect Darcy.

Of course.

I didn't have a lot of family around now, obviously, but I'd grown up hearing the stories. Darcys who were senators and CEOs and leaders in their community, who were a shining beacon for all of us. Who married well and had tastefully sized families, who played instruments and painted (but only for pleasure, of course, never for profit). Fitz was the clear next incarnation of the perfectly accomplished Darcy.

That had never been my path. Fitz was always so good at being a Darcy that I hadn't had to be. He'd met with the lawyers after Dad died and used the authoritative voice I'd assumed was genetic to tell them exactly what we needed. He'd been the best student Pemberley had seen in years, a rising star by all accounts. And I'd lurked behind him, Fitz's sister. I never needed to worry about being the perfect Darcy. I had one in front of me.

I'd let Fitz take care of me, ever since he'd found me and Wickham. He'd coddled and protected and smothered and it hadn't worked, had it? Fitz couldn't protect me from everything. That's why I was here, breaking curfew, miserable as I stood in front of Wickham, who stared like he knew he could control me. Why wouldn't he think that? I'd been controlled my entire life.

But a real Darcy didn't let anyone control her.

I had to control myself.

"Let me prove it." The words rushed out of me fast, my breath producing a puff of smoke. "You think that I need you as much as you need me? Let me prove that I don't. I can win this school back by myself. I'll be the perfect Darcy, make everyone respect me again. And if I can do that, you leave me alone."

"How?" He laughed, cruel. "Going to make your brother do your homework for you?"

"I'll manage." I straightened my shoulders, stood up as tall as I could. If I was going to do this, I may as well start now. "And when I do, you're going to leave."

That was it. That was the last card I could play. I wasn't some weak kid to be manipulated and coddled and hated. I was a Darcy, and the whole world would know it.

It would be easy, of course, for Wickham to say no. To threaten to go straight to my brother anyway, to make sure I stayed in his clutches. But I knew him, just like he knew me. I knew he liked to play with his food.

"You've got some sort of measurable level of Darcyness I can track then, right?" His bemused skepticism was clear in his expression, but he hadn't said no. "What's the Dow Jones equivalent? Is there an app somewhere I can follow your progress?"

"You'll know."

"No. Not good enough." He leaned back against the tree trunk, thinking. Wickham was always leaning against something. "How about this?" He pushed off the bark, closed what little distance there was between the two of us. "You become the perfect Darcy, fine. Great for your self-actualization or whatever. But you want me to leave?" He reached a hand out toward me, caught a curl that had fallen loose from my ponytail and tucked it behind my ear. I shivered. "Get your brother to admit it. And if you don't, I'll either tell him all the ways you failed myself, or you work with me. Because if you let things get that far, I won't just tell him that we talked, Georgie. By the time we're done, he'll think that everything we did together was your idea."

The wind whipped around us, biting.

I should have said no, that there wasn't a chance in hell. Because Fitz would never admit I was crushing it; in his mind, I never could. And what did Wickham want me to do, set him and Fitz up on a Zoom call? If Fitz found out Wickham was at Pemberley, I was done for.

But I didn't have a choice, did I? If this was what Wickham wanted, the only way he'd give me a chance . . . It wasn't like I could back out now. And Wickham hadn't said Fitz had to admit it to *him*. Just admit it. Fitz didn't need to ever know Wickham was involved. Maybe, the least logical part of me wondered, I actually could prove myself to my brother, to the school, to everyone. Sure, the stakes were high if I failed . . . but that just meant I couldn't fail.

"Deal," I whispered, because he was close enough that I didn't need to be any louder. But then he stepped back, finally, and held out his hand. As we shook, the contact sent an electrical current through me. His expression told me that he knew.

"I'll be checking in." He squeezed my hand before he dropped it, stepping back. "And when you fail, you'll work with me without complaints." A chill went through me. That was the other half of why he'd agreed, probably. Half to watch me flounder and half to ensure my eventual cooperation. He stretched his arms over his head, revealing half an inch of skin where his T-shirt rose up beneath his unbuttoned jacket, and I hated myself for looking. "I'm not going to wait forever, kid. You've got a month, maybe, before I need to kick this into high gear."

"What are you doing, exactly?" I felt a mix of morbid curiosity and dread. Whatever Wickham's new business venture was, I doubted it boded well for me. "What are you selling now?"

"Oh no." Wickham shook his head. "You want information? Earn it. But if you need someone to talk to, I'll be around."

"I won't need you."

"Sure." Wickham laughed, shoved his hands into the pockets of his coat. "You'll be emailing me again before the week's out. And I'll be waiting for you. Maybe then I'll tell you what I'm doing. If you're good."

I held my breath for a second, unsure what he'd do next, but he just turned toward the fence to move the loose pole aside. I didn't wait for him to turn back, to throw out one more pithy one-liner designed to intimidate me. I spun on my heels and marched away.

I would not do this again.

My mind whirled with the formulation of a plan as I continued my march, back through campus and up to my dorm room, where I snuck back in via a conveniently placed tree. Without even taking off my coat, I sat down at my desk and opened my laptop, and began to type furiously, ideas pouring out of me and onto the white expanse of my waiting document like I was writing a fic.

I would be everything that I was born to be. Fitz would see it, and Wickham would see it, and he'd know I was *good*. I was fine without him.

Just fine.

CHAPTER FOUR

The next morning, my first day of classes, I moved through my classmates in a haze of gossip and stares, head down toward the floor, just trying not to get tripped. I'd spent the last few weeks terrified about what this day would hold for me, sure that someone would stick gum to my chair, that I'd have to hide in the bathroom to eat lunch, that someone would graffiti my locker.

And I mean, they did. The marker someone had used to write NARC on my locker seemed to be permanent, too, which was going to be a pain in the ass to get off. Couldn't wait to live with that for the rest of the year.

But with my new plan in place, it seemed a little less horrifying. More *Cabin in the Woods* than *Saw*.

In service to both my plan and my near-expulsion, my day had started with a guidance counselor meeting.

"You want to switch *all* of these classes?" Mrs. Ryder looked up at me with skepticism from the sheet of loose-leaf I'd handed her as soon as I'd entered her office. "This is your entire schedule, Georgiana."

"I just don't think my previous schedule really pushed me to my fullest potential, you know?" I ignored the use of Georgiana. Priorities. The list of Ideal Darcy Accomplishments I'd typed up last night included the very best grades in the very best classes, so I needed to up my academic game pretty much immediately.

"But I don't . . . you want to go from *no* AP classes to *all* AP classes?" Mrs. Ryder hadn't yet recovered from the initial shock of me walking in here with a purpose, and the purpose itself seemed only to unsettle her further. "That's quite the change."

"Band isn't moving." I reached over the desk to point out the one block on my schedule that didn't shift. "Are you telling me you don't think I could do it?"

I raised an eyebrow at her, this small white woman with pink-framed glasses who surely had bowed to the demands of Darcys before. After a moment, she gulped, then nodded.

No wonder Fitz treated people like this. It was *super* effective.

"But I'll be keeping an eye on your grades," she warned as she shifted her chair toward her computer, inputting my new schedule. At least, it sounded like she meant it as a warning. "We don't want to see you fail."

That would make her the only one, I thought, but I just smiled as I grabbed my new schedule from her. "Don't worry," I called over my shoulder as I grabbed my backpack and booked it toward my first class, which was now AP government and met across the campus in ten minutes. "I won't!"

I kept repeating that mantra—*I won't fail, I won't fail, I won't fail*—as I blurred through the dark wood-paneled halls of the school, which looked more like an elite ski lodge than any of the average high schools I saw on TV. I made it through my first couple classes of the day without causing too much of a scene—Mr. Jacobson, my chem teacher, wasn't even going to assign lab partners until the end of the week, so I had a few days before I had to deal with that inevitable humiliation. (*"Georgie's my lab mate? No, Mr. Jacobson, I'm allergic to people I hate!"*) I'd kept my head down and doodled in my notebook while he muttered about our course objectives, chanting the steps of my plan in my head. They were weirdly comforting.

And I needed all the comfort I could get as I headed toward the band room. Somehow, this place that should have been a safe haven was even scarier than AP calc.

For all that the rest of the school hated me for what went down with Wickham, the members of the Pemberley Academy Marching Stallions hated me most of all.

It hadn't always been like that, obviously. Freshman year, I'd been gently accepted, as all the new weirdos were, allowed to float at the periphery of the band's social circle and pretend that meant I had real friends. With Fitz still at Pemberley, that had been enough. And last year, when I was a sophomore, I'd gotten closer to a couple of the trombones, made some half-hearted advances toward genuine human relationships . . .

And then, Wickham.

He'd caught the entire band's attention in an instant because, for all of his moral failings, Wickham was one of the best trumpet players I'd ever seen. He had the innate talent of someone who didn't care enough to try but was nonetheless extremely good, and the whole band knew it. They'd fallen for his charms just like I had, even if he was always a little too anti-establishment to return their feelings. He showed up for practice when he felt like it, and when he did, he didn't talk to anyone besides me. Still, the rest of the band high-fived him in the hallways, jostled against him at the back of the stands, hooted for his solos. I knew none of them could quite figure out why he'd chosen to hang out with little old me.

So when he got expelled, and the entire school knew I had *something* to do with it? Yeah, that didn't exactly buy me a lot of goodwill with the others. The school hated me for supposedly turning in their drug dealer. The band hated me for allegedly turning in one of their own.

But still. I leaned against the wall next to the band room, counting down the minutes until practice started. I needed to go in, needed to remember the plan. All the Darcys who had ever come through Pemberley—aka, basically every Darcy—excelled in extracurriculars. Fitz had been a champion debater. And I was a decent trombone player, if you were evaluating musical talent and not my popularity. I needed the band to accept me for my plan to move forward.

I had to go in. It wouldn't be as bad as I thought, probably. I just had to go in, pick up my foot, step through the door, *don't be a coward, be a Darcy.*

Dread crept through my chest, took hold in every crevice.

Wickham stood in the doorway of my dorm room, and Fitz shouted like I'd never heard my brother shout before. His eyes were wild, his dark curls standing straight up from his head, and he held a small Ziploc bag full of pills—

"George!" I turned with a start at the sound of my name, half-expecting to be pelted with a Slurpee or something. But when I saw Avery Simmons walking toward me, hand up in a wave, it kind of felt like being drenched in a Slurpee, anyway.

Avery was a year above me, a fellow trombone and one of the few people I had managed to count as a friend before everything in my life blew up. We weren't super tight or anything—I didn't know how to be super tight with anyone—but he'd always been cool, and we'd sat together on the bus to all of our away games and parades. Decorated lockers side by side and made weird jokes that no one else in the section seemed to understand.

He was also another victim of my mistakes.

It had started small, as all of this had. A missed sectional, a study date rescheduled, the sort of thing I did more and more as Wickham and I got closer and closer. Avery wasn't the type of person to question me or my shoddy excuses, even as they got shoddier, but by the end of the year I'd stopped answering his texts entirely, even when they seemed worried. (By then, admittedly, everyone's texts had seemed worried.) And then Fitz came and got me, I lost all of my communication with the outside world, and I hadn't heard from him since. All I had was a screenshot of our last texts, from May, which I'd grabbed off my old phone in a desperate act of masochism.

AVERY: George! Still good for 4? Audition video?

AVERY: Gotta send it in tonight by midnight so text me back

AVERY: kind of need you here friend

AVERY: I'll be here till 7 but then I have a shift at the front desk can you text me back

AVERY: You're not with him are you

AVERY: Come on you promised you'd help

AVERY: George?

Then he'd called. I hadn't answered, too entrenched in Wickham's arms to see my screen light up.

Yeah, I didn't exactly expect this to be a joyous reunion.

But there he was, even taller and lankier than he'd been at the end of last spring, with shaggy dark hair that flopped over into his eyes as he closed the distance between us. I braced for the impact of whatever was to come. A mocking remark, or the coldest of shoulders. I had to get used to it. That was going to be the next couple hours of rehearsal, until everyone got it out of their system and I could fade to the background, me and my trombone as a pounding bass line and nothing else. Once I proved to them that I was good enough, they wouldn't think about how much they hated me anymore. Maybe they'd even forgive me.

Maybe.

"We missed you at band camp." Avery held onto the straps of his backpack as he beamed at me. No one had beamed at me in . . . months. Fitz wasn't a beamer. "Mrs. Tapper basically tried to murder us. If you were there, we would have had an extra person for the human pyramids."

"Did you really do human pyramids?" The shock of his pleasantries sent my guard crashing down, and the question slipped out of my mouth before I could pull the walls back up again. *Any* sort of conversation that didn't start with "get out of my way, asshole" was a surprise today, but Avery had more of a right to hate me than anyone. He'd actually earned it.

"No." He shook his head and leaned against the burnished wood paneling next to the band room door, his smile bright. "But if you were there, we could have. What did you do this summer?"

"Um." What was . . . what was any of this? This was easily the longest conversation I'd had IRL with someone who wasn't my brother, an authority figure, or Wickham since school had ended last year. I wasn't sure I remembered what to do. Half of me wanted to throw my arms around Avery, sob into his embrace in gratitude for an actual pleasant human interaction. But the other half, the half that had developed after The Incident and took over most of my interactions, warned me to stay back, be cautious. Wickham had beamed at me, too. "Just hung out with my brother." Avery didn't need to know about all the Fitz-mandated family fun activities I'd been forced to participate in. He was, clearly, just being polite. Any second now, someone who hadn't completely abandoned his friendship for a guy would show up, and Avery would be gone.

"Cool." He nodded. I shifted the weight of my backpack from one shoulder to the other, tried to look like a normal person, and not one who was panicking about the implications of this deceptively simple human interaction. "I had to work the whole time. Lifeguarding. They let me take time off for band camp, though, and not every job does that."

I couldn't take it anymore. "Do you need something from me?" *Smooth, Georgie, smooth,* but no one could blame me for being suspicious.

"No?" He smiled through his quizzical look, all straight white teeth. "Besides," he added, like it was an afterthought, and not an extra addition to the collection of daggers that had been shoved into my heart over the course of the school day, "I hear I have to get my Adderall somewhere else now."

Slurpee, all over again, dripping down my metaphorical neck and mixing with the sweat that made my shirt collar stick to my skin.

"I didn't know about the drugs, Avery." I immediately ran past babble and into a full-on blather, with the speed the words rushed out of me. "I swear, I didn't know anything, and I didn't turn Wickham in, I just—"

"George." He held up his hand to stop me, not unkindly.

Honestly, at that point, he could have knocked me out cold and I wouldn't perceive it as unkind. "It was a joke. All my meds are strictly doctor-prescribed."

"Right." God, this was an unmitigated disaster. We'd been *friends*, Avery and me, and I didn't even know how to talk to him. "It's possible I've lost my ability to distinguish those."

"Well, didn't you spend the whole summer with your brother? Riding zebras, or whatever it is Darcys do on their vacations?"

"I'm pretty sure riding zebras is illegal."

"Either way." He shrugged, and I felt the smallest trickle of hope pierce my armor. Despite how poorly this conversation had started, Avery hadn't walked away. I would have, if I were in his shoes. "I don't exactly remember Fitz being the class clown."

"No. Not so much." I bounced back and forth on my toes, just a little, a childish habit I'd spent years trying to correct that still came out whenever I got nervous. The silence between us lengthened, quickly nearing uncomfortable territory.

"I can let you go," Avery said, finally, completing misinterpreting my quiet to think I had somewhere better to be. "I'm sure you want to catch up with the others."

I should have taken the out, maybe, but I didn't.

"You're allowed to hate me, too, you know." A little voice in the back of my mind was shouting at me to shut up, to take this modicum of human kindness Avery was throwing me and not ruin it, but I'd never been good at listening to that little voice. "You deserve the chance more than the rest of them." And I'd count this conversation as a one-time thing and go back to crushing loneliness.

"Why would—they don't hate you." He pushed his hair back from his eyes when he spoke. "Pemberley loves gossip, that's all. You know that."

I was self-aware enough to know that it was a complete and total deflection of what I'd said.

"If it helps," he continued, looking down at his shoes briefly, "I think the school's a lot better off without Wickham Foster in it."

"Right." Avery had been one of the few people not to fall under Wickham's spell. In retrospect, amazing judgment, though that didn't help me now. Other students streamed into the band room, but at least no one stopped to make a mean comment toward me, even as they stared at us. "Well. Whatever. Maybe another senator's kid will get arrested for money laundering."

Avery shrugged. "Look, if people are going to be dicks to you because of last year . . ." He drummed his fingers along his backpack straps. "I don't know. There's nothing you can do about that. But I'm not going to be. And hey, I guess it happened after you left, but Mrs. T made me drum major this year. So I've got a lot of authority, or whatever."

"Really? Congrats." I meant it. Avery was one of the best musicians in the band, and chill with everybody. He was a great choice for drum major.

"Thanks." Avery smiled, his head tipped down. "We should go in. I've got a precedent to set, and all that."

"Right." I nodded. "Gotta go major those drums."

"Wow, you must have read a book about drum majoring over the summer." Avery held the door open, and I pushed through my dread to step into the room. The chatter inside didn't stop when I walked in or anything, which I guessed was a relief, though I definitely got a bunch of side-eye. "You have an amazing grasp on the lingo."

"I'm extremely well-read," I told Avery as the door closed behind us. The band room was loud with the bustle of a hundred kids trying and failing to tune instruments, a sound, I realized in the moment, that I'd missed. "It's possible I've read two books."

"Nice." Avery laughed as he dropped his backpack next to the conductor's stand, where he'd be stationed for practice. "Hey, you should let me know how I do, after this. Tell me if I suck."

"I'm sure you don't."

"But if I do, you're the only one honest enough to tell me to my face." He shoved his shoulder against mine, and I nearly let myself smile, until my eyes drifted to the back of the room. "Always have been."

My gaze fell on the trumpets before I could respond, all the way in the back. Muscle memory, I guessed. That was where Wickham sat, when he bothered showing up. Second chair—he was good enough to be first chair, but skipped way too much for Mrs. Tapper to give him the position—pushed back out of the row a little, so he could put his feet up on my seat in front of him. Kick at my chair until I giggled too much to keep playing.

And then my gaze drifted forward, where the entirety of the trombone section was staring at me as if I'd grown an extra head.

Braden, a senior, sitting in the first chair, all bleached-blond hair from his summer back home in Florida, with a look dirty enough that I almost called the janitor; Jackson, a Black sophomore who had his arms crossed over his chest like he needed to block my energy from getting anywhere near him. The two freshmen—I assumed they were freshmen, since I didn't recognize them—watched me nervously. And Emily, a Korean-American girl in my year with dark, straight hair that fell in front of her face, who sat in the middle of the row, and kept darting looks at me out of the corner of her glasses like I wouldn't notice. She was the only other trombone I'd really hung out with, besides Avery. From the way she looked at me, that wasn't something she planned on repeating.

"Oh, right." Avery followed my gaze, his tone slightly less jovial than it had been before. "And Braden is your section leader. You probably got an email from him, too, about what you missed at camp. We got most of the routine down for our first show. Mrs. T had all the section leaders make videos for anyone who missed it."

"Right." I had received no such email. Of *course* Braden was section leader. Braden, whose stare toward me was the iciest of all, who hadn't liked me much before The Incident. Our families had known each other a little, growing up, and the once or twice a year we ended up at dinner parties together, he'd followed Fitz around like a puppy dog, desperate for his attention and approval.

The problem with Fitz, though, was that he rarely gave anyone his attention or approval. It had apparently festered in Braden, and he'd spent the first two years we were in band together making thinly veiled remarks about me. Now that the whole school hated me, there was no need for thinly veiling anything.

If they had the first show down already, I was even more screwed than I'd thought. I was way better at music than I was at marching, and tended to need every rehearsal we had to get the steps down with the precision Mrs. T required.

It was fine. I'd just have to . . . I'd practice. I was reasonably bright, according to my various tutors. And yeah, I already had about three times as much homework as I'd ever received just from my first couple of AP classes, but I'd make it work. Being a Darcy meant making it work.

"Um." Avery sounded uncomfortable, though it was most likely just a fraction of what I felt. "I'm guessing Braden didn't send you the videos, did he?"

"Not a chance." I kept my gaze fixed on the section. I felt like they might all attack if I had the audacity to look away.

"Right." Avery nodded toward them, seeming to understand my hesitation. "Go on. I'll forward them to you after practice."

I should have said thank you, but my throat had closed up

enough that I couldn't actually manage it, so I just nodded before I gripped my backpack tighter and headed toward the cluster of chairs in the second to last row that was supposed to be my home.

"Hey, guys." I *sounded* scared as I said it, unpacking my trombone, which didn't bode well for the rest of the hour. "Good to see you."

"You can sit at the end of the row until you actually know your music," Braden snapped as I put together my instrument, since apparently basic niceties were reserved for other people. I did my best to look unfazed. I'd been third chair last year, and while I'd figured I'd have to perform for Mrs. T again this year to earn my place like everyone else, I hadn't anticipated this much open hostility. My mistake. "We learned it at camp. You know, *mandatory* camp? Serving a prison sentence doesn't excuse you."

"I clearly wasn't in prison," I muttered, as one of the freshmen passed me a pile of sheet music with a shaking hand. "And I'll learn the music."

"Good," Braden scoffed. The rest of the section kept their gaze forward, like they couldn't hear him. Cowards. "Because I'm not going to let you bring this section down."

I wanted to defy him, to tell him that bringing down the section was the last thing I'd ever want to do, but there was no point. He'd never believe me. From the way the rest of them ignored me, I started to think that none of them ever would.

I'd thought, heading into rehearsal, that if I was just a good enough musician, I'd be able to earn back their respect. Show them that I wanted to be there. But I was starting to think otherwise.

I pictured Wickham for just a second, leaning against the back of one of the black metal folding chairs. Smooth smile, suggestive eyebrows at the way the freshmen moved their slides up and down. The false sincerity that dripped from his voice whenever he spoke.

I told you. Imaginary Wickham smirked, a stab in the heart. *I told you no one would ever care about you besides me. Don't you remember that I'm always right?*

I did my best to will him away, to stay in tune as Avery raised his hands and began to lead us in scales, but Wickham's ghost didn't leave me. He never really did.

Screw you, I told Imaginary Wickham. *I can do this.*

Can you? His mocking smile was the most familiar thing in my life. *You don't need to put yourself through it, kid. I'll take you back. I promise.*

It shouldn't have been more appealing than band practice. Band should have been a place where I felt safe, where I felt comfortable, where I couldn't see Braden staring down the row at me like he was hoping lasers would start shooting out of his eyes to demolish me into dust.

If Wickham really was here, and this was last year, it wouldn't have mattered what Braden thought of me. I'd only have had eyes for Wickham, who filled out a Pemberley uniform better than anyone else in school. Who chose me when everyone else wanted him. He may have been kicked out (or "asked gently and lovingly to leave," as he'd said) of a non-zero number of military schools, but it had given him an air of something he'd never had before. It wasn't just confidence, an area in which Wickham had never lacked. It was like . . .

Magnetism.

If the trombone section was a magnet, on the other hand, it was one of those opposite ones that pushed me away instead of pulling me in close.

Close was how Wickham had always liked me, when he'd take me to lounge under trees even after it got way too cold, where we'd push against the boundaries of both curfew and what we were to each other.

"You don't have to lie to me." Wickham's voice was low and smooth, and I felt it in my bones. *"I know it's fucking freezing out here."*

"I'm fine." I was not fine. It was the middle of October and I was, in fact, fucking freezing, but Wickham had asked me to come meet him and there was no way I was going back to my dorm just to get a better jacket. *"I don't mind."*

"Come here." He held his arms out toward me, and when I hesitated, he stepped toward me instead, held me against his chest. *"I can keep you warm."*

He didn't say anything else, but I didn't want him to. Because every now and again he said something like that and I thought . . .

I thought I might just have a chance.

He finally tilted his head down, back toward me. Eyes warm with a glow I longed for.

"I'm glad I came to Pemberley, kid."

I was, too.

It had been intoxicating, to have someone look at me like that. I missed it.

I'm going to make them respect me, I told imaginary Wickham, the version I knew now, with a fierceness I never managed when he was actually in front of me, *and you can fuck right off.*

But I had the sinking feeling, as warm-ups began around me, that just being good at music wasn't going to win the band over. And yeah, there was nothing in my list of accomplishments about making BFFs—Fitz certainly never had—but a Darcy was respected among her peers. I needed to figure out a way to make that happen.

I caught Avery's eye, conducting us from the front of the band room, and he grinned. Grinned like he didn't hate me.

There was a chance, though, a small possibility . . . that I just might have a way in.

CHAPTER FIVE

I had to make my way through the rest of the school day before I could continue my grand scheme, which was honestly a disgrace considering how much my brother paid for my tuition. You'd think saving my reputation would rank high enough on the list of academic priorities that I could have exchanged my gym requirement for an extra study hall.

Still, I did my best to pay attention in my classes, for once. I took notes on all my lectures, even though most of them were just introductory, and even used my lunch period to order myself some cool new notebooks from a stationery store in town. Organization was the key to success, according to my brother. Sure, I'd never taken AP classes before, but Fitz always had. I'd manage.

Academics, check. But on the band side, the respect of my peers' side . . . it had become extremely clear that I needed some extra help in that direction. And there was only one person in this school who had given me the time of day.

Which was why I found myself hustling back to the band room after dinner that night, trying to summon up every ounce of courage within me for the task ahead.

The academic buildings, besides the library and a few research labs, were technically off-limits to students after the school day was over, but the band room was on the first floor, with windows I could reach from the sidewalk. As soon as I was close enough to see a light on inside and hear the quiet hum of a recorded marching band, I rapped on the glass, hard.

The music stopped, suddenly, and Avery appeared at the window. He hovered in front of me with a perplexed expression, his purple-and-white tie crooked around his neck, white button-down shirt all wrinkled. I waved at him, a little more frantically than was perhaps strictly necessary, tilted my head to the back door of the band room to indicate he should let me in. To his credit, he did so without hesitation, and I let out a sharp exhale once I was safely inside and out of the cold. Avery looked me up and down, one eyebrow raised.

"What's up?" His uncertainty was warranted, since it was almost nine o'clock and I should have been studying at the library or ignoring my roommate in my dorm, not harassing my drum major because he'd had the basic human decency to say hello to me. I probably looked as wild as I felt, my cheeks flushed from the cold and the wind, my hair huge. It was going to be a pain in the ass to detangle later, but I reminded myself that any number of knots was worth my dignity.

Or something like that.

"I figured there was like, a fifty percent chance you were in here." I looked around the room, which seemed weirdly empty without the entire band packed into it. "Practicing?"

"I hear it's important." He shrugged, his smile vaguely concerned. Again, warranted. "Mrs. T worked it out with administration. I've got like, a perfect record with following rules so they let me use the room after hours this year. It helps me wind down."

"Strangers banging on the window probably helps you relax, too, right?" I was speaking too quickly, still out of breath from the cold. He laughed.

"I think you earned me an extra hour of a relaxation podcast before bed, but whatever. You okay? What are you doing here?"

"Would you believe I *also* have permission to wander the school buildings after hours?" Deflecting, that was what I was doing. Like one of my mom's more polished mirrors.

"Remember the part where I said my disciplinary record was clear?"

Right.

Just like before, an uncomfortable silence settled over the room. But this time, I didn't let it linger. I was, after all, a girl on a mission, and if I waited too long to shoot my shot I was definitely going to lose my nerve, so I opened my mouth and let myself say something that I really, *really* hated saying.

"I need your help."

"What?" Avery, who had been looking politely down at the floor, whipped his head up so fast it was lucky he didn't need the school's on-call chiropractic team.

"I need your help. I need you to like . . . be my friend again." If I slowed down, I'd lose my nerve, or worse, give him time to shut me down before I got everything out. And I couldn't let that happen, because I clearly wasn't going to be accepted by the band without Avery and if I wasn't accepted by the band, my entire redemption tour was toast. "I was a jerk to you last year, and I'm sorry. I completely ditched you when I got wrapped up in Wickham and

I was, truly, a completely shitty person, but I'm hoping you can forgive me because frankly, no one else will." Points for honesty at the end, I guess. Maybe too honest.

Avery glanced down at his shoes again, well-worn and a contrast against the freshly replaced carpet. When he looked up, I couldn't read his expression.

"What are you doing, Georgie?"

"I just . . ." I threw my hands out, glad that the heating in here at least meant my fingers didn't feel like they were going to fall off anymore. "I don't want last year again, okay? I don't want to have nothing and then fall into the first something that comes along. I'm trying to find my own something."

"That's . . . kind of confusing."

"Yeah, well, it's been kind of a long day," I snapped, then winced. Avery didn't waver, though. "You said before that if people were going to be dicks to me because of last year, there was nothing I could do about it. This is me trying to do something about it, okay?" I let out a long breath. "Please, Aves."

The notes in my voice leaned too close to desperation, but that made sense, because I was desperate. Desperate to break the cycle of Wickham, to prove to him that I could do this, to prove to my *brother* that I could do this.

Freshman year Georgie: attached to her brother's hip. Sophomore year Georgie: attached to Wickham's mouth. Junior year Georgie? So far, a royal fuckup with no one to codependently cling to. All the AP classes in the world wouldn't keep me from Wickham if I was still completely alone.

I just wanted like, one regular friend.

And I could be pretty stubborn, when I wanted to be. Fitz would only slightly sarcastically say it was one of my better traits.

"You seem to hate me less than everyone else does," I rambled on as Avery stared. God, I was actually getting a little too warm now, but that could be the fire inside of me. "And I have this . . . this is stupid. I have this plan, right? To be someone here my brother could be proud of. To prove to everyone who thinks I'm nothing that I can be something. Winning the band back over is my best way to do that."

"I don't hate you."

"Prove it." I licked my lips, my whole throat suddenly dry. "Help me show him what I'm made of."

"Is this about Wickham, by any chance?" To his credit, he managed to keep his tone light, though he looked back at the floor when he mentioned Wickham's name.

"Did he . . . You know he's back." It wasn't really a question on my part, but Avery nodded anyway.

"I've seen him around. Skulking." He stuck out his tongue in distaste. "In town, before the semester started. Didn't talk to him, obviously. But is that who you really need to prove yourself to?"

"Maybe," I hedged. A dark expression flashed across Avery's face. "Does that change things?"

"Are you . . ." He coughed, eyes back down at his shoes again. "You're not with him again, are you? Because I'm not trying to get caught up in some sort of weird thing between the two of you."

"I'm doing this to get *rid* of Wickham," I said, pushing away thoughts of the kiss. It wouldn't happen again. My voice sounded weaker than I would have liked, but what else was new? "I think it's the only way I can."

Avery watched me in the fluorescent lights of the band room, mixing with the moonlight that streamed in through the windows. He seemed to study me for a second, and this was totally a "so much depends on the gangly drum major, glazed with indecision, standing beside the broken girl with a cry for help" moment, and I didn't know how it was going to go.

But the thing I'd forgotten about Avery, I guess, was that he came through.

"All right." He smiled, all hints of darkness gone from his expression, and even though it was smaller than one of Avery's trademark giant grins, it maybe meant more. "But you owe me like, a million hours of listening to me ramble on about drum major techniques."

"How many different techniques are there?" I needed to get back to my dorm before curfew hit, but I wanted to hold onto this moment for a second, a moment where I reached out and asked someone for help and they didn't turn against me. Take that, Fitz; take that, Wickham; take that, every short-lived therapy appointment I'd ever had. I wasn't a total recluse who refused to let anyone into her inner circle.

God damn it, I was going to get *better* this year, or I was going to die trying.

"You would be surprised." He reached behind us, grabbed his coat off the back of his chair. "Come on. I'll teach you all about them on the walk back to the dorms."

"I also need to catch up on everything we learned at band camp." I spoke fast again, before the momentum could die, before my better judgment caught up with me. "That should be right up your alley, right? You're Mr. Big Fancy Drum Major now. They probably named the band room after you." I pushed open the door, held it for him as he followed me. He locked it carefully behind him, dropping the key into the pocket of his jeans before he patted them, just once, like he wanted to make sure they were in there.

"They only do that for the rich kids, Madam Matthew Darcy Science Wing." I saw his grin even in the dark. Felt it, anyway.

"But I can do that. We can hang out after practice on Thursday? Make sure you've got everything set for the homecoming game. Cool?" We walked through the tree-lined paths, where the rustling branches blocked the worst of the wind from hitting us.

"Cool," I repeated, as we approached the side of my dorm. We both laughed, and it felt . . . almost okay. "I should go. Rodney's got to show up eventually." Our school's one security guard was too slow to be effective, but I was trying to be good.

"Yeah." He shivered. "I'll see you at practice, I guess. Or meals this week. Or whenever."

"Whenever." That was a clear signal to leave, but I didn't yet, shifted from one foot to the other. Avery watched me, easy, before I asked my last question. "Why'd you say yes, Aves?"

He tilted his head as he considered it, but weirdly, I wasn't nervous for the answer. There was something to be said for being around someone who didn't make you nervous.

Finally, he shrugged. "Maybe I like a project."

I laughed.

"See you, George." He waved, and I waved back as he turned and faded into the darkness, moving briskly to get back to his own dorm as I continued in the opposite direction, back to my building and my tree. Once I checked that the coast was, in fact, clear, I stepped onto the lowest branch, pulled myself up a few more branches, and slipped in through the window I'd left open next to my nightstand. I hadn't quite hit curfew, could have come through the lobby, but old habits die hard.

Sydney was sitting up in her bed, staring at me.

"Just making my monthly full-moon run." I may have needed to make friends, but no one said they had to include Sydney, whose nose wrinkled in disgust at the idea of casual lycanthropy.

Or just me, maybe. It was hard to tell.

"Whatever." As she laid back down, turning over to face the wall, I slipped quickly into my pajamas—monogrammed and *Sage Hall* inspired, a gift from my brother—and crawled into bed, smiling to myself. Not even imagining the way Wickham would smirk at the idea of *more* band practice—of actually liking more band practice—could push away my brand-new nugget of hope.

CHAPTER SIX

Saturday morning, and I was exhausted. In addition to adding on practice time with Avery and actually trying in my classes for once, I needed to attempt to maintain the bare minimum with my brother, while also super not mentioning that I'd had any contact with Wickham.

Not complicated at all.

At some point, I'd need to figure out the final part of the plan—not only becoming the perfect Darcy, but getting Fitz to admit it without knowing Wickham was in any way involved. Maybe I could start a Twitter account under his name, sing my own praises on the internet.

Well. I had time to figure it out.

I jumped the last couple of stairs going out the front door of my dorm and headed into the brisk September air, lowering sunglasses onto my face as Fitz waved at me from that expensive but still too-sensible car of his. This time, at least, I was going in with a plan. I would tell Fitz about my all-AP schedule today. Earn some brother brownie points, pave the way for him being proud of me and getting Wickham out of here for good.

"The prodigal sister returns." He watched carefully as I buckled my seat belt, waiting until he heard it click before he eased the car into drive and moved slowly out of the parking circle.

"Pretty sure you're the prodigal one." The leaves had started to change, which meant the campus was only days away from being flooded with tourists who came to see the historic buildings and the dying chlorophyll. "Eventually they're going to throw you a parade here."

"Oh, they've reached out a number of times, but I've always declined." Fitz kept his eyes exactly on the road, not looking at me. "You know I hate pomp and circumstance."

"Yeah, you're the picture of modest living," I muttered. "Still no new cup holders, I see."

"Like you said. Modest living. How was your week?" He adjusted the collar of his button-down, another possession that didn't look flashy but I knew cost hundreds. He did appreciate good tailoring.

"Pancakes first, then talk." I pressed my fingers against the bridge of my nose, trying to wake up. I'd kind of figured that if I just paid attention in class, the excelling academically part of my plan would come easy, but that had not been the case. Turned out Pemberley had earned at least some of its prestigious reputation by being academically challenging. Who knew? Every hour that I hadn't spent on the field with Avery, or rehearsing my music in one of the practice rooms on campus, I'd been locked away in the library trying to understand calc and chem, which had both taken sharp turns toward the difficult. (Those were, of course, both subjects Fitz had been great at, like everything else in his life.) Even English, usually a reliable subject, had zoomed past my levels of comprehension as each class centered on readings I didn't have time to do. "And bacon today, too. I need the protein."

"Haven't you previously argued that whipped cream has protein from the dairy, which was why I should allow you to keep consuming it at the levels you do?"

"I mean, it definitely does." We passed through the gates of Pemberley, headed out on the winding road toward the outskirts of town. "I just need extra today. That's all."

"Sure." Fitz sighed. When I looked at him, it seemed as if he had more to say, but whatever it was, he kept it to himself.

It was after we'd settled into our booth, pancakes ordered with both whipped cream and a side of bacon, that the full force of Fitz "Not Your Dad but I Am Your Guardian Now" Darcy turned on me.

"Your English teacher emailed me."

"She *what?*" Fuck. The whole point of Pemberley, according to all of their literature, was to teach us the responsibility we needed to succeed in college and beyond. I was pretty sure no college professor ever emailed their students' parents to tell them they'd flunked a quiz. They *definitely* didn't email your big brother. I should write a letter to the school complaining, I decided. Even though they'd probably used up all their leniency points on not expelling me in the first place. "How does she even have your email?" There went my plan, because while I was going to tell Fitz about my classes, I was *not* going to tell him about my current grades in said classes. Yet here I was, stuck on the defensive. Again.

"It's on all your school forms, Georgie. I'm your contact— emergency and otherwise." He took a sip of his coffee, and didn't even wince at the heat or the pure, unadulterated caffeine. "She's concerned about you."

"It was one assignment." I tried to take a sip of my own coffee—I mean, way watered down with milk and sugar, but still technically coffee—in the same cool, disconnected way that Fitz did, but it was way too hot, and it was all I could do not to gasp as it scalded my throat. "We've been in school for a week. I'll make it up." Somehow. It had been a stupid assignment to miss, easy reading comprehension stuff, but you needed to do the reading to comprehend it. I didn't tell Fitz that the idea of finishing the assignment, on top of all the other ones that had piled up, made my palms sweat and my pulse race, the same feeling that, last year, would have had me calling Wickham to come over so I didn't have to be alone with my thoughts.

"Which is why missing papers right now has an even bigger impact on your GPA. You don't have any other grades to cushion it." Fitz didn't let up, just pushed and pushed and pushed, like he always did, like a Darcy always did, and sometimes I understood why I had broken.

"Well, it doesn't exactly matter, does it?" I had never been good at taking a Fitz lecture. My blood boiled, a fun mix with the anxiety. "I'm sure she mentioned something about this being a dangerous pattern of mine, right? Because I missed all of those assignments before you pulled me out last year."

"She might have." Fitz spoke through gritted teeth. "The fact that it doesn't surprise you isn't exactly a good sign."

All of the waitresses here knew well enough to steer clear of our table right now, with a full-on Darcy-family-brawl in the works.

I shrugged, as casually as I could, swirling my coffee around. I'd never been like this around Fitz before he went to California.

We'd fought, sure, but we'd always been on the same team. It was only once he decided that his ideal future was more important than me that we'd formed our own teams of one.

His face in my room, the way he'd held up that little plastic bag like a question he knew the answer to.

"Is this seriously the attitude you're going to take toward this?" Fitz drained the rest of his coffee in a single, impressive gulp. "Honestly, Beanpole. I'm trying to treat you like an adult here—"

"Ha!" I barked out a laugh. I saw our waitress hover at the edge of my vision, clearly torn between her desire to fill up Fitz's mug and to leave us the hell alone. "If you wanted to actually treat me like an adult, you wouldn't come and check up on me every week." I was so close to shouting. Dangerously close. "I promise, Fitz, you're treating me like a complete and total child. And guess what? You're *not* Dad."

I took a deep, heaving breath, stared Fitz down. He held my gaze and didn't answer me right away, just extended his mug out to the side for the waitress to fill up. She ran in so fast it was a wonder she didn't spill coffee everywhere, filled up his cup, and backed the hell out of that situation.

Fitz and I had been best friends before he'd left me. It sounded weird, with our age difference, but it was the truth. We weren't exactly rolling in company growing up, isolated in our huge house up in Rochester, homeschooled through middle school by tutors until it was time to go to Pemberley. We knew Wickham, and had some casual acquaintance "friends" who were actually just the close-aged kids of my parents' business associates, but our closest friend was always each other, until it wasn't.

Fitz kept sipping at his coffee, kept watching me as I tried to catch my breath.

I had thought, when Wickham showed up in the hallway of my

dorm a year ago, when he texted me later, asking if I wanted to catch
up, when I had someone who responded to my texts when Fitz was
too busy with school and friends and building a better life without
me, that he might fill in the gap between where Fitz ended and I began. But all he did, in the end, was widen the crack, push us farther
apart, and then slither himself out, so that Fitz and I were left with a
huge gaping hole in ourselves with nothing to connect us.

I needed to make Fitz proud of me, somehow. If I ever wanted
Wickham to leave, I needed to wrench that look of disappointment from my brother's eyes and turn it into something else.

I still didn't regret what I'd said.

Finally, Fitz put down the coffee.

"I'm going to take you back to Pemberley now." He signaled
for the check, the first time he'd looked away from me since I'd
exploded. "I'm going to take you home, and then I'm going to go
back to Meryton, because I've got a study group at four. You can
call me after that's over, and we can try to have an actual conversation about this. If you don't want to, then just don't call me. Okay,
Georgie?" A flicker of emotion crept into his voice, quickly and
immediately snuffed out. "Just don't call me if all you're going to
do is fight with me."

I tried to tell myself that didn't hurt.

As Fitz paid the check, I followed him out to the car, kept my
head down, avoided the gaze of everyone in the diner. I wouldn't
cry, definitely not. I wouldn't give them—or Fitz—the satisfaction.

And as Fitz drove me back to campus in silence, I could almost hear our relationship cracking farther, farther, farther apart.
It splintered as it fell, a messy break, a vase dropped on the floor
where half the pieces ended up under the couch and you'd never
find them again, never be able to make things whole.

Fitz didn't even want to make things whole, I thought as I

watched the trees out the window. He just wanted to get through this, move past it. To get back to the life he'd built without me.

I had no doubt that Fitz loved me. He was my brother. He didn't have a choice.

But I was starting to think, as I watched him drive away after dropping me off in front of my dorm, my denim jacket pulled tightly across my chest to block out the bitter morning wind, that he didn't like me very much, not anymore.

ell

I was halfway back to my room for some good old *Sage Hall* despair-bingeing before I remembered Sydney.

Crap. It had been so much *easier* to sulk on my own last year, when I'd had a single. Before Fitz had declared in front of the headmaster and anyone else who could hear him that I'd "lost the privilege" of a single, like he was the arbiter of my entire life. Whenever the world got too loud around me, I could hide out in there, surrounded by *Sage Hall* posters and no one else.

But now . . . I had Sydney. Joy.

Wickham would make fun of Sydney, if he knew her. Mock her flags and her color-coordinated bows and the way she over-enunciated any word with a t in it.

He hadn't emailed again, which surprised me. It would have been on-brand for Wickham, constant taunts mixed with cold half-compliments. Maybe he was withholding on purpose, knew that I'd be on edge every time I checked my in-box. Not that I'd checked since I got back, and I didn't know if I was saving it as a reward or a punishment for myself. Even if there was an email from him in there, I wasn't about to respond just to make fun of Sydney. That wasn't what I did with him anymore. Obviously.

I unlocked my screen, stared down at the email icon. No new messages.

I worried, too, about whatever this new business of his was. Whatever he was doing here, besides trying to torture me. If it wasn't drugs—and I suspected it wasn't, because The Incident was a closer call than Wickham was comfortable with, and I was also pretty sure a new supplier had already popped up to take his place—it had to be something else. But what?

I guess it didn't matter, as long as I could get him to leave.

I dropped my phone back in my pocket, turned and headed back down the elevator. I didn't know where I was going, but I couldn't manage to interact with Sydney, to go into my room and see the pure judgment coming off of her and her friends in waves. I just needed to adjust and go . . . somewhere else. The library, maybe, even if the librarian was probably tired of seeing my face at this point. I'd catch up on my homework, try to understand what a factorial was and read as much Nathaniel Hawthorne as I could stomach. Avoid future lectures from Fitz, as if that were possible.

This stupid denim jacket I had on really wasn't warm enough. I pulled it tighter around me as I headed back into the school's main quad, like that could somehow stop the wind that went straight through it to my T-shirt underneath. The *Sage Hall* scarf around my neck helped, but not much.

In my pocket, I felt my phone vibrate.

I scrambled for it, because what if it was Fitz? What if he felt bad about how we left things, and he was speeding back to Pemberley to hug me or something? When I saw his name come up on my screen, I let out a sigh of relief I didn't know I had in me.

"Fitz?"

"Hey there." A female voice I only vaguely recognized twanged out over the phone, overly loud. I winced. Not Fitz, for sure. "Is this Georgie Darcy?"

"Yes? How'd you get this phone?"

"This is Jenn from Townshend's." Joy. "Your brother left his phone and wallet here. Your number was most recent, and I thought—"

"Thanks." I hung up the phone immediately, even though it was super rude, because this day was just getting better and better. Fitz was going to be so mad if he had to drive all the way down here again, and who would be blamed? Yours truly.

I wanted to scream, to throw my voice up into the air of the quad until all the trees trembled with it, but there were other students around and I didn't want to have to go to the school psychiatrist again.

Homework would have to wait. I could always call Jenn back, tell her to look up Charlie's number and call him instead, but the weight of being useless and a burden on the family bore down on me. A perfect Darcy didn't shy away from her family responsibilities, even when she felt like they were suffocating her.

I just needed to figure out a way to get to Meryton and luckily, I did know one person on campus who had a car and didn't hate my guts. Sure, this was maybe a bigger leap in our friendship than just extra band practice, but there was no harm in trying and also, I didn't have another choice.

I switched over to my contacts and, with a deep breath and a lot more courage than I thought I had in me, called Avery.

CHAPTER SEVEN

*A*very's car should have been condemned.

Not to judge or anything. Though I was clearly judging. It was just that I wasn't sure it was even road-safe, at this point. Did you legally *need* bumpers on a car? Or was that just a suggestion? Not having a car of my own, I didn't know, and from the way Avery looked at me when he pulled up in front of my dorm, only twenty minutes after I'd called him, he was aware of the situation. But I didn't want to test the tenuous waters of a newly rekindled friendship by asking.

It did, at least, have enough cup holders in the front seat. That was something.

After I gave him the extremely simple instructions on how to get to Townshend's—Lambton, the town outside of Pemberley, was so small it was basically nonexistent—I sat back in my seat to watch him drive.

"You're lucky you have a car." I ran my hands over the torn siding on the inside of my window, next to the crank to raise or lower it that Avery had instructed me not to touch. "You must take it out all the time."

"I mean, I do have to go to class and stuff." Avery's driving posture was basically the exact opposite of Fitz's. He sat twisted in his seat, left leg tucked under his right, only one hand on the wheel. It would have given Fitz a heart attack, even if Avery's gaze was alert. "But when I've got the gas money to spare, yeah. It's chill to see the world outside Pemberley."

"I wish I could get away." The road wound around in front of us, and Avery slowed as we hit the curves. "The beaches of Aruba sound pretty nice right around now."

"Well, that's not exactly where I've been going, but sure." He glanced over at me. "Do you want to talk about it? Whatever's going on with you. We don't have to," he added, fast. "But you can, if you want. Now that we're officially friends again. My sisters used to give me a nickel to let me psychologize them when we were kids."

"Do I need to adjust for inflation?" I could picture him as a kid, too, crowded by little girls—I had no idea how many sisters Avery had, but I invented three—just a shorter version of him now, but in a white coat. "Because I've only got a quarter on me."

"You pay it forward for the next one." Avery held his free hand out in my direction, and after some digging through my wallet, I pulled out a quarter and dropped it into his palm. "The doctor is in, etcetera."

"You're so weird." I leaned against the window; let my head rest against the streaked glass.

"Good weird?" He glanced over at me, fast, since we were still on the winding roads headed out into the mountains, and I nodded.

"Yeah." I sighed, still staring at the winding roads. You could get carsick on these roads, if you weren't careful, but I felt a lot less nauseated with Avery than I had with Fitz. "Good weird."

We got to Townshend's in just a couple of minutes, and I ran in and out as fast as possible, the better to avoid interactions with anyone there. Luckily, it was (mostly) painless, and soon we were headed out into the mountains proper, toward Meryton.

Where, it started to hit me, after about fifteen minutes of driving in companionable silence, I'd have to actually face my brother again.

"It must be nice." Avery, with his eyes on the road, clearly missed the panic in mine as we got closer to our destination. "Having your brother close by. My whole family is back in Ohio."

"I'm sure it's better to have them far away in Ohio and loving you than close by and hating you." Hot air blasted out of the vents unevenly, triggering nausea. Ah, there it was. "He isn't even supposed to be close by. He's supposed to be in California, getting as far away from me as possible."

"Why would he want to do that?" The corner of Avery's mouth twitched into a frown. "I thought you guys were like, super close. You hung out all the time your freshman year."

"Yeah, and then I went ahead and ruined everything." We passed vibrant red splashes of trees against the greens and browns, their colors starting to come in. "I fucked up and he got stuck here. Just like he's always been stuck with me." I sighed, closed my eyes briefly. "Hence, the plan. I need to become the ultimate Darcy."

"Ultimate Darcy sounds like a very specific Frisbee game."

"That's the first time 'Darcy' and 'Frisbee' have ever been uttered in the same sentence." I laughed, despite myself, like I kept finding myself doing around Avery. "Seriously, my family is . . . they're perfect. They always have been. I need to channel them to get the school to respect me again." I settled my head against the headrest—worn but comfortable—and kept watching the trees. It would be nice to drive up this way again in a month or so, once the leaves had changed entirely. If I hadn't scared Avery off by then, maybe I'd suggest it. "Pemberley has always respected the Darcys."

"Your brother doesn't sound so perfect if he completely bailed on you, and if you're too scared of him to have him drive back and get his phone himself." The corner of Avery's mouth turned down into a frown, just long enough for me to catch it as I glanced toward him.

"You can be a dick and still be respected." My chest squeezed. "Not that Fitz is like that. He's just . . . It's complicated. I messed up so bad, Aves, and I just—"

"Hey." Avery reached over with his right hand, placed it on my arm for a moment to stop my rambling in its tracks. Right. He was right. I managed a deep breath, and he smiled and placed his hand back on the steering wheel with care. "It's all good, George. You don't have to explain yourself to me."

"Fitz has just always managed the Darcy veneer better than anyone." Maybe I didn't have to explain, but I wanted to. "That's what I need, to get the school back on my side. To get Wickham out of here."

"A hard outer shell?" He sounded uncertain, but I nodded. "Exactly."

"And how does Fitz play into this?" He took a quick look over his shoulder, switched lanes to get around a slow-moving truck. "Are you going to make him give you Darcy lessons or something?"

"Please," I scoffed. "If he knew I was doing this, he'd vacillate between horror at how bad I was at trying to fulfill my family destiny and telling me that I just need to be 'true to myself,' or whatever other crap he pulled out of this week's parenting book."

"I'm guessing you don't find any merit in that idea."

"You saw me last year." A lump welled up in my throat, but I pushed it down. See? I had some Darcy in me, after all. "Do you really think I should ever try to be myself?"

Avery didn't reply. I gripped the armrest as we came around a curve in the road, the cliffside dropping way, way down below. We'd lost cell phone service completely at this point, which always happened as soon as you hit the mountains, so I couldn't even pretend to distract myself with scrolling.

"I just need this to be done with." I pressed my fingers against my temple, feeling a headache coming on already at the idea of seeing Fitz again. "And then we can get back to Pemberley, and we can practice the show music or something."

His expression softened.

"Okay." He nodded as he straightened the car out at the end of the curve, and I let out my breath. "I don't—I'm not going to pretend I understand your family situation. Or your family at all, to be honest. But I know that in like, an hour, we'll be done. Over. And then we can concentrate on your plans for Pemberley domination. You think you can make it through an hour?"

I considered, then nodded. "I think so."

"I think you can, too." And Avery looked over at me, just for a second again, and grinned before he turned back to the road.

cll

"We're looking for the Lucas Library," I instructed Avery. We'd found the visitor parking lot at SUNY Meryton without too much trouble—it was a super-small school, smaller even than Pemberley. Fitz had told me it was mostly a commuter campus, which was why he and Charlie had an apartment just outside of town. Luckily, thanks to the shared Google Calendar, I knew where Fitz's study group was, so we didn't have to spend hours searching every building on campus for him.

"There." Avery nodded ahead, to a library that looked a lot less impressive than the ones in pictures of Caltech I'd seen, back when Fitz was applying. My heart sank again. Look, nothing against Meryton, but my brother had been at one of the best engineering schools in the country. It didn't feel great to look at where he had ended up and know that he had only transferred because he didn't trust me on the East Coast by myself. "I guess we just wait outside?"

"Yeah, they probably don't let you in without a school ID." I wrapped my scarf tighter around my throat, tucked the ends into my jacket.

"That's a cool scarf." Avery leaned on the wall of the building next to us, one foot up behind him as we settled in to wait. I smiled.

"Thanks." My hands went up to it instinctively, following the diamond pattern with my fingers. "It's from this show I'm into."

"*Sage Hall*?"

"Yes!" Something stirred in my chest, a jumpy feeling. "How'd you know?"

"From you?" He cocked his head to the side. "You talked about it constantly on the bus last year. And the year before that. Damn. You really repressed our entire friendship, didn't you?"

"I'm impressed that you didn't." A few students wandered past, but they didn't take a second glance at us, didn't seem to realize we clearly didn't belong. "Honestly, I don't know anyone who thinks my *Sage Hall* ramblings are worth remembering."

"Why?" He pushed his hands into his pockets, rocked back and forth on his heels. "You care about it."

I wanted to point out how little literally anyone thought what I cared about was interesting, when Fitz pushed through the double doors at the front of the library, and I was pretty sure my heart stopped entirely.

"There." I just barely got the word out. I should have waved, or called to him, or something, but I couldn't manage it. "There he is." Avery waited for my lead, but I just watched my brother.

He wasn't alone. Bursting out the doors with him, locked in intense conversation, was a shorter white girl with auburn hair who talked with her hands. A girl with similarly colored hair walked with another tall guy behind them. I recognized the guy, actually. Charlie. So the girl he was with, that had to be Jane, right? The one he'd met at the party last weekend and gone full-on obsessive with. Which meant that the girl Fitz was currently arguing with . . .

Lizzie Bennet.

It wasn't Lizzie herself that stopped me in my tracks, though. It was the way Fitz looked, the way he stood, the way he held himself.

I was so used to seeing Fitz perpetually worn out, always anticipating some sort of blow, braced for what was to come. He'd internalized, since Dad died, since Mom left. Took everything that had been on the outside and hidden it way down deep, where it couldn't get hurt.

That wasn't how he looked here. Instead of closing off, he'd opened, used his hands almost as much as Lizzie did, occasionally pointing back to Charlie, who stepped back, hands up in defeat as he laughed. Even though Fitz was frowning, clearly fighting with this girl, his eyes were lit up like I hadn't seen them in . . . forever.

They were close enough that we could just overhear them, with their voices raised.

"That's an absolutely ridiculous argument." Fitz's voice even sounded lighter as I pressed myself back against the wall, like that would somehow keep my brother from seeing me across an open courtyard. Luckily, there was no way he'd look away from Lizzie.

"Just because it isn't your experience doesn't make it ridiculous."

"I'm not . . . It's a problem set, Lizzie." Fitz's voice cracked, revealing his frustration, but not Georgie-frustration. It was different. I didn't know how to describe it, exactly, but it was different. I knew what my brother sounded like when he didn't like a person, because I'd heard it directed at me just this morning, and this wasn't it. "It doesn't matter what your experience with it is. There's one right answer."

"Even if that *is* true, you don't have to be a dick about it."

"I wasn't aware that following the principles of mathematics to the letter made me a 'dick.'"

"Why don't you just go ahead and apply some of your super-sound mathematic principles on the test Friday?" Lizzie challenged, as she turned and poked Fitz in the chest. He stepped back, more from the emotional shock, I had to imagine, than the actual force of a single finger. "And then we'll see who's right."

"We're—we're going to," Fitz replied, and she stalked off with Jane right behind her, an apologetic look in the boys' direction as Fitz started after her again. Charlie stepped in front of him, speaking in a voice too low for us to hear. After a second, Fitz nodded, though he never took his eyes off Lizzie's back, before he turned and followed Charlie back toward the library. As he did, I caught a glimpse of his face. He was smiling.

Whoa.

Unfortunately, that smile quickly fell off his face when he saw me across the courtyard.

It was night and day, the way my brother had looked a second ago and the way he looked now, as he sent Charlie inside and then took off at a jog toward me, irritation written all over his features. As he approached, Avery had the sense to step back.

"What are you doing here?" Fitz crossed his arms over his chest, the collar of his peacoat turned up like some sort of Regency viscount's. "I told you I had a study group. You can't just— and how did you even get here?"

"You left your phone at the restaurant." I held both the phone and his wallet out toward him, declining to drag Avery into our conversation. "I brought it back. I thought it would be helpful."

"You shouldn't be leaving campus without my permission." It was like he'd aged ten years from when he was talking to Lizzie. Even though he'd argued with her, too, he'd seemed younger, closer to his actual age of twenty than the way he was acting now, like some middle-aged miser who only existed to make my life harder.

Is that what I did to him? Did I make him like this?

He'd been having—well, not a good time, maybe. I didn't know how much enjoyment Fitz got out of arguing with Lizzie. But it had been, without a doubt, the most chemistry I'd ever seen two people exhibit.

And one of them was my *brother*. Which was kind of gross. But still. Maybe my brother did have a chance at happiness.

The only thing standing in his way? Me.

"Are you listening, Georgie?" Fitz ran his fingers through his hair, making it stand straight up. "You need to go back to school. How am I supposed to trust you when you do things like this?"

I bristled, suddenly snapped back to attention. I had just been trying to help. All I was ever trying to do lately was help. To be better. To figure out the secret to being a put-together person and just *do it*.

Part of me wanted to explain my whole plan to Fitz right there. That it was impossible to predict what would disappoint him because it seemed like everything did. Tell him that all I was trying to do was be a worthwhile member of the family, and that it wasn't my fault if our family standards were impossibly high. That I'd figure it out, I'd make this all work, I would get better if he just gave me time. But what did that prove? That if I groveled in front of Fitz, if I showed that really, I was a good kid—I was doing my best! I was going to be just fine!—*then* he should trust me?

He was my brother. The only family I had.

I shouldn't have needed to earn his trust and frankly, I wasn't sure I could again.

So I needed to pivot my plan, didn't I? To get Wickham out, I needed Fitz to be proud of me. But he'd never be proud of me like this, watching over my shoulder, waiting for me to make a mistake. If he was distracted, and if he was happy, somehow, maybe I could pull this off. *Then* he might be willing to admit I was a worthwhile member of the family. When he was too preoccupied to look closely.

I'd discovered the best way to kill two birds with one stone. There was something—*someone*—here who not only might bring Fitz some happiness, but would serve as an amazing distraction. The best way to get Fitz away from my life was to make sure he had one of his own.

And so my plan had suddenly become a two-parter. Part one, turn myself into an accomplished Darcy worthy of the family name. But part two?

I could help Fitz Darcy be happy, for once in his goddamn life.

"You're right." The words were so unusual from my mouth that Fitz blinked, stepped back in surprise. "I'll leave."

"You'll—good." Fitz collected himself quickly, as he always did. That hard Darcy shell. "You'll text me when you get back." I nodded, and without another word he'd turned and stalked back toward the library, where he'd undoubtedly stew over what a terrible sister he had.

That was fine. He wouldn't be stewing for long.

"You okay?" Avery broke through my reverie, and I jumped. I'd almost forgotten he was there, in all of that. "That was harsh."

"Don't worry about it." My mind raced. "I've got a plan." I took off at a jog back toward the main office we'd parked by, both due to my excitement and to get some blood flowing to my legs. Avery followed just behind.

"Okay?" I didn't blame his confusion. But I needed to get the idea together in my head before I said it out loud, or I'd lose it halfway through. "Another one?"

"More like an addendum to my first one." This could work. It *would* work. It had to, right? The chemistry Fitz and Lizzie had was undeniable. All they needed was . . . a little push. "Because did you see him back there? He looked happy. And then the second I showed up, I ruined it."

"George."

"No, it's okay." I shook my head, fast. "I get it. I broke everything for him, right? It makes sense, in his weird overprotective pseudo-parent way, that he won't leave me alone. But I'll never be able to get better at school and stuff with him breathing down my neck. And that girl, that Lizzie, she makes him happy. He thinks he hates her, but he obviously doesn't."

"What are you talking about?"

"I'm going to get them together." The autumn sun was warm against my face, and I had a purpose, something that could actually be a good thing for my brother instead of ruining him even further. "I'm going to get them together, and then Fitz is going to be happy."

And yeah, he was going to be happy without me, but the way things were looking, happy with me was no longer an option.

This would do just fine.

very seemed slightly less sold on the entire thing.

"Do you have an actual plan for this?" He caught up to me as I marched toward the car. Oak trees framed our path, acorns scattered underneath us. "Can you even matchmake remotely?"

"Patience, young Padawan. I'll figure something out. It sounded like they're in math together, don't you think?" I felt charged, frantic, and that was excellent, because the more I threw myself into this idea, the less I'd think about how I was personally responsible for everything bad in my brother's life.

"Um." Avery looked confused. Reasonable, I supposed. "Sure?"

"So, we start there, and we work backward." I pulled my phone out of my pocket as Avery unlocked first his side of the car, then mine. I climbed in as I scrolled through my calendar. "That's what this study group was for. See, differential equations. Which sounds like math for sure."

"I don't think I should look at your screen while I'm driving." Avery backed out of his parking spot carefully, making sure there was zero chance we'd scrape any of the surrounding cars. "We're headed back to Pemberley, I guess?"

"What? Oh, yeah." I opened my internet browser and entered the site where Fitz's email was hosted, luckily getting the password right on the first go. (My birthday, which I'd guessed over the summer and he hadn't changed since. Predictable Fitz.) "They're in a class together, and I've definitely heard Fitz mention that they have breakout groups for it. He complained about it like, three days ago."

"Okay?"

"So, I don't see why those group assignments can't be gently changed for our purposes." I searched his in-box for a list of assignments, though as the emails were loading, guilt tickled the back of my brain. I turned to Avery, paused carefully at a stoplight, who looked back at me with wide eyes. "I'm not being . . . this isn't completely absurd, is it?"

"You need to give me like, thirty percent more information for me to make that analysis."

"These groups change all the time." There was the list, emailed from a guy named Collins who seemed to be the class TA. "If I— aka Fitz—request a switch into Lizzie's discussion group, they'll be forced to spend way more time together."

"Which will . . ."

"Make them fall in love, of course!" I rolled my eyes. Avery clearly hadn't spent an entire summer locked inside his family home watching period dramas. His loss. (About the TV stuff, anyway. In every other respect it was obviously his gain.) "They were literally *crackling* with chemistry back there, Aves. Anyone could see it."

"It looked like they hated each other."

"That's how all the best love stories start," I said dismissively, opening a reply to the email. There was no reason for me to feel guilty. Fitz needed this. I needed this.

"I don't know, George." When I looked up at Avery, finally, he looked way more uncomfortable than I expected. So uncomfortable that I actually put the phone down and shifted in my seat so I could face him better. Shit. Maybe I *was* being an idiot. "There was a lot of . . . yelling. You don't think it would be better to find your brother someone he was friends with, if you wanted to pair him off with someone?"

I shook my head.

"Fitz doesn't *have* friends," I explained. It was, admittedly, kind of a Darcy trait, but I didn't want to make the conversation about me again so I moved past it. "And he doesn't argue with people like that, either. He generally just kind of exists to baby me. People either have to force their way in—that's his roommate, Charlie, the other guy who was with him—or they have to fight." I half-smiled. "Lizzie looked like she knows how to fight."

Avery considered for a moment. "So you get them in a group together and . . . what? They yell at each other until they kiss?"

"I'm hoping there will be more nuance than that," I managed, with more dignity than my bare scrap of a plan allowed. Rome wasn't built in a day. "But that's the underlying principle. It's a start, Aves. We'll add more things as we go."

"We?"

Shoot, I hadn't meant to say that. "If you want. I don't want you to get involved in anything you don't want to. I can handle this on my own." I could handle anything on my own, I reminded myself sternly. That was what being a Darcy was about. Being alone and being strong enough to take it.

I hoped he'd say yes.

He watched the road as we merged back onto the highway, leaving Meryton and heading back toward Pemberley. The little traffic we'd hit in town cleared out, and it was just me and Avery and the open road, driving toward . . . something.

He grinned, brighter than the sun that scattered over my shoulders, and I loosened my grip on the armrest.

"Are we doing anything illegal?" he asked.

"Not in New York State, at least."

"Then what the hell. You're emailing the TA?"

I nodded, too relieved to speak, and typed out an email as fast as I could as we approached a cell phone service dead zone, trying out my best Fitz affectation.

> *Dear Collins,*
>
> *I know it's late notice, but if it is possible, I would appreciate if I could be switched into Breakout Group 4. I'd rather not go into my reasoning, as it is extremely private. Please respond posthaste and post hence.*
>
> *Yours, most sincerely,*
> *Fitzwilliam Darcy*

"Does your brother really talk like that?" Avery asked after I read it out loud to him.

"I mean, it's close enough." I hit send before I could overthink it. There. I'd done it. I'd taken a step toward making a positive difference in the world, toward making Fitz look happy again for the first time in months. Toward making up for what I'd done. "Once, when I was little, I asked him if he'd wandered out of *The Muppet Christmas Carol* by accident."

"Did he?"

"Jury's still out." My head buzzed with anticipation. "We're going to crush this, Aves. Fitz is going to be happy, which is going to give me the room I need to turn everything around at school. And then he'll see how well I managed on my own and probably declare on the spot that I'm the perfect example of the Darcy legacy." *And I'll record him saying it, and then Wickham will leave*, I thought, but didn't add it out loud, because Avery looked happy and I wasn't going to ruin that by bringing up Wickham.

Avery shook his head. "Is this a Darcy thing? Intense, immediate dedication to a cause? Or is this a you-specific trait?"

"Both." I nodded forward. "Eyes on the road, mister. We've got a lot of work to do."

"Aye aye, Captain." Avery managed a salute before he replaced both hands on the wheel, and I pulled out my phone, jotting down notes.

This was a three-pronged plan. A trident. Reclaim my spot in the social scene at Pemberley, all while forcing my brother into admitting he was in love and getting off my back to be happy, for once, which would put me in a position to succeed at Pemberley unencumbered by his ever-watchful eye. I'd thrive, Fitz would admit it, and as a result, I'd send Wickham packing. (Maybe the recording-him-saying-it part wasn't such a bad idea. I could always livestream it.) Sure, each element of the plan added its own charming complications, but I'd basically trained for this my whole life. I could figure it out.

It was the sort of thing my mom had occasionally tried to show me, before she decided I was too much of an odd duck to bother teaching formal social etiquette. But back in my younger years, when she thought I might just grow up to be the debutante I was destined to be, she'd always stressed the importance of multitasking. *Anyone of above-average intelligence has the capability to focus*

on two things at once, Georgiana. She always called me Georgiana, the only person who did. My dad and Fitz always called me
Georgie, and now Fitz had picked up Beanpole.

Avery was the only one to call me George.

But she would elongate all the syllables, like my name had
weight. *Georgiaaaaaana.* She'd tell me this as she was directing
Fitz's tutors with one hand and writing out a list of meals for the
cook with the other. *Are you of above-average intelligence, do you
think?*

I was pretty sure I'd just shrugged, my head deep in my book,
and she'd sighed. Even though I hadn't seen my mother in years,
her sigh was still imprinted on my mind, a permanent sign of
her displeasure. It mixed with Wickham's smirk, with Fitz's disappointed looks.

But they'd see. They'd all see.

Fitz's in-box pinged, and I almost dropped the phone when I
saw that a reply had already come through.

Fitz—
Sure.
—C

"Yes!" I punched my fist in the air, almost dropping the phone
in the process. "Oh my God. It's working. It's actually working."
I danced in my seat as Avery watched me, his ever-present smile
playing across his face. "Can you believe it?"

"From you, George?" His smile only widened, and mine did,
too. "Yeah. I can." He raised his hand up for a high five and I met
it in the air.

"We're going to be the *best* matchmakers." I'd have to wait
till we got better service again to start my frantic googling, but I

could brainstorm in the meantime. Honestly, this was way more interesting than trying to pass chemistry. "I'm thinking dancing telegrams, chocolates, tricking them into sharing a plate of spaghetti while an accordion player sings in the background à la *Lady and the Tramp* . . ."

"You," Avery said as he laughed, and I continued to dance, "are so weird."

"Good weird?" I asked, as I added in more elbow-work and a head bob. (Though I made sure to delete the emails first, so Fitz wouldn't see them. He'd just get the new group assignment and figure it was because of non-meddling-sister reasons.)

"Yeah." He looked back toward the road, but I could still see he was smiling. "Good weird."

CHAPTER NINE

The Friday of our first football game, less than a week after Avery and I had driven up to Meryton, I woke up at four a.m. in a cold sweat. I didn't have the strongest memory of the dream I'd had, but I knew it involved getting stabbed in the heart by a twirling flag decorated in our school colors. What a metaphor. I stayed in bed for another two hours before Sydney's alarm went off, my eyes on the shiny color guard uniform she'd laid out over her desk chair. It was 100 percent taunting me, and even the three separate *Sage Hall* one-shots I meandered through on my phone couldn't distract me from it, especially since JocAndrew seemed to be everywhere in fic these days and I could do without Wickham-like characters taunting me through my screen. In the end, I just spent an hour cleaning out my email, deleting messages from my mom I wasn't going to read. Still nothing from Wickham. If this was a ruse designed to get me to think about him obsessively, it was working.

"Do you need the sink?" Those were the first words Sydney had managed toward me all week, and they came just after her alarm when she sat up, turned on the light, and noticed my vacant stare. "Can I go?"

"Sure." Our room had a little sink room just off of it, with a mirror and a medicine cabinet and stuff. She nodded before averting her gaze back down to the floor.

As I brushed my teeth after Sydney and changed into jeans and a violet marching band T-shirt (we didn't have to wear our uniforms on game days, because yay school spirit or whatever), I tried to summon up an ounce of the excitement I'd felt for games the last couple of years. Pemberley got way into football, with huge cheering sections even for away games like today. The energy in the air was incredible, and before, I'd eaten it up, reveled in being part of it. It was the one part of school pride I liked.

This time, I knew *all* eyes were going to be on me, and not for good reasons.

But, I reminded myself, I had my plan. Not only had I spent the entire week practicing my trombone, memorizing all of the music I should have learned over the summer, and running marching drills with Avery on the football field, I had a little something extra up my sleeve, something I hadn't even told Avery about. I wanted to surprise him.

I pulled my curls into a messy topknot and added a tortoise-shell clip while next to me, Sydney secured hers with a big purple-and-white bow. She'd gone full adorable-chic in honor of the first game, with an oversized shirt knotted at the waist over leggings and knee-high boots. I should consider myself lucky, I guess, that our room wasn't filled with half a dozen girls who also hated me, all applying face paint to each other.

I tried to maintain a sense of some optimism for the rest of the day, passing through classes I was desperately trying not to fall behind in and ignoring the whispers of students in the hall that I'd heard a million times before. Somehow, even after almost two weeks back in classes, I hadn't grown used to it.

"George!" I turned to see Avery bound up behind me in the golden retriever way that only he could, as I waited outside the band room at the end of the day. We had a quick changing period scheduled before we loaded onto the bus to head to the game, and I'd gotten in the habit of waiting outside the door until the last possible second to avoid the stares inside.

His grin lit up his whole face as he leaned against the wall, arms crossed over his chest. He had on the same Pemberley Academy Marching Stallions T-shirt as me, though it fit him way better, his arms and shoulders more toned than last year now that he spent most of his time waving his arms at us across a field. "You pumped?"

"Yeah." My voice cracked, which took away from my attempts at sincerity. "Let's go, Stallions!"

"Wow." Avery's expression was deadpan as he nodded, his feet tapping against the tile floor. "That was amazing. I don't want to lose your talents in band, but you should really consider going out for the cheer squad."

"Don't tell the other trombones." I tried to laugh. "They'll fill out the application for me just to get me out of their section." I'd meant for that to come across as self-deprecating in like, a fun way, but even I heard how sad it sounded. Avery didn't manage to hide his wince from me. "Sorry."

"It's all good." He shrugged, though he dropped eye contact, staring down at my soft brown boots. Mom had sent them to me from Italy a few years ago. The quality was high enough that, with any luck, they'd last me forever and I'd never have to take a gift from her again. "You're going to kill it out there, though. The amount we've been practicing? It's been like, ten band camps combined. I'll have to keep an eye on the trombones during the show."

"Yeah?" I crossed my arms over my chest. "Why's that?"

"Because I need the best section in the band to inspire me, obviously." He grinned again, and I had to remind myself that he grinned like that at everybody. "Besides. I'm going to be freaking out up there."

"Yeah, okay," I scoffed, but I felt better. It was weird, how he kept doing that. "You're going to be amazing. You're way better than Daniel."

"That's because Daniel was constantly baked."

"That *did* get in the way of his conducting." It had taken me a few months of my sophomore year to realize why our drum major at the time had always been half a beat behind, with an unfocused look in his eyes. At least I knew his particular brand of drugs hadn't been dealt out of my room. Probably. "Either way. You're almost guaranteed to be better than him."

"Almost?"

"You want me to jinx you? No way." I shook my head, tucked a stray piece of hair behind my ear. This felt almost normal, this back and forth with Avery. Almost like I wasn't about to walk into a roomful of enemies.

Though maybe my surprise inside would help.

"Fair." Avery shifted, his back against the wall, foot propped up against it, hands shoved deep into the pockets of his jeans. "Hey, I meant to tell you. I had a matchmaking idea. For your brother."

"Spill."

"Could you send an anonymous note to Lizzie or something?" He spoke fast, like he would chicken out of the sentence if he didn't say it quickly enough. "Not a full-on love note. But some sort of secret admirer thing."

"Ohh. That's good." My mind whirled as I pulled out my phone, grateful for both the idea and the distraction from all of my band-terrors. "But what if we bump it up to the next level? There's got to be a flower delivery service in—yep, boom." Thank goodness for Google. I showed my phone screen to Avery, where I'd pulled up the site of a florist in Meryton. "We can set up weekly deliveries from this place and not even worry about it. Tell them to sign them all from an anonymous admirer."

"That, um, are you sure?" For some reason, Avery didn't seem pumped about this idea, which was ridiculous, because it had been his in the first place and all I'd done was make it even more epic. I shuffled my feet beneath me. "It seems kind of expensive."

"Don't worry about that." I waved my hand. Fitz never bothered checking my credit card statements. "I'd rather pay the money than have to remember to do it every week."

"Positive?" Okay, Avery was definitely uncomfortable. Shit. What did I do? Why couldn't I get through a single interaction with a human without ruining it?

"I was." Shit again. I dropped my gaze down toward the floor. "If you don't think it's a good idea . . ."

"No! Sorry." Avery shook his head just as I looked up, and he transformed in an instant from weirded-out Avery to the regular, smiling version. "It'll be fine. It's a good idea."

"I don't know."

"George." He rolled his eyes. "Don't be weird because I was weird."

"Isn't our whole thing that we're both super weird?"

"The weirdest." He pulled out his own phone and glanced at the time. "We should go inside. But get the flowers, okay?"

"Okay." Before I could lose my nerve again, I entered my credit card number—Fitz made me memorize it years ago, in case of emergency—and submitted the order, to be delivered to the classroom Lizzie and Fitz shared.

That taken care of, I looked back up at Avery, tried to settle into my feelings.

"After you." He reached over my head to push the door open, giving me a closer glimpse of his arms, which I immediately ignored again because friends didn't look at their friend's arms. Avery had proven once again that he was my friend. My only one, maybe. I wasn't about to mess that up.

Besides, he was about to be blown away by what I had inside.

I stepped into the band room before him, then shifted to the left so he could come in after me. Just as I'd hoped, his jaw dropped basically to the floor when he saw what I'd done.

The back wall had been set up with three long buffet tables, each with a tablecloth in our school colors dangling over its edges. Chafing dishes crowded the top of the table, each still covered, but the smells of spicy meats permeated the room. I'd gone for a Mexican theme, because it was the one type of food our dining hall could never manage to pull off, and our family had a catering company on retainer that really killed it in the enchilada category. A couple dozen of my classmates stood around the tables, staring curiously at a team of caterers, the closest of whom nodded when he saw me.

"Miss Darcy." His voice was sharp, polished, and I beamed back at him, glad to finally be doing something *right*. "Shall we open the line?"

"Go ahead." I nodded, and the caterers stepped forward as one, pulling the lids off the chafing dishes to reveal a mouthwatering spread of dishes. Next to me, I heard Avery gulp. No one else moved, which was weird, because I'd seen the way a hungry band room could descend on food before. This was decidedly out of character.

Then the trumpet section leader stepped out of the crowd toward me, a senior named Alex whose transition lenses never quite got the lighting right, and who had, I remembered with a sinking heart, a particular fondness for Wickham.

"You did this?" His voice was sharp, and even though we were far enough removed from the rest of the band that not everyone could hear us, I could see the kids closest to us straining to listen, the whispers already passing down the chairs.

"Yes?" This wasn't how I'd wanted this to go. This was supposed to be something fun. Bonding! Snacks! But from the way everyone looked at me, from the way *Avery* looked at me, I'd made a fatal error in my calculations. "Was there like, a vote that I missed this summer or something? Do we all hate Mexican now?" I tried to make it sound like a joke, but I wasn't entirely kidding. With the way this was going downhill fast, it felt like exactly the sort of thing the band would have decided just to spite me. "It's just food."

Except it wasn't, was it?

"No one should eat that much right before we play." Alex turned away from me, headed back toward his section to unzip his uniform bag. "And it's blocking the tuba lockers."

I watched with rising dread as a freshman clarinet walked up to grab a plate that had been laid out next to the food, but one of her upperclassmen stopped her, and no one else tried after that. And I just stood there, frozen in the doorway, unable to fix what I'd done, doing my best not to cry.

"People need time to get ready." Avery's voice was distant, and even as I glanced over at him, he didn't look at me. Great. That meant this was more than just the band already hating me. "We don't have that long before the bus leaves." Somehow, I'd managed to fuck up in a new, fun, Georgie Darcy trademarked way.

It figured.

This was why I didn't try anymore, not really. Because no matter what I did, no matter what I attempted, I never quite managed to pick up on the social cues that made Pemberley run smoothly, that made a family run smoothly, that made a relationship run smoothly. I didn't know that having a crush on someone because you thought they might actually like you back meant they were a shady asshole who wanted to rope you into some scheme, that it only took one mistake to cost you your best friend, and that the Pemberley Academy Marching Stallions didn't forgive easily.

People used parties and feasts all the time to solve problems in *Sage Hall.* Not for the first time, I wished I could escape back into my favorite show. But if I ran out now, I'd only ruin things further.

Beside me, Avery put his hand on my shoulder, patted it like some sort of absentminded uncle, and that only made me feel worse.

"Right." I gave a weak thumbs-up to Avery. "Get ready. Of course." He smiled half-heartedly before he cut away from me, into the crowd.

Get ready for even further humiliation, more like. Tonight couldn't possibly get worse.

cll

"Has anyone seen my pants?" I called out, fruitlessly, over the cacophony of an entire marching band trying to change in the same room at the same time. My only answer was getting shoved by a percussionist as she tried to pass through with her quads, even though she had about a million feet of space on her other side. I resisted the urge to shove her back, into the wall of still-untouched Mexican food.

"Nice one, Scrooge McDuck," she muttered. What was that even supposed to *mean*?

A couple of minutes later, I found my coveralls hanging on the back door of one of the practice rooms, the snaps very carefully ripped off. That felt like a place I definitely wouldn't have misplaced them, especially considering how no one in my section would make eye contact with me when I made it back to my chair, but it wasn't like I could go around accusing the collective trombones of theft and vandalism. Even Emily, who I'd hoped would be less aggressively unkind than the rest, only stared at her shiny black shoes. I grabbed a couple of safety pins from Mrs. T's desk, my head still down, my gaze still down, everything about me still down.

And that was just the tip of the iceberg. Once I'd finally gotten dressed—coveralls zipped up to my bra-line, huge feathered helmet in its case under my arm, purple-and-white jacket over my shoulder, trombone case in my hand—and headed out to the bus, I realized that there was no way I was going to have a desirable seat partner. Avery had been cornered by one of the tuba freshmen who had a million questions about what it was like to be the drum major, and when she'd sat down next to him, he'd given me an apologetic look that forced me to keep on walking down the aisle.

"Don't have a limo to take you to the game tonight, hot stuff?" Braden called out as I walked past him, and the guys sitting in the rows around him snickered. If I hadn't been so utterly humiliated by the catering thing, I could have attempted a comeback about the limo I saw taking his parents to divorce court, but I wasn't going to earn points by being mean. Not that I was going to earn points by doing anything.

Whatever.

I found an empty seat in the back, threw my jacket on the space beside me to make it look like I *wanted* to be completely and totally alone when everyone else was sitting with their super-special band friends.

Yeah. It was swell.

Eventually, we made it the hour-long drive to the site of to-night's game, Oakham Mount, and I guessed I had to take it as a victory that no one had tried to put gum in my hair. Still, Braden's speech as we filed into the cool metal stands on the visitors' side of the field made me want to rip my own ears off so I never had to hear him talk again.

"We have to kill it tonight, people." Braden held his trom-bone in the air like the world's longest gavel, one he undoubt-edly wanted to pound down on all of our heads. He had a scarf wrapped all the way up to his chin and tucked under his jacket in a way that undermined the inspirational-sports-movie-coach vibe he was clearly going for. "This is it! This is our shot!"

"What is it our shot for, exactly?" Emily adjusted her glasses as she slid in next to me on the bench. Even though she avoided eye contact, I was at least moderately grateful that she didn't flinch when our thighs touched, which was literally something one of the freshmen had done earlier today.

"Glory!"

"Yeah, but this is an away game. And Oakham sucks." She looked at Jackson for support, and he nodded. "I don't think we need to like, rouse the troops." I felt my fifteenth twinge of regret of the night as Emily spoke. Besides Avery, Emily had been the closest thing I'd had to a friend my first few years here. The only girls our year in the trombone section, we'd stuck together, sat beside each other in the stands, her seat always right behind mine and Avery's on the bus so the three of us could chat.

At least until news of The Incident came out and Emily, who wanted to go to Brown, had apparently decided that associating with me was too much of a risk for her college acceptance chances, a decision made obvious in the way she'd been avoiding my gaze ever since school had started back up.

Emily would respect what I was trying to do, though. She'd see that I was trying, see it when my grades rose and I killed it on the field. She may not have eaten any of my catering, but that wasn't the only trick I had.

"Can I go to the bathroom?" one of the freshmen, whose name was either Corey or Rory, asked, his voice small and hesitant. Braden rolled his eyes and nodded, stepping back as the kid snuck out of the row.

That was our section, at least the core of it. We'd lost Avery to drum major, and two of our sophomores, who were both named Eric and were deeply in love, had decided to play doubles tennis this year instead of band. We were small, but as Braden had reminded us in an email at midnight the night before, we were mighty. We were, he had written with no sense of irony, a *family*.

He actually didn't send *me* the email. Avery had forwarded it.

Emily kept her gaze straight ahead. Well, fine, I didn't have to look at her, either. Maybe if I kept my eyes on the Astroturf, I could let it blur until it became the wooden floor of a ballroom, disappear right into an episode of *Sage Hall* for comfort.

I remembered the first time I'd come to watch one of these games with Fitz, his freshman year. I was only in the sixth grade, at that age where high school kids looked like gods, full-blown adults who had it together way more than I could ever imagine. Fitz had bought me a Pemberley scarf and hat, and Mom and Dad drove me up to spend time together "as a family." We ate bad popcorn and Fitz let me stand next to the band, where I stared at this sick trombone girl the whole time with unabashed awe. I'd just picked up the instrument the year before and was still epically bad at it, but she did things with a slide I'd never even seen.

In retrospect it was probably like, the fight song, but it seemed amazing to me. Fitz had gotten me a bunch of the band's trombone music that year for my birthday, and I'd spent hours practicing, pretending I was the girl with the feathered hat that reached straight up for the starry sky, lit by the bright lights of the field as she stepped high.

But those feathered hats were five years older now and so was I, and I felt just as droopy as they had started to look.

From behind I felt something hit against my helmet, hard enough to make me wince. Great. The game hadn't even begun and we were already throwing things? I turned around carefully, only to see the trumpets two rows behind me, glowering.

"Hope you're having so much fun," a senior girl muttered, tossing a piece of wrapped hard candy up and down in her hand. I turned back around quickly, vowing to keep my helmet on for the rest of the night. I'd heard Wickham's absence from the trumpets every time we rehearsed. Apparently, I wasn't the only one.

I paid semi-attention to the game as the first quarter started, even managed to cheer as we ran the ball down the field for four touchdowns in a row—seriously, Oakham did suck—and jumped to my feet to play our victory song with everyone else. God, though, it felt gross and empty, just going through the motions, and as I pressed my mouthpiece against my lips, memories flashed of other stadiums.

The first game Wickham had been at last year, when he rolled his eyes every time the rest of the band cheered but absolutely killed it whenever we played the fight song, his tone clear and pure above the rest as he jumped octaves with ease. The way he'd brushed off my compliments afterward, said that it didn't matter, and the more he said it, the less it mattered to me, too.

The practices he'd convinced me to skip with him, when he'd wrap his arm around my shoulders and walk me to the edge of the field when we got a ten-minute break in practice, like he'd wanted to show me something, and then he'd just keep walking until we were in our own little world again. He'd even met me for lunch in the stands back at Pemberley once or twice, near the end. When I was too wrapped up in him to want to be around anyone else, we'd gone there. Because he'd convinced me that he mattered more than band ever did.

And even though these were different stands, and even though I was one of a thousand people here instead of one of two, that old, hollow feeling still had a hold over me, the one I'd had at the edges of Wickham. That we were just playing at something. That I was just playing at something.

Back then, I'd pretended to be someone desirable, someone wanted. Now, I had to pretend it didn't matter that I wasn't.

Avery caught my eye as we lowered our horns, the latest iteration of our fight song complete, and I tried my best to remember why I'd wanted to come back here. Why I'd spent this whole week trying so hard, enthusiastic as anything, when this place had only ever burned me. The smell of popcorn wafted through my memories, twisted them up into a messy tangle.

I needed to, I reminded myself. This was the only thing I'd ever been halfway decent at, and if I wanted to earn the respect of the band, to stay on my path toward undeniable accomplishment, I needed to prove I was worth keeping around. This was how I was going to get *rid* of Wickham. Once he was gone . . . there was no rule I had to do this next year. I just had to get through it. And I could. I had to.

As we neared the end of the second quarter, I tuned out Braden's latest pump-up speech. It wasn't like I needed it. Since Braden had stuck me in the middle of the section, muttering about how I couldn't be trusted to be in a point where I moved independently of anyone else, I barely needed to pay attention to the memorized drill—I could just follow the line, and no one would be the wiser. Avery and I had run the routine in full three or four times the last few days, laughing in the darkness of the football field, which felt far away now.

"Let's go, everyone!" Mrs. Tapper called into the stands, and as we filed out and down onto the field, most of the band chattered with excitement. We didn't normally do a halftime show for an away game, but Oakham was too small to have a band, so we were happy to step in. What could go wrong?

Hello hubris, my old friend.

The beat of the drumline resonated in my chest as we marched onto the field, knees lifted high and our gazes straight ahead. I resisted the urge to look back toward the stands. Last year, my brother had flown out for my first game, but there was no way he would be here tonight, not with our current radio silence. Besides, Braden would murder me if I shifted my head and broke formation. Once we took our spot on the field, adjusted to face the crowds in the stands who cheered for us, I was too far back to easily make out any faces in the bleachers. Not that I would need to, because again, there was no way he'd decided to come. Why would he? No one wanted to drive two hours on a Friday night to catch a glimpse of their useless sister in the middle of a line of trombones. I'd just have to—

I saw Wickham.

Not in the stands. He was never a "pay for admission" kind of guy. Instead, he leaned against the metal at the bottom of the bleachers, arms crossed over his chest. Watched me, and from the way he raised his hand to wave, clearly knew I'd seen him.

I drew the sharpest intake of breath.

Wickham was in the doorway of my dorm room, and Fitz was there, too, and I hadn't expected him, hadn't expected either of them, and Fitz was screaming at Wickham, screaming at me, and I didn't know where to look or what to do—

And then I missed the first beat.

Normally, not a big deal. I'd skip over the first note—my part had a rest for the first couple of measures anyway, it was fine, it was chill, I could manage—and pick it up. All that required was elementary counting skills. I tore my attention back to the field, away from where Wickham had stepped out of my nightmarish reminiscing and into real life.

Except that I'd forgotten that the trombones basically took off at a run on the first downbeat, booked it across the field in double time to mimic the frenzied pace of the music, and I'd gotten so in my head about Wickham that it caught me entirely by surprise. I booked it to keep up and pursed my lips as I began to play, but I could tell I was behind, and from the look one of the freshmen—Corey? I really thought it was Corey—gave me as he passed in front of me, everyone else could, too.

It was fine, I thought as I took steps as big as possible, which were more like leaps, to catch up to the others. I just wouldn't play. I could hold my trombone up and march and because we were so far in the back, no one would notice I wasn't moving my slide unless they were watching carefully. And sure, it was super hard to remember the marching without the music, because I'd memorized them together, but I was literally in the middle of a line. When I tried to visualize the drill, to picture the little number that marked me on the field, I didn't think I had anything weird coming up. I'd figure it out, and the show would be over soon, and then I could determine what the hell Wickham was doing here.

The drums pounded, and the woodwinds next to me trilled, and I ran across the field with the other trombones at a frantic pace. We turned 90 degrees onto the thirty-yard line and began to march in place, as I tried to catch my breath, tried to remember what came next.

That was when the whole section started to march backward.

Back marching isn't exactly complicated, not when you know it's coming. I should have been able to handle it. In fact, Braden's exact words, when we'd gone over this in the drill last week, had been, "And Georgie . . . you just step backward. You know, backward? It's the opposite of forward? Okay? Do you think you can manage?" Which was aggressive and mean and I'd ranted about it to Avery for like, an hour that night, cutting into the time I should have been writing an analysis of *The Scarlet Letter*.

In retrospect, Braden's condescending attitude had, in fact, been called for.

Because the back march caught me by surprise, and somehow, I tripped.

The back of my shoe caught the edge of the turf, and I stumbled, throwing my arms above my head so that I wouldn't smash my trombone beneath me as I fell. And I didn't just hit the ground. No, the trombones were all standing close together enough that when my hands went up, I heard the clash of metal against metal, heard Emily scream as she collapsed beneath me.

We'd gone full Rockettes toy soldier Jenga line. Collapsing in the sort of horror show that would undoubtedly make it into a top five compilation of disastrous marching band moments on YouTube, I landed, half on the field and half on Emily, and behind her I saw the two freshmen trip, too, and fall, the line of flutes that were about to intersect with us scream and high-step out of the way. Braden jumped back just in time, but from the look of pure contempt on his face as he marched in place just a few strides away from the damage, I kind of wished he had fallen, too.

"Get up!" Braden hissed, his eyes straight ahead, his knees still lifted high as he marched in place. "Come on!"

I scrambled to my feet, face burning, bits of rubber from the Astroturf coating my coveralls. Shit shit shit. I didn't need to look into the crowd to know what Wickham was doing. Smirking, maybe a slow clap. Whatever would be the *least* helpful in the situation. I didn't look toward Avery, either. I couldn't handle the shame.

I stumbled back onto the thirty-yard line with the rest of the trombones, who had righted themselves. Emily's helmet was askew but she was up, at least, her eyes red-rimmed with tears, which was either from embarrassment or pain. Probably both. And it was all my fault.

I just wanted to do one goddamn thing right this year, but it turned out that was impossible.

The song ended, and we finally stopped moving. I had never been as glad for an abbreviated halftime show as we marched off the field. Even if it was to a furious Mrs. Tapper.

"What the hell happened out there?" she whisper-shouted, stepping in front of the trombones to block our escape as we came off the field. "Is everyone all right?" I would have personally preferred the order of those questions reversed, but whatever.

"We're fine," Emily muttered, as she wiped tears off her face. "It's nothing." I glanced over at her, surprised. Braden would have thrown me under the bus, and from the look on his face, he was about to, before Mrs. Tapper spoke up again.

"Whatever it was . . ." She looked between me and Emily, eyebrows raised. "It better not happen again. Got it? This band has a reputation to uphold. You need to remember that."

A reputation to uphold. Yeah. I knew what that was like.

I managed to nod even as she stormed off. Shit. And now I had to make it through two more quarters surrounded by my section, who stared at me with utter contempt as they brushed away Astroturf. Band sure was a safe, fun place where I'd found my true family, all right.

I thought Avery might come find me, tell me it wasn't my fault, shield me from the glares of the trombones. But he didn't.

Instead I just heard Wickham's last words to me echo in my head, the words he'd spat out as Fitz pushed him out of my door for the final time.

"You think you're anything without me, kid? The only interesting parts of you are all the parts I made."

CHAPTER TEN

It was bad enough having Wickham in my head. But now, stumbling off the field, when I let my gaze drift to the right, I saw him watching me. Tilting his head to the side, indicating I should come over.

I shouldn't. Obviously. But no one was looking, so I slipped away from my section, darted back beneath the bleachers. He met me there, in our old familiar spot. Different stands, sure, than the ones at Pemberley. Same isolation. Same desperation.

"Beautiful work." He had new jeans on, and I hated that I noticed. They looked expensive. "Really holding up the family legacy out there."

"I don't want you here, Wickham." My voice trembled, but I tried my best to be strong. To be something.

"I figured you needed someone in the stands to support you,

kid." His shrug was easy, unburdened. "It's not like Fitz was going to show up."

"You didn't know that."

"Yes, I did." He laughed. "Don't forget, I knew him first. I know your big brother better than anyone."

I wanted to argue with him, but the truth of the matter was that Fitz hadn't shown up, so my ammunition was exactly nil. My hands tugged on the edge of my uniform sleeves, pulled them down over my wrists.

"You didn't tell me you were coming." I changed the subject, the only thing I could pretend to control. "Thought it would be better to just appear out of nowhere?"

"I like the element of surprise." Wickham's hair was down around his shoulders today, a little rough around the edges. "And if you were really going to prove to me that you had your shit together, well, I wanted to see that in action. Again, really killed it tonight."

"Shut up." I managed to keep my eyes dry, because I wouldn't give Wickham the satisfaction, but my voice still caught. Stupid traitor voice. The moment he heard it, Wickham leaned forward, hand on my shoulder. I almost jerked away, but I didn't.

"Hey." His voice was quiet, caring. He was so fucking good at that. "What happened?"

"You saw."

"There's something else. Come on." He reached out and righted my helmet, gently, where it had gone all askew from my fall. "Talk." His hand lingered near the side of my face, and I exhaled. Closed my eyes.

It was how well he knew me, after all, that let him break me. But what was I, if not already broken?

"I tried to make this like, grand gesture." I tossed my hands up, helpless to both the situation and Wickham. May as well tell him. May as well let him know how much I'd screwed up. "I got dinner for the whole band, full catering spread, and they just . . . rejected it. Like I'd poisoned it or something."

I didn't know what I'd expected Wickham's response to be, but I didn't expect his laugh, barked out short.

"You got catering?" He stepped back from me, hands on his knees, the laughter spreading through his body in a way that made my stomach twist. "Fuck, kid, you really are such a Darcy."

"What's that supposed to mean?" I crossed my arms over my chest, defensive, hurt.

"It means that you're so obsessed with the idea that all your money can solve your problems that you don't think of anything else." He stood up, finally, but laughter still played across his face in a way that I hated. That wasn't what being a Darcy was. I had a literal list describing the desired traits.

"We do not."

"Why do you think everyone hates you, kid? Really? Because of me?" Wickham's laughter faded as he shook his head. "Georgiana Darcy, they hated you before, too. Pemberley Academy might be full of rich kids but there's no one like a Darcy, who can throw money at any problem, no matter how big or small. Who freezes out everyone who isn't like them. Why do you think they were so surprised when we hung out last year?"

As always, Wickham's words stung. He always did that, found the place where it would hurt deepest to twist in the knife. But I didn't leave, because I never did that, either.

"That's not true. I'm not like that."

"It doesn't matter if it's true or not." It was infuriating, how easy Wickham's smile was as he stabbed toward me. "Let's take a little history lesson, Georgie. Your brother spends four years here, and we all know what he's like. Talks to the teachers, maybe one or two other students he deems worthy, no one else. Gets a wing in the fucking library named after him just because he can. Then you come along, and what do you do? You attach yourself right to his hip and don't stray any further."

"Stop it." My heart turned and squeezed in my chest, like Wickham's hand was in there, ruining me.

"He graduates, and does little Georgie Darcy do anything to show the school she's not like her brother? No, she keeps to herself, all *Sage Hall* in her single dorm, and she's the iciest of ice queens, until I came along." His voice got smooth. Low. "And I could have given you a life here, Georgie, a real one, if you hadn't let your brother fuck it up. You wonder why everyone still hates you? Take a good, hard look at yourself, and then tell me, truthfully, that whatever I can make you isn't better than whatever it is you've managed to be."

Whatever he could make me.

I wanted to make myself a Darcy.

If I believed Wickham, that would still lead to my failure.

A whiff of popcorn caught in my nose, and I was back at Pemberley, back in last year, spring, when things were getting bad. Wickham had been hanging out under the bleachers during a lacrosse game and wouldn't tell me why, but he'd let me come once I begged enough.

"Why are we even here, Wickham?" It was too cold for a skirt, but I'd worn one anyway, because Wickham had told me a week ago that I shouldn't hide my legs. They practically shook in my thin tights, but I did my best to hide it, to look like I belonged here, at Wickham's side.

Even though I doubted it every day.

"Don't tell me you don't like lacrosse." He hadn't looked toward the game once since it started, but there was no hint of a joke in his voice. The way he watched me was unsettling. "It's the Ivy League's favorite pastime."

"Yeah, but why are we here?" I wouldn't push, I never pushed, but the cold and boredom had started to get to me. A kid I recognized from the library—back when I'd gone to the library, I hadn't gone to the library in weeks—edged up on me and Wickham, but backed away quickly when Wickham caught his eye and shook his head in a sharp no. As soon as he had, Wickham turned the full force of his attention back on me.

It was electrifying, to get that much attention. I almost drowned in it.

"And where else do you have to go?" His voice didn't get sharp with me often, but whenever it did, I flinched. "You've got someone else you want to hang out with?"

"No," I answered quickly. Avery had asked me to study with him, but Wickham wouldn't like that answer.

"Then chill out, will you?" His tone had changed from sharp to flippant so fast I might have missed it, and he walked over toward me, put his arm around my shoulder to pull me in to his chest. "Why don't you get some popcorn, kid? On me." He pulled out his wallet, peeled off one of a thick stack of twenties. "Got my hush money yesterday." That was what Wickham always called the stipend that his dad, absent but guilty, sent him every month.

"Okay." I nodded, taking the money, and he squeezed my shoulders before dropping a kiss on the top of my head.

"That's my girl."

His girl.

And it didn't matter that everything else felt like it was slipping away from me. That my brother hadn't called in a week and a half *and Emily kept giving me weird looks in the hallway and Mrs. Tapper wanted me to come into her office to talk about my performance.*

I was Wickham's, and I didn't need to be anything else.

I wrenched myself back from his grasp, wishing I could smell anything besides that stupid popcorn. Above us, students stomped and cheered in the stands. The rest of the trombones wouldn't be concerned that I was gone, but at some point, Mrs. T would ask about me, and they'd start to look out of necessity if nothing else. My uniform threatened to choke me, the collar pushed against my neck.

"I have to go," I managed as I brushed the sleeve of my jacket against my eyes. "And you need to leave."

"You should be proud, kid." He smirked. "You said you wanted to be the perfect Darcy, right? Far as I can tell, you've got it in the bag. Just get your brother to admit it and we'll be all set. Or you could just . . . give up."

"I can't do that."

"Sure you can." His most gentle voice was back, and now his eyes were in on the action, soft and made only for me, which I'd spent months reminding myself was a lie. It got harder to believe here, with Wickham in the flesh, still the only person who wanted me. "Work with me. This school hates Darcys. But kid, trust me, it loves a Wickham."

I held my breath for longer than I was proud of. Let the spell of Wickham last longer than it should. I could always say yes. Find out what, exactly, Wickham was doing here. Pretend to go along with it, then turn him in. Or not. I could always just . . . get swept away in it.

I blinked, fast, and the real world came back into focus.

"Leave, Wickham." I jerked my head toward the parking lot. "Please."

"I'll see you at homecoming, then." He stepped back without trying to touch me, but I flinched all the same. "See if you've changed your mind. Maybe I'll bring flowers."

He left before I could say anything else. Not that I knew what else I would say. I crept out from under the bleachers and made my way back into my row near the top of the stands, sat down at the edge without trying to push my way past any of the other trombones who wouldn't want to look at me, anyway. Next to me, one of the freshmen pulled his leg in toward himself, to avoid touching me.

Wickham in the doorway. My brother, holding up the pills. The dean, telling me that I was very, very lucky.

If being the perfect Darcy wasn't even the answer, what the hell was?

I blinked back definitely-not-tears in the bright lights of the stadium, and I prayed that the night would be over soon.

CHAPTER ELEVEN

You're canceling?" I sat straight up in bed the next morning, phone pressed against my year, even as Sydney shot me a dirty look from her own bed before pulling her pillow over her head. "You're not in the hospital, are you?"

"I promise I'm not hiding a life-threatening illness." Fitz's voice was dry as he referenced one of my favorite *Sage Hall* episodes, one he'd seen me watch a dozen times over the summer. "But I need to put in the extra hours on this term paper. Besides, don't you have a calculus test this week? You can use the extra time to study."

"I deeply regret telling you about that." I tried to ignore the sinking feeling in my chest. Fitz was definitely canceling, like he said, because of his term paper. Not because he was still ticked off at me from the last time.

Might have been a nice lie if I could have brought myself to believe it.

Since Sydney had developed a truly murderous look in her eye from my phone call at eight a.m. on a Saturday, I jumped out of bed and headed into the sink room, closing the door behind me. "But sure. I can study." I didn't tell Fitz that my calculus teacher had started grading our homework, too, and my average was currently living solidly below the C mark, despite my best efforts. He'd find out soon enough. I tried to pump some cheeriness into my voice. "You won't miss me too much?"

"I've got your picture in my wallet if it gets bad."

"Good." I was glad he didn't ask how the game went the night before. Maybe he knew, using some sort of brother Spidey-sense, how horribly it had gone. Or maybe he just assumed everything in my life went poorly these days. He wouldn't be wrong.

"Bro!" I heard a different male voice through the phone, muffled on Fitz's end, like someone was shouting from a distance. "You coming?"

"Who's that?" I asked, as hurt spread through me. That voice didn't sound like homework. "Your term paper?"

"What?" Fitz already sounded distracted. "Oh, no, sorry, that's Charlie. We're going to the library together."

"I thought you needed to work."

"I do," he snapped, and I winced. "I'm just meeting up with some people from my class to work together. Is that all right with you?"

Lizzie, I thought. Oh. Well. That was something, right? Maybe my plan was working. That part of it, anyway. Since the rest of my life was clearly spiraling into a shitshow, I should be happy that this aspect of the plan hadn't gone up in flames.

"I just didn't know you and Charlie shared any classes," I lied. This would all be easier if I could see Fitz and Lizzie together again, to get a sense of how their relationship was progressing. My brother wouldn't tell me in a million years. Maybe I could do that, instead of homework. Figure out a way to get up to Meryton or something, see the two of them in their natural habitat, accidentally release a flock of doves in the library in a way that seemed super romantic . . .

"Oh. Yes." If Darcys every apologized, there would be a hint of it in Fitz's voice. "We don't, actually. Not technically. We just share some professors. But he's decided he's in love."

"With . . . the professors?"

"No, Beanpole." Fitz sighed, and I held back a retaliatory comment, before I told him not to use that stupid nickname. "With Jane Bennet. I'm in a discussion group with her sister, so Charlie keeps insisting we all study together. It's absolutely ridiculous. We hardly get anything done with the two of them making eyes at each other, and Lizzie has never met a point she couldn't argue with."

"Sound like she challenges you." Progress, right? My mood buoyed, at least a little. It seemed that Charlie was helping even more than the flowers. Thank God because really, I was just one person. "Didn't you tell me once that complacency was the root of the disintegration of justice?"

"Did I?"

"Maybe. It sounds like something you would say." I leaned back against the wall, letting my head rest on the cool plaster. "She can't be that bad."

"Trust me." Fitz sighed. "She is. I really do have to go, though."

"Yeah." That sinking feeling again. I tugged at the bottom of my pajama shirt, ran my hands over the satin. Remembering what Wickham had said last night, about our money, I wrinkled the fabric in my hands. "I know."

"I'll call you tomorrow, all right?" I could hear him push me off the phone. "Maybe we can get dinner later in the week, if there's a night you don't have practice."

"Okay." Or a night I did have practice. With the way the band looked at me now, that would be perfectly acceptable. "Good luck."

"Thanks, Beanpole. Bye." Fitz hung up before I could say anything else, and I leaned back farther, used the back of the door to slide down to the ground and sit.

No Fitz this morning, then. Fine. All fine. I didn't even like those breakfasts, didn't want to be interrogated about my grades and my friend(s) and how band was going. This was better. Part of the Georgie Self-Improvement Plan was based on getting Fitz together with Lizzie, and more time spent with her could only be a positive. It wasn't like he needed to spend time with me—his opinion there was already extremely well-formed.

The only thing was that without my brother, I was down one of my major sources of human interaction for the weekend, and that kind of sucked. It wasn't like Sydney and I were going to braid each other's hair and gossip about how the game went down.

I didn't want to spend the day in the library, studying calculus concepts I didn't understand. And there was no way I'd be able to go back to sleep, now that the adrenaline of all my failures had pumped its way into my veins.

I needed to suck it up and study. Just taking the AP classes wasn't the key to being the perfect Darcy—success in them was. And so far that was going . . . decidedly not well. In addition to calculus, I'd completely blown a chemistry lab earlier in the week, missed turning in a report for gov because I'd been practicing with Avery the night it was due, and was now a full three-quarters of a book behind in my English reading.

My chest ached as I longed for the *Sage Hall* universe,

where school wasn't a torturous thing. Oh, to live in a world where high school hadn't been invented yet. They had more scurvy, maybe, but way less of all of this.

Although *Sage Hall* hadn't been much of a comfort this past week. The fandom was abuzz about the amount of scenes the actors who played Jocelyn and Andrew had filmed together recently, with call sheets leaking to the internet and wild speculation about what it could mean for their relationship. Which was all well and good, for people who weren't reminded of the friendly local irredeemable asshole in their life every time Andrew convinced Jocelyn to slip away from polite society.

I mean, obviously I was still watching, but I could have done with fewer scenes between the two of them.

Before I had to choose among failing my classes at the library, failing my classes from bed, or falling down the *Sage Hall* rabbit hole of major emotional projection, my phone buzzed. I grabbed at it, desperate for something to take me out of my anxiety spiral, even if it was another admonishment from Fitz. Hell, I'd take an email from Wickham, if it meant someone talking to me. Acknowledging me.

That was a dangerous thought, and I shook my head to clear myself of it as I swiped my phone open.

A picture from Avery waited for me, him on the podium at the front of the field, arms high with a baton in his hand, feathered hat standing tall and proud. I allowed myself a smile. It was clearly a professional photo, and whoever took it had captured the look of madcap excitement I saw in his face whenever he conducted.

The text below it read:

*They're running this in the school paper Monday
Not bad, right????*

Not bad, I responded, even as my blood spiked through me at even the mention of last night. Honestly, Avery was the last person I should be talking to. That picture had certainly been taken before my trombone-dominoes mishap, a mishap we hadn't yet discussed. I'd avoided Avery after the game, not wanting his false reassurance that it was fine, really.

Or even worse, hearing him judge me for it.

Of course, that was when I thought I'd talk to another living soul sometime this weekend. And I did want some social interaction, damn it. Wanted to do something besides spiral into further self-doubt.

We should celebrate. I sent the text before I could lose my nerve. *You want breakfast off campus? I'll buy.*

I half-regretted it the moment I hit send, because maybe I needed to be more careful about tossing out money after the Mexican Food Incident. But it was too late now. His reply came through just a second later.

Pick you up in an hour?

I sent a thumbs-up in reply, and felt some of my anxiety ease away.

cll

"You know you said an hour," I said, once I'd met Avery on the sidewalk in front of my dorm, both of us bundled up in peacoats with the collars turned up against the wind. Bright red leaves drifted through the air around us, and I brushed one aside as it landed on my head. "It's been an hour and five minutes."

"So you do know how to keep time," he replied, but as the

smile fell off my face at the reference to last night's game, he sucked in a quick intake of breath. "Sorry, I didn't mean . . . I thought you'd want to joke about it. You usually do."

"Right." I bristled as I shoved my hands, stupidly gloveless, deep into my coat pockets. This was exactly what I was afraid of. Avery was, first and foremost, the drum major. He was pissed at me for ruining the show, probably, and trying to hide it under humor. "Maybe we should skip, anyway. I've got a ton of homework." He was well within his rights to be annoyed at how I'd royally fucked the band over last night, but I was well within my rights to not want to hear about it. It was one thing to hear it from Wickham, or even from Sydney, or the other kids in the band. But I didn't think I could take it from Avery.

"George." Before I got the chance to turn around and head back into my dorm, Avery stepped behind me, arms held out wide like he was trying to conduct. My breath caught on the bitter air as he framed me inside of him. "Hey. I'm sorry. We don't have to talk about it."

I stopped myself within the confines of his arms, took a deep breath. I had to get ahold of myself. This was Avery. *Avery.* We were friends. As tempting as it was to run away from every possible chance of a confrontation, I needed to give him the benefit of the doubt. Sometimes a joke was just a joke.

"It's fine." I forced my shoulders to relax. "It's freezing out here. Let's go, okay?"

"Okay." Avery's face split into a grin, and as he opened the passenger door of his car for me, I slid inside. "Tell me about these pancakes."

The racing pattern of my heart evened out as I buckled my seat belt. "Have you not been to Townshend's?"

"Only when we stopped to get your brother's phone. I don't

eat off campus much." Avery shrugged as he got into his own seat, buckled his seat belt before he pulled out of the lot. "And I work in the dining hall most mornings, anyway."

"Work-study?" I'd forgotten. Wickham would smirk at that, say it was typical, that it was a sign of how self-absorbed I was, but I pushed his voice aside. I snuck a sideways glance at Avery, whose gaze was on the road as it led off campus.

"Yeah." Avery nodded as his fingers drummed against the steering wheel, presumably to the beat of whichever one of our songs was stuck in his head. "Four days a week. I do the regular breakfast shift for three weekdays, and then on Saturdays it's usually six to ten. But I got off early today."

"Oh. Cool." That sounded horrific, but Avery's chipper attitude didn't change when he talked about it. "Do you . . . like it?" I'd never had a job, and I couldn't imagine juggling classwork plus band *plus* a job on campus.

This time, Avery did glance over at me.

"You don't have to get all weird about it." He laughed, but it wasn't as full as it sometimes was. "It's just a job, George. A lot of students have them."

"I wasn't trying to be weird." God, this day. I sighed, leaned my head against the passenger-side window. "Can we start over again, please? Hi. I'm Georgie. It's nice to meet you. Want to get completely regular, non-emotionally-charged pancakes? They put whipped cream on them."

"I'm actually vegan."

"What?" Maybe I should have just opened the door and jumped out now. We were only going thirty, forty miles an hour. Chances were I wouldn't die. It worked in *Lady Bird.* "How did I not know this?"

I lifted my head off the window to look at Avery, completely distraught . . . and saw him laughing.

Oh.

Tension I didn't know I held released inside of me.

"You're literally the worst," I informed him as he cackled, gasping for air. "Seriously."

"You've seen me eat meat!" Avery snorted, and soon I was laughing, too. I couldn't help it. No matter how much better I thought I liked the world in my head, Avery always seemed to bring me out of it. "God, you're gullible, you know that?"

"Just drive." I tried to keep my voice stern, but the laughter that bubbled out again betrayed me, and from the look Avery gave me out of the corner of his eye once he'd recovered, full of mischief, he didn't fall for my stern attitude, either.

CHAPTER TWELVE

"Okay." Avery stabbed his fork into another pancake, his third plate of the morning. I was impressed—he could actually keep up with my pancake consumption pace. I was living for the looks of dismay on Jenn the waitress's face each time she came around to refill our platters, which had started when I showed up without my brother and only got worse from there. "What did you want to be when you grow up?"

"What do you mean, did?" My mouth was muffled around a huge, syrupy bite that Avery applauded when I managed to swallow. "My brain hasn't stopped functioning *that* entirely, dude."

"No, like when you were a kid." Avery cocked his head to the side across the booth from me, and the red vinyl squeaked as he shifted. "For example. I wanted to be a stop sign holder."

"The metal pole that holds up a stop sign? Weirdo." I didn't remember the last time I'd been at the diner without feeling constantly on edge. That felt kind of disloyal to Fitz, but whatever. He was the one who'd canceled on me, and all I ever did was make him miserable. Maybe it was okay to admit that sometimes, the feeling was mutual.

"No, that's an inanimate object, George, come on." Avery cut through another pancake, tossed a handful of M&M's onto his plate with a practiced hand. "I wanted to be the person who *holds* the stop sign. Like, when you pass a construction site on the road, and there's a sign that says STOP on one side and SLOW on the other? Someone has to hold that sign. And that person controls the entire flow of traffic. They're extremely powerful."

"I'm sticking with the weirdo label, dude. You missed out on some prime firefighter longing." I snorted, tucked a piece of hair behind my ear to keep it from trailing into my syrup. I was lucky I didn't get syrup up my nose, too, from all the laughing.

"I've always prided myself on my individuality." He smirked, and I laughed. Again. I laughed more with Avery than I did with anyone else. Admittedly, I didn't *talk* to anyone else.

Still.

After the bumpy car ride (metaphorically, not literally, as Avery seemed to be the world's most careful driver, probably to make up for how his car was barely held together), breakfast had been . . . good, so far. Last night's disaster of a performance, the Wickham situation, and all the leftover catering I'd donated to the custodial staff seemed in the distant past. Mostly, I focused on how many pancakes I could shove in my face at once, plus how Avery still looked cute with his cheeks chipmunk-full of whipped cream.

Friend-cute, obviously.

"I will grant you individuality." I raised my coffee mug in his direction, and he tapped it with his own. "What did you do for career day? Make a cardboard STOP sign to bring to school?"

"My mom found one of those orange safety vests at a thrift store." He spread whipped cream over his pancakes, creating an even layer. "Hard to explain to the other kids, though. And my teacher thought I wanted to be one of those dudes who sang 'Y.M.C.A.'"

"That tracks." I nodded. "Do you still have the vest? Do you wear it around the house when you're feeling nostalgic? Sneak out onto the street and try to conduct traffic? Wait." I pointed my fork at him, all accusing, as he grinned. "Is that why you're into conducting now? Because it's the closest thing you have to following your dream?"

"No way." He shook his head before he cut off more pancake. "I conduct because I like having power over all of you plebeians. You're completely in my control."

"Maybe we'll riot and rise up against you."

"Please. I've listened to *Hamilton*." Avery's hair fell in front of his eyes again, and he pushed it back with his fork-free hand. "You don't have the resilience needed for a coup."

"Challenge accepted." Across from us, a big group of senior girls gathered tightly into one of the booths, more girls on each side than was necessarily safe. They clustered in a way that had BFF written all over it, and a year ago, hell, a month ago, I might have spent the whole morning staring at them in a jealous seethe, unable to obtain what they had.

Right now, though, I kind of felt like I had everything I needed.

I pulled myself out of the booth, stood next to the table for a moment as I buzzed with the feeling of actually being, you know, *happy* for once. "I'm going to go to the bathroom and definitely not plot to ruin you while I'm in there."

"I'll build up my strength," Avery replied, nodding toward his incoming plate of pancakes. I did my best to keep my smile to a normal, human level as I crossed the restaurant, humming the *Sage Hall* theme under my breath as I passed spread-out legs and sticky high-top tables. It was a busy morning, which normally made me feel claustrophobic, but I was starting to think that was just the influence of Fitz. Maybe I could come here with someone else and not leave feeling like literal, actual garbage.

Wild.

I pulled out my phone as I used my shoulder to push my way into the bathroom, pausing before I entered a stall to check my notifications. Yikes. I had half a dozen from *Sage Hall* fan sites, and they were only growing. Something big must have gone down. Maybe one of the actors was pregnant or something? The only thing that showed up on the notification was BREAKING and a bunch of ellipses, so I leaned back against the bathroom counter, careful to avoid the wet spots, to click through and see what was up.

And what was up was . . . a lot.

BREAKING NEWS:
SCRIPT LEAK CONFIRMS JOCELYN AND
ANDREW ROMANTICALLY INVOLVED
MEETING THEIR KISS QUOTIENT:
THE FANS GO WILD FOR CONFIRMED KISS

Oh wow.

Oh no.

I'd experienced *Sage Hall* spoilers before, of course. You didn't follow as many fan sites and Twitters as I did without stumbling across the occasional spoiler. Besides, the show was broadcast on the BBC, so half the time British fans had seen their episodes a day or two before they got uploaded over here. It was part of the territory.

None of those previous spoilers made me feel like my world

was collapsing around me in the bathroom of a roadside diner in the middle of nowhere New York, but I guessed it was just a matter of time.

Breathe. Breathe, Georgie. These were fictional characters, after all. Just because I'd accidentally completely associated Jocelyn and Andrew with me and Wickham didn't mean that I needed to keep doing it now. It was just a kiss, on TV, in my favorite show.

I should have been thrilled. This was the dream. The dream of every girl who ever pined after a rarepair, everyone who'd ever searched JocAndrew on AO3 and was forced to read the same half a dozen fics over and over because there was nothing else available.

I should have run out of the bathroom to grab Avery's hands, spun him around the diner and celebrated with a whole can of whipped cream. I should have been screaming.

But I just kept thinking of Wickham, and the times he'd kissed me, and how excited I'd been for that, too.

God damn it. I'd thought I was *past* this, past trying to breathe in a bathroom, past thinking a day was going maybe kind of actually okay and then boom, there was his face, there were his lips, there were his whispers and his promises and his hands on the back of my neck, a caress that didn't feel like a lie yet. His smiles just for me and his comments about how mature I was, his requests to hang out in my room while I went to class and my ignorance of what he actually used the room for.

Breathe.

I gripped the counter behind me, allowing the wet splotches of soap to ground me back in reality. I'd been having a nice day. An okay day, at least. A nice past hour. I was moving past Wickham. I was moving past everything that had happened last year. I was going to suck it up, go back to our table, and act like a normal person in front of Avery, who I didn't want to see me like this, quivering like this was something that mattered.

Obviously *Sage Hall* mattered. But this didn't have to. I could make it so it didn't. Probably.

Avery wasn't some rogue trying to steal me away from my family and my propriety. He was a nice, funny guy who enjoyed spending time with me, for whatever reason. If I just got myself back into the dining room, I knew his whole face would light up when he saw me, because that was the kind of person he was. I just needed to give it a chance. Put down the phone, ignore Regency England and its scandals, and go.

Another deep breath, water splashed on my face. There. I looked . . . about as presentable as I had when I came in, I reasoned, watching myself in the foggy bathroom mirror. Not like my happiness was always one insignificant-to-the-world headline away from being torn apart.

I put my hand over my heart, as if I could force it to slow down if I just pressed on it hard enough, and took a few more deep inhales before I quickly used the bathroom, washed my hands, and headed back to our booth, determined to keep it together in front of the boy who maybe cared about me.

"I still want to know your answer." Avery picked our conversation back up without missing a beat as I slid into my seat. He reached across the table with his fork to try and spear one of my pancakes. I batted his fork away with my own while I tried to act like everything was fine, totally fine. "Childhood dream. Go."

"Right." I shoved images of JocAndrew out of my brain as I knocked his fork aside. He was seriously persistent, and I was suddenly seriously tired. "It's not as interesting as yours." Maybe if I just talked, talked over my own internal monologue that was still panicking, I could distract myself.

"You are a much more interesting person than you realize. I promise."

"Yeah, right." My anxiety had started to mix with self-doubt, to rise up like a high tide to a moon. I felt Wickham's presence all around me, closing in tightly. Saw his face last night as he'd laid into me, like I was watching the whole thing play out from above, saw how I hadn't left. How I'd just stood there and taken it. "The most interesting things about me are the bits people made up, Avery, I promise."

"Seriously?" He took a sip of his coffee, then winced and added another generous pour of milk. It was already closer to white than it was to black, but I welcomed the difference in the person across from me, was glad to be here with someone who didn't just accept that the bitterness of life was his to swallow. And I *was* with Avery. Not Fitz. Not Wickham. Avery was safe. Avery was okay.

If I listened to the pounding of my heart, it didn't feel that way, but I tried to will my head to take over.

"Is it something embarrassing?" Avery pushed as he ripped open a packet of sugar, then dumped it into his what-could-no-longer-be-called-coffee. "Because I told you my STOP sign holder story. If your big, dark secret is that you wanted to be a stockbroker since the age of two, you can admit it. I'll only judge you the normal amount."

"I'm pretty sure stockbrokers need to pass high school math." I should just answer the question. Maybe if I gave a real answer—and I knew what the real answer was, even if I tried to avoid it—I could distract myself from JocAndrew and Wickham. Could dredge up some new, fun childhood trauma.

Wickham wouldn't expect me to answer Avery. He'd remind me that I never wanted to talk to anyone, except him. Just like a Darcy.

But as Avery watched me with dark brown eyes, shaggy hair falling in front of them, I wanted to let him in. Wanted to let *someone* in, so that it wasn't just me in my brain, where all of these thoughts and fears battled against me. And it wasn't just to rebel against Wickham and his expectations. It was for me.

"I . . ." I took a deep breath, ignored the flutter in my chest. As he leaned into me, I picked up a whiff of cinnamon and soap that brought back two years of riding on buses, memories of laughing and falling asleep on his shoulder that I'd thought I'd lost. "I wanted to be a pit musician."

"Cool." Avery nodded, nonchalant as ever, unaware of what a huge admission I'd made. "For musicals?"

"Yeah." I only had half a pancake left, but I pushed it around on my plate, my gaze on the trails of syrup it made. "My, um, my dad took me and Fitz to see a bunch when we were kids. Like, I was younger than you should be to see a Broadway show." I started to group the M&M's by color on my plate, reds separated from yellows separated from browns, as I tried to keep my voice even. "We went to see *The Lion King* when I was . . . three? Four? And my dad knew the conductor, so he took us down to meet the pit, and they were super cool to me. I wanted to be just like them."

I remembered it perfectly, even though I hadn't reached for that memory in years. My dad, picking me up by the waist to see down into the pit. The conductor who'd let me hold onto his baton as the violins played a perfect A on my cue. Fitz and I had both gasped when the music eventually started up, when the drums hit their beat from the boxes above us and a giraffe bowed in our direction. The way my dad had smiled, then hired a private piano tutor for me the second we got home.

I'd loved the way music made me feel. The ultimate distraction.

"That's awesome." When I glanced back up at Avery, he smiled, though his eyes searched mine. Like he knew there was more to the story. "Do you still do that? When you're home and stuff?"

"Not since my dad died." And he would have hated this place, I didn't add. Dad may have seemed like a salt-of-the-earth down-home guy compared to my mom, but he still wore suits every day and never ate anywhere that didn't have a wine list. Fitz and I didn't go to places he would have liked anymore. "Fitz tried to take me to a show afterward, like, a month after the funeral, and we were both so wrecked that we ended up leaving at intermission."

I'd never told anyone that before. I still didn't go into the details—how I'd gone into the bathroom at intermission and had a panic attack in one of the stalls, and one of the ushers had gone to find Fitz, and she ran into another usher who had been coming to find me, because Fitz had locked himself in a supply closet and couldn't stop crying. The two ushers reunited us, Fitz drove us all the way back home, and we'd never, ever talked about it.

We didn't show each other our emotions now. The funeral was the beginning of that, and Wickham was the end. I lost my dad, and my mom left, but I also lost my brother, who had decided he needed to be my parent and not my friend.

I missed him.

"Right, sorry." The grin had fallen off of Avery's face when I looked up, his expression serious as he blinked, stumbled over his words. "I didn't know. I mean, I knew about your dad, but not—sorry."

"How would you know?" I shrugged. I didn't cry over it anymore. I'd gotten that all out of my system years ago. "I didn't tell you. It's fine."

"Right, but like . . ." There was a flash of frustration in Avery's voice, an unusual sound, for him. "We're friends. Good friends. Right?"

There was a vulnerability to Avery, then, that I wasn't used to seeing in him, but that I recognized. Knew it from myself, in my deepest parts that I often ignored.

I did my best to smile as I raised my hand to grab the check from Jenn, who delivered it with so much speed that she must have had it already printed out, in high anticipation of this moment.

"I'm pretty shitty at being friends with people, Avery. I wouldn't blame yourself. I don't talk about this stuff with anyone."

"You're telling me now, though." It wasn't a question.

"Yeah." I threw down a pile of cash and scooted out of the booth, shrugged on my coat even though I already felt surprisingly warm. The JocAndrew kiss wasn't here yet. And in the meantime . . . like I'd said, not everything was garbage. "I am."

His smile, a beam down at me from on high, from someone whose friendship I almost certainly didn't deserve, hit me hard.

Something itched at the back of my mind, a desire I hadn't felt for a long time. A hint of an idea. A beginning of something.

cll

The first sentence came easily. I didn't usually write original characters in my fic, but this new character, a friend for Jocelyn, wouldn't get out of my head, and for once I didn't want to write about Andrew. Rogues were easy to write, with their smirks and dashing comments. I had a strong and sudden interest in someone who was just . . . nice. A good person.

Jocelyn had been closed off from other people for so long, she barely even noticed when she had stopped.

As I continued to pound at my keyboard, the words flowed out of me like water.

Jocelyn was perpetually surprised by Henry. And why shouldn't she be? Everything she'd expected about him . . . it had come out twisted. When she expected him to be cruel, he was kind. When she expected dismissal, she received acceptance.

When she'd come to him in the night, tired and lonely and worried about her sister, he had hugged her.

He hadn't asked why she was there, at his manor on the hill at a time that no respectable lady should be out and about. He'd seen the look on her face and laid his hand over hers, led her to a bench in his elaborate garden. He dismissed the servants, who stared at her with wide eyes, who all tutted to themselves about an inappropriate match.

But Henry never said a word against her. He sat next to her while she poured out her fears and her dreams, and when she stood up to go, to sneak back into her too-quiet house where no one would speak to her, only of her, he looked her in the eyes, waited for her nod of consent, and wrapped his arms around her, over her shoulders so she had to breathe into his neck.

It didn't feel natural, or easy. Jocelyn was not well versed in natural or easy. But it felt undeniably correct.

I sat up from my laptop, rubbing at my eyes. It was nearing midnight. Wherever Sydney was, she would be back soon. I needed to go to bed.

I saved my document and closed my computer, then crawled beneath my covers and shut my eyes, the smells of cinnamon and soap heavy in my nostrils.

Chapter Thirteen

ield practice was not going well.

We'd been out here for an hour and a half, and not only was it freezing, we were sucking. *Majorly* sucking. We all marched with the approximate skill of a bunch of freshies on their first day of band camp, and Braden's persistent shouting didn't help.

"Emily, pick your feet up! You want to drag your shoes through the mud, do it on your own time."

"There isn't even any mud here," Emily muttered next to me. If I hadn't known better, I would have guessed she was talking *to* me, but that was scientifically impossible. "You don't get mud on Astroturf."

"Do you have something to share with the class, Emily?" Braden glowered down at her from his spot on the end of the rank. We were tucked into the top left corner of the field, way out on the ten-yard line, too far for Avery to offer me any comfort. On top of everything else, we were getting pelted with precipitation. Closer to mist than rain, but still unpleasant enough to ruin any semblance of enjoyment field rehearsal might have otherwise held. All the woodwinds had run their instruments back inside at the first sight of a cloud, but we brass held strong, the metal of my trombone freezing against my hands.

"No. Sir." She muttered the last word again. I glanced over at her, tried to catch her eye, but she just stared down at her bell. Braden had moved her next to me permanently ("someone clearly has to supervise you," he'd said) after the crash-disaster last week, and we still hadn't spoken. She just sort of spoke . . . near me.

"Good." Braden nodded. For once, I was jealous of how overprepared he was for the weather. Between his puffy coat, ski gloves, and pom-pom'd hat, there was no way he felt the cold. "We're only a week away from homecoming. We screw up again, we'll never hear the end of it."

Like anybody really cared about six trombones, I thought, clenching my hand over my slide as I tried to think warm thoughts. Avery looked like an action figure on his ladder at the front of the field, chatting with the drum line. I wondered what they were talking about. They looked a lot warmer than we did.

God, it was miserable out here. But it wasn't like I had a choice. Even if I could have pulled some sort of "cough cough I'm sick" routine and gotten away with it, I was still trying to figure out how to prove my worth to the band after last week's debacle. I'd briefly considered asking Fitz to make another donation to the school, but Wickham's comments about everyone hating me and my money not helping hung heavily on my mind. For once, this wasn't something that could be solved by throwing the Darcy family money at it.

Probably, anyway.

I jumped to attention when I saw Avery raise his arms, nod in our direction. Braden was still going on and on about tradition and dignity from his end of the row, until Jackson elbowed him and pointed toward the front of the field. Braden shut up mid-word, like he wanted to trap a fly in his mouth, as Avery lifted his arms even higher and we began.

Left eight, forward eight, hold two three four. The drill wasn't super complicated at this point in the music, a weird medley of pop songs that Avery had called "These Fools All Dated Each Other." The trombone part in "Sucker" had looked cool on paper, but the sound was . . . not great. I could distinctly hear dissonance from the end of the rank, a blaring horn against the rest of us.

The answer to "Who the hell sounds terrible?" presented itself to me as the trombones turned a corner at the twenty-yard line, the shining brass of instruments the only color in the gray mist that surrounded us.

Braden.

Well, shit. The only one who could correct Braden on his notes and tuning was Braden. I was pretty sure he'd murder anyone else who tried, and who would dare? Braden was a senior, and he cared a lot about band, even if his musicianship had never been the best. I totally got why Mrs. Tapper had made him section leader.

That didn't mean he sounded good.

In front of me, two rows of flag corps, led by Sydney, careened into each other. Perfect. (I subtly took a step back, just to make sure it didn't look like my fault.) I tried to get into the music, to lose myself in the pumping bass line of the song, but all I could hear was Braden's uneven wails. I wanted to rip the trombone out of his hand and beat him over the head with it. Honestly, what he was doing was a dishonor and a travesty to trombones everywhere. The Jonas Brothers hadn't poured all of their reunion energy into this song just for him to play the wrong notes.

I winced as we hit the final beat, bells popped into the air for emphasis. We looked okay, but that *sound*. Braden was the section leader. The freshmen looked to him for guidance. What if they thought that was the right note, and adjusted to match him? Then half the section would be wrong, and you'd *definitely* be able to tell from the stands, and poof, there went the alumni donations that made all of this possible. There went our trips to parades and exhibitions.

I mean, with the way my grades were going there was no way I'd be able to participate in travel anyway, so it wasn't any of my business. But I wanted the band to be good. I wanted to prove to them that I cared about what we did here, how we sounded. I wanted to prove to Mrs. T that I wasn't a detriment to the section, and I wanted to prove to Avery that he hadn't made a huge mistake in believing in me.

I didn't think that was too much to ask.

Maybe I should tell Braden. It was a bad idea. But what did I know? Most of my ideas had proven to be terrible, even if I thought they were great. Maybe *thinking* this idea was bad actually meant I was onto something.

"That's it for today," Mrs. Tapper announced into her megaphone. I eyed her gloves with jealousy as I shivered, even colder again now that we had stopped moving. *Note to self: have our housekeeper send me a few extra pairs from the house.* "Keep practicing." Was it my imagination, or did her eyes purposely swing back to the trombones when she said that? She had to have noticed. She had to.

I stayed on the field for a minute longer as the band filed off around me, the freezing mist battering against my face. I should just keep my head down. Pretend nothing was wrong. Be a good girl, stay under the radar. Be the perfect, stand-against-the-wall-while-the-world-went-on-around-me Darcy.

Before I knew what I was doing, I ran to catch up to Braden at the edge of the field, blocked his entrance back into the band room.

"Hey." I tried to take a deep breath at the same time that I spoke, which meant that I choked halfway through, coughing loudly. Braden stared down at me, his expression unreadable as he waited for me to not die. Or *to* die, probably. "Can I talk to you for a second?"

"I guess." His voice dripped with disdain. Super fun. I loved being treated like an inconvenience because I dared to converse with my section leader, whose literal job it was to take care of me. "Make it quick. It's freezing out here."

The rest of the section had stopped to watch us, which put me even more on the defensive than usual, but I took another deep breath, tried to sound like a reasonable person worth listening to. "I just think you may have been out of tune or something. You sounded off."

"I was not." The color drained out of Braden's face as his eyes narrowed. "And how would you even know? You don't exactly have a history of playing well with others."

"Well, you were." I ignored his jab as I shrugged, my arms crossed over my chest to keep in any warmth I could. "Trust me. I have ears, is the thing. That's how I knew." Okay, maybe harsher than I'd intended, but it was a lot harder to keep up a façade of politeness when Braden insisted on being a dick. A sharp intake of breath next to me, which sounded like Emily, but I didn't turn around. I wasn't going to break Braden's gaze. If he wanted to have some sort of trombone power struggle, I'd dance.

"Last time I checked, I was the section leader." Color flooded back into Braden's face as he turned red with anger. "And you're just some reject nobody, so why don't you leave me the hell alone? You don't like the way I play, or the way I conduct my section, fine. We don't need you here, Darcy."

"I'm trying to help, Braden." As much as I wanted to shrink down, I held my ground. The rest of the section must have agreed with me, whether they'd say it or not, and I was determined to make myself heard.

"And I'm trying to tell you." He stepped up, real close, close enough to smell the peppermint on his breath, which made me wince. "We don't need you, and we don't want you. You might have wormed your way back into this band by virtue of your dead daddy's money, but that doesn't mean I have to treat you with respect that you've *never* earned."

Now it was my turn to go colorless as I looked toward the other trombones. Surely, at this point, when I'd stuck my neck out for them *again*, when I'd done my best to prove that I cared, surely someone would say something. Stand by my side. This was different than the catering thing. This was me, a person, trying to make my band better. Someone had to respect that.

No one did.

He didn't stop there, either.

"Besides, it's kind of funny you pretend to care about the way we sound," he said, riding on the high of no one interrupting him, no one stopping him in his onslaught, "because you're the one who got our best trumpet kicked out, aren't you?"

It always came back to Wickham. Always came back to the squeeze of tightness in my chest and the way I felt so small.

I backed away. I wanted to say something else, to throw out a biting retort, but all I saw was the rest of the section around Braden, who didn't bother to refute him. Who didn't step up and say that they wanted me, actually, that I wasn't that bad, that the rumors about me were untrue, that Braden didn't know what he was talking about and I *was* just trying to help. They just watched me, with expressions ranging from disinterested to antagonistic, and none of them moved to stop me as I turned and fled the field.

Screw them. Screw all of them. Clearly they had no interest in accepting me. Wickham was right, even though I hated to think it. He'd always been right about me, and about the people around me.

I grabbed my backpack from the band room without stopping, abandoning my trombone as I ran out of the room and down the long hall of the music wing.

This wasn't because of The Incident. People made mistakes all the time. This was a deep-seated dismissal I'd never fully grasped, because this was the first time I was at Pemberley without the safety net of my brother or Wickham or my own false bravado. These were the people who were supposed to care about me specifically saying that they didn't want me. I knew what they all thought, after all. The band would have been a lot better off if Georgie Darcy had gotten expelled instead of Wickham Foster.

I wanted to email Wickham. I wanted to feel wanted.

I ran faster, pushed open the door of the arts building and ran across the quad, rain be damned. I wished I could go back to my room, put my head under the covers and sleep forever, but Sydney would be headed there, too, and I didn't want to deal with her, either. I turned toward the library, the only spot on campus that would be open late. I could stay there until curfew, then slink back to my dorm and pretend I was alone. Pretend that it was last year, or the year before, before everything went to shit. Or even better, pretend my dad was still alive. That my mom was still around. Pretend that I still had a whole family who loved me and cared about me.

Wickham was in the doorway of my dorm room, and it was hot for April, almost sticky outside, and there was Fitz, holding up the bag of pills and asking what they were, and Wickham laughed and tried to play it off until my brother slammed his fist against my desk and screamed that he wanted answers.

I still didn't have them.

The library was, blessedly, almost entirely empty as I signed in at the front desk, my hands shaking. And it was warm in here, cozy. The dark wood that permeated our campus actually worked in this space, with the building's high archways and long, floor-to-ceiling windows that showed whatever weather you were currently hiding from. Glowing lamps were scattered around the floor, and tucked in between the shelves were nooks and hidey-holes with gathered plush chairs.

There was an alcove here named after Fitz, technically a wing, where he'd spent his whole four years studying. We'd worked in here together, during our overlapping year. He'd made the donation as his graduation present to the school, and the plaque was still shiny and new. I stayed as far away from it as possible.

At least my favorite chair was open. In view of a window, but not close enough to let the chill in, it was squishy and red and tucked away by itself. I pulled another chair over to prop my feet up and took advantage of the real boon to the spot—the outlet hidden behind the chair's tall back. With my laptop plugged in and my headphones on, curled up as I watched the mist turn into full-on rain in front of me, I could stay here for hours.

Or at least the five hours before the library closed for the night, when I'd have to trudge through the rain back to my dorm room. But on a day like this, I'd take what I could get.

I grabbed my phone as I settled in, pulled up my contacts without really thinking about it. Opened the contact for Fitz. He wouldn't want to talk to me. I didn't know why I suddenly felt so compelled to call him. He'd just yell, or worse, he wouldn't answer.

And I wouldn't email Wickham. I would not email Wickham.

I put my phone back in my pocket.

CHAPTER FOURTEEN

very found me.

It was possible he had some sort of Spidey-sense where I was concerned. I didn't want to seem ungrateful as he picked his way through the shelves toward me, hand up in a hesitant wave, but didn't he have other friends? Other obligations, besides my comfort?

Being me, that was the first thing I asked him.

"Don't you have anything better to do than track me down at my worst?" I asked, as he pulled over an extra chair—he didn't ask to take the one I'd put my feet up on, which I appreciated—and plopped down next to me. "You have to have other friends." I felt a twinge at words that came out harsher than I'd intended.

His smile faltered for just a second before it reappeared. He was like the Cheshire Cat. If he ever started to fade away around me, that smile would be the last thing I saw.

"You're not the only one who'd rather keep to themselves sometimes, George." He propped one elbow up on the armrest closest to me, leaned his head into his hand to bring it even closer. "Not many people appreciate my amazing sense of humor."

"Or your modesty?" I offered. Avery was . . . okay, not popular. The school wasn't big enough to have true popularity contests, but if it did, the drum major of the marching band, who wore a constantly wrinkled uniform and made weird jokes about feelings, probably wouldn't be at the top of the list. "For real, though. If you have other people you'd rather hang out with, it's okay. I'm not offended."

"George." Less of a grin, that time, more of a smile that edged into sadness. "Who are all these people you've seen me hang out with? Can you tell me about them, please? Maybe give me their phone numbers?"

The rawness, the exposed nerves of his feelings on his face, hurt to look at. I didn't want to look at it.

"Anyway," he continued with a shrug. "I tried to catch you after practice. With . . . you know. But I was caught up talking to Mrs. T and I couldn't get away. Took me forever to find you here. If you want me to leave you alone . . ." He let his voice trail off. Watched me.

I shook my head, and he smiled, ran his hands over the leather of his chair.

Welp. I took a deep breath. I guess I wanted to talk about this after all. "You have super-special drum major powers, right?"

"A couple. Still can't fly, though."

"Can you fire Braden?" The words came out a lot faster than I meant them to, and Avery raised an eyebrow. "He's just . . . he's a shitty section leader." This was total narc behavior, but whatever, the whole section already hated me.

"Ouch." Avery settled into his chair, in for the long haul. "You want to tell me what you guys were yelling about?"

"Oh, the usual." My laugh came out all darkness. "I tried to offer like, one iota of advice on his playing—which needs more than an iota, but I acknowledge no one cares about what I have to say—and he totally blew up at me. Called me a . . . a reject nobody who was coasting through on my dead daddy's money." I blew a curl out of my face. "Then he decided to remind me how talented Wickham was for good measure. And if that's the sort of thing he says to my face, can you imagine what he's saying behind my back?"

I leaned my head back against the crushed velvet fabric of the chair. Avery didn't say anything for a minute, and we both watched the rain, which was coming down in sheets outside.

Then he spoke.

"Can I say something?"

"You can say as many somethings as you want, as long as they aren't lectures on responsibility or decorum. I'd call my brother for that." My hair was frizzing up, I could tell, and I tried to push it back out of my eyes. I needed to buy more hair ties.

Avery took a second to consider his words before he spoke. "Why do you care?"

"What?"

"Why do you care?" he repeated, like the four single-syllable words were what I'd had trouble understanding. One of the librarians crossed behind him, seemingly oblivious to my emotional well-being or lack thereof. "Braden, he—I shouldn't say this, because I'm drum major or whatever. But he sucks. I know you know that. Why do you care what he thinks?"

I struggled to put into words what I was feeling. I wanted to make Avery understand, but I wasn't sure I could, because thinking about it, why *did* I care what Braden thought? So he hated me. I mean, it sucked, but what did that *do*? Nothing. It was just words. That was all anyone in this school could ever throw at me. Words and threats and empty promises. It was just like when the Hawkins family—the main societal rivals to Jocelyn's family on *Sage Hall*—showed up in Bath at the same time as them one season, and spent the whole time trying to make it look like Jocelyn was sleeping around.

She didn't even need Andrew's help to get out of it, either, though he offered to run her off to Scotland for a hasty elopement and frankly just got in the way of her own empowerment by moping around the whole episode. She stood tall, proud, and rose up against the rumors, proving them untrue.

Just like Jocelyn, I knew what everyone said about me was a lie. She didn't let those lies hurt her.

I wasn't sure why I let mine hurt me.

"I don't know." I was evading the question, but I wanted to let my thoughts simmer for a while. Figure out how much of my hurt was me caring about what *Braden* thought and how much of it was my own broken psyche. "Sorry. I sound stupid."

"Eh." Avery shrugged, and I grinned, both of our eyes turned toward the rain. "Being drum major isn't everything it's cracked up to be, either, if it helps."

"Lonely on your platform of power?" I'd meant it as a joke, but it didn't come out sounding like one, and Avery just shrugged.

"I don't know. Turns out it kind of sucks, being all by yourself up there. Not sure if you're doing a good job or completely screwing up every chance you had at a future." He sighed, then reset his face into an immediate smile. It was like he had practiced it, practiced pushing down any bad emotions fast enough that there was no evidence they'd ever been there. "Do you want to watch something?"

"What?"

"Like, a show." He nodded to the darkened screen of my laptop. "I don't feel like doing homework, and it's pouring out there. And I just . . . we could both use some distraction, right?"

Part of me wanted to let him push his feelings aside. But I knew Avery well enough, was relearning him well enough, to know that he wouldn't have let me get away with that, if our roles were reversed.

"Nope." I shook my head, sat up a little as I crossed my legs underneath me. "Come on. I can play psychiatrist right back at you, no quarter required. Does your whole future really rest on being drum major?" I'd meant it as a rib, but Avery shrugged again.

"Unless you've got twenty grand a year lying around to pay for my college, then yeah, it kind of does."

The weird thought occurred to me that I did, if I wanted it. But it didn't feel like the right thing to tell Avery, whose gaze had shifted behind me again, out the window at the pouring rain. His dark brows pinched in the center, his face lined with more worry than I'd ever seen on him before.

"How does band factor in?" My voice was hesitant. If there was one thing I didn't know how to talk about, it was money. That was one of the earliest memories I had of my mom, actually. Her constant reminder that the only money talk that needed to exist was no money talk at all. But then again, everyone I'd grown up around had it.

"There are plenty of schools that give band scholarships through athletics." He played with the strings on his worn-out hoodie, adjusted them to the same length. "It tends to be schools with big football programs, too, which is good for me. I want to study sports medicine. A lot of colleges like that have practical opportunities available for undergrads."

"Wow." I knew, technically, that I needed to start thinking about college this year, but after The Incident it was so far removed from my consciousness that I'd managed to ignore it. But Avery, for all of his joking about being a STOP sign holder, knew exactly what his path forward was. Envy shot through me. I may have known money wouldn't be an issue, but I would have traded that for certainty. "Medicine, huh? Didn't know you were secretly a genius."

I wish I knew how to put more sincerity in my voice, how to talk about something serious without hiding behind layers of banter and jokes and sarcasm, but then again, this was Avery, and he and I spoke the same language. He grinned as he looked back at me.

"I didn't want to intimidate you, that's all." As he ran his fingers through his hair, it stood straight up from his head like a mad scientist's. "But to go to those schools, I need scholarship money. Even if I stay in-state back home, go to Ohio, I'll need something. And it's a lot, holding your entire future in the palm of your hand like that, you know? Like, if I do a good job I can have everything I ever wanted. And if I ruin it, I'm done."

I watched Avery, the first person I'd let into this secret corner of the library with me in forever. Watched him open up to me, and I couldn't help but think that he was one of the bravest people I'd ever known.

I'd lost a lot, after I fell in with Wickham. But I was so, so grateful I hadn't lost Avery, too. For once, I didn't hear the voice of Wickham in my head, telling me I was wrong.

"If it helps, you're looking at someone who did fuck up their life." I indicated myself with my hands, and Avery laughed, broke the spell we'd both fallen under, lulled in by rain and intimacy. "I'm hoping there's a chance at redemption."

"I'll keep my fingers crossed for both of us," Avery said, then reached over and squeezed my shoulder, just for a second, before he cleared his throat and sat up fully in his own chair. "For real, though, do you want to watch something?"

Surely we'd gotten emotional enough for one night. The rain continued to pound down outside, and I smiled.

"Sure." I woke my computer back up and pulled up my web browser. "Preferences?"

"We can do *Sage Hall*?" Avery offered as he leaned over to see my screen, and my chest squeezed tight. "I've seen an episode here and there. And a lot of GIF sets on Tumblr. You can catch me up on whatever episode you want."

"Sure," I replied, my voice catching, which was completely stupid. Just because no one had ever offered to watch *Sage Hall* with me IRL before—Fitz had watched it with me, but only at my distinct coercion—didn't mean anything. Jocelyn, a fictional character, certainly wasn't sending me a sign. "Let me see what's up."

I popped over to the web page for streaming episodes. I had a few episodes saved on my hard drive, but I'd watched them all so many times this summer that I needed a palate cleanser.

As the page loaded, my whole body tensed up. The web host had tweeted earlier that he probably wouldn't get this episode up until Friday, but here it was. The newest episode. The JocAndrew kiss.

Oh my God.

"Is that a new one?" Avery pointed at the screen, seemingly unaware of how much my hands were shaking. "We can watch that, if you want. I don't want to deprive you of the latest content."

"Um." My face went ashen, my hands trembling harder than they had out in the cold. This wasn't supposed to happen here. This was supposed to be something I watched on my own, in my dorm, with the covers pulled up over my head so that Sydney wouldn't see it if I cried. This was supposed to be something I got through alone, because this was my own private shame I was trying to carry like a Darcy, pushed deep down where no one but me would ever find it.

My vision of how this would go didn't include Avery, staring at me in confusion.

"Hey." Avery had finally noticed how freaked out I was, which proved less about his observational skills than it did my visible panic. "You okay?"

"It's just . . . um." I took a deep breath. "I'm pretty sure what's going to happen in this episode? Is both going to be extremely narratively rewarding while also bringing up stuff from my past I generally try to never ever think about. And I'm going to have to think about it like, a lot, when I watch this. I don't know."

"I'm guessing skipping it entirely isn't an option."

"Of course not!" My voice was louder than I'd meant it to be, and I half-expected a librarian to run over and shush us, but we were far enough in the back that no one came. "Sorry. I just . . . I mean, I have to watch it."

"Okay." He nodded, considering the problem with a seriousness I didn't deserve. "Do you . . . if you'd rather watch it by yourself, I completely get it. For real. But I can also watch it with you, now, if you want. And then you won't have to be alone for it? We don't have to talk about it or anything," he hastened to add. "This doesn't have to be more therapist hour. But sometimes things that are hard are easier with someone else there, you know?"

I didn't. But maybe, I thought as my chest squeezed tightly again, I could find out.

"Are you sure?" I would give him as many outs as he needed.

"Come on." Avery's gaze flickered down to my hands, then

back up to my eyes. "You can explain who everyone is, too. And I'll ask as many annoying questions about the timeline as you want."

"Which is zero?"

"Which may be zero," he conceded as I passed him an earbud, feeling something that, surprisingly, wasn't dread as I pressed play. "But may be one or two. I'm only human."

"Shut up," I muttered as the title sequence passed across the screen, all carriages and moonlight, and God, I loved this show. "It's starting." Avery grinned at me and we both settled back to watch, the laptop perched between both of our armrests.

cll

It was actually happening. I could feel it.

They were about to kiss.

It was unclear if the quick beating of my heart was from romance or anxiety. It was probably a fifty-fifty mix of both.

The scene blurred in front of me, memories of Wickham popping in among the Regency setting.

"Come to the carriage," Jocelyn begged Andrew, her hands pressed against his face in desperation. "Before I go. I'll . . . I'll prepare early. I'll wait for you, there, and we can go away together. We can go wherever we want."

"Why should we wait?" Andrew murmured, as his hands reached up to grab hers. "Why should we wait a single second more?"

"Come on, kid," Wickham said, standing in the doorway to my room.

"I just don't want Fitz to get mad." I shrugged, only inches from him. We'd been hanging out for weeks, walking around campus and

sneaking into town together, but I'd never let him into my room. It seemed . . . I didn't know. "You know how he gets."

"And I also know he's all the way in California, and I'm pretty sure he doesn't have cameras in your room," he said as he nodded toward the corners. "Let me in, G. Come on. I missed you tonight."

"You saw me at dinner an hour ago," I said, but I stepped aside, and as he crossed the threshold into my room, closed the door softly behind him, a thrill zipped through me. I'd been in love with Wickham Foster since I was a kid. Now he was in my room, my single *room, and he was looking at me like I was the world.*

"Maybe food wasn't all I was hungry for," he said, and my heart jumped.

"Here?" Jocelyn asked, and she didn't take her eyes off Andrew as she spoke. "Andrew, if someone sees . . ."

"Let them see." He leaned his forehead against hers, and both of their eyes closed. "Let the world know that I want you."

"Can I sit?" Wickham nodded toward the bed. "I remember that blanket. It's from Rochester, right? From back home?"

"Yeah." I tried to stand up as straight as possible, to look older. I'd put on eyeliner after he texted to say he was downstairs. It looked okay.

"Come on." He patted the space next to him on the bed. "Come sit with me."

I moved like I was floating in a pool, each motion smooth and weightless. We sat together, our thighs pressed close as he turned to face me. I did the same, my heart beating like a hummingbird's in my chest.

"I love the nest of your hair, you know?" He touched my hair, and I cataloged his touch to remember forever. "It's wild. You make me wild."

It was happening. It was actually happening.

"May I show you how much?" Andrew asked. "May I, please, Jocelyn, may I show you?"

Andrew asked. Wickham didn't.

As Jocelyn's and Andrew's lips crashed together, all I could taste was peppermint, the gum Wickham had been chewing when he'd kissed me, when he'd pressed his mouth against mine and lowered me down, his weight on top of me, and I'd had a hard time breathing under the pressure but I didn't want to breathe, anyway, because this was all I had ever wanted.

We'd stopped at kissing. My phone had buzzed with a text from Fitz, and Wickham had gotten up and winked as he told me he'd see me later, and we began a year of laters, a year of kisses and secret meetings and me giving him the spare key to my room to meet me, a year of me forgetting to respond to Fitz's messages and Wickham telling me I shouldn't, anyway, because he wouldn't understand us. A year of learning the wrong way to love someone before Fitz burst into my room to find all the little pills in baggies, where he didn't believe me even as I said I'd never seen them before. That I didn't know what Wickham had been doing. That I'd thought he loved me.

Wickham in the doorway.

It all tasted like peppermint. All of it.

I ripped the headphone out of my left ear, let it fall as I buried my head in my hands. I hated that stupid taste. I hated Wickham and I hated peppermint and I hated everything he'd ruined for me, and everything I'd ruined for myself.

"Whoa." At Avery's voice, I looked up, saw his face over the screen that separated us, the concern there. "George. It's okay. It's okay." He put one arm around my shoulder and pulled me in, awkwardly over the armrests, and I let myself be pulled because I couldn't remember the last time someone had offered me comfort without judgment. "I'm sorry. We shouldn't have watched."

"Wickham was who I always imagined, when I wrote fics about those two." I nodded at the screen, at the frozen image of Jocelyn and Andrew, moving on from their kiss into the gazing-into-each-other's-eyes portion of the evening. "Which is stupid, I know." I inhaled, a deep, shuddering breath. "I had this . . . this huge crush on him growing up. He was always nice to me." Avery didn't say anything, just held me against his chest. It was nice there. Warm. "I thought I was the luckiest girl in the world, when he transferred here."

"George."

"And once we were together . . ." I spoke as fast as I could, so that I wouldn't get scared and take the words back. I was tired of being scared. Of taking words back. Of pretending that the things I felt were a lie. "You saw what happened. I stopped doing home-work. Barely went to class. And he just . . . I didn't know about the drugs, Aves. I didn't, and I should have, because it's honestly more embarrassing that someone calling me pretty completely blinded me to their literal criminal activities. But I didn't know. I don't even know what he's doing here now."

"George." Avery's hand caught my face for just a second, though he dropped it like my skin was burning hot, and I turned to look at him, suddenly aware of my babbling. God. He was going to totally ditch me now, wasn't he? This was why I didn't open up to anyone. No one wanted to hear it. No one cared *why* the rich girl ended up with a drug dealer in her bedroom. All they cared about was that it had happened and that I'd deserved it.

I did, too. I didn't tell Avery that part. That I was small and worthless and deserved everything that had happened to me, because why would all this shit keep happening if I didn't deserve it? I'd been born into a world of privilege that I wasn't good enough for, and I didn't blame the dozens of students who wanted to take my place there. They deserved it more than me, who didn't work hard enough and wasn't smart enough to be loved. That's what separated me from Jocelyn. She was good and kind and deserved the things she had, and I, simply, did not.

I kept that to myself. I had to. For all that Avery was literally the best, he'd leave me after I told him that. I'd be alone again. And even though I could handle it, even though I'd been doing it for years . . .

When I was with Avery, I didn't want to.

"Sorry." I shook my head. "I'm rambling."

"You weren't—well, maybe you were, but it seems justified." Avery laughed, and from anyone else it might have sounded cruel, but Avery had no cruelty in him. "You had a lot to say."

"That doesn't make it worth hearing."

"That's bull, and you know it." He leaned back, his hand drifting from my back to my shoulder, and looked down at me. "I know you know it."

"Right." I'd pretend. "The rain is letting up." I hadn't looked at the window in the last hour, and in that time the heavy rain had turned back to mist, just cloaked in darkness. "We should go. Curfew, and stuff." Curfew didn't hit for another thirty minutes, but what were Avery and I supposed to say after I poured out everything I had?

"Yeah." Avery stood up, then helped me to my feet, held out his hand to pull me up from my chair. "Curfew."

I didn't regret talking to him, weirdly. Didn't wish that I had watched *Sage Hall* in the safety of my own room. It would have been safer. But I didn't think it would have been better.

cll

I didn't think I'd want to write that night, expected to fall straight to sleep when my head hit the pillow, but I didn't, so I pulled out my laptop and let the words go.

"*You don't have to stay, Henry.*" *Jocelyn shouldn't have come to town, not without a chaperone, but she'd needed to get away from her home, away from the oppressive crush of expectations that surrounded her there.* "*I can see myself out.*"

"*And let the gossips ran rampant with the knowledge that Jocelyn Tetherfield went into town alone?*" *Henry feigned shock, and Jocelyn let out a laugh she hadn't expected.* "*But if you don't want me here, simply say the word. I shall depart at once, and tell everyone I meet that your trip to town was untouched by scandal. Remind them that the Bible prohibits gossip.*"

"*Does it?*" *When she was with Henry, the world fell away. It scared Jocelyn, but she couldn't stop going back for it.* "*Really?*"

"*I haven't the faintest idea.*" *Henry's smile was the warmest Jocelyn had ever seen. The kindest.* "*Shall I go, Miss Tetherfield? Shall I leave you?*"

"*No.*" *Jocelyn spoke decisively, quickly, and she felt something shift between them as she did.* "*Stay.*"

And so, he did.

Chapter Fifteen

he kiss was all the fandom could talk about.

I didn't blame them, obviously. And once I isolated the kiss from the context—thank you, Tumblr GIF sets—I memorized the blocking enough that I could swoon and squee with the best of them. I was getting through.

I'd spent the first half of the week keeping my head down, making as few waves as possible. I'd barely spoken to Fitz all week, but I figured that was for the best. The floral company I'd hired to deliver Lizzie flowers hadn't reported any issues, so I had to assume that was working.

I wanted to do something more, bump up my efforts even further to let Lizzie know that *Fitz* was in love with her, not just some rando. Matchmaking my brother was a lot more fun than trying to figure out why I'd failed another chemistry test, so I poured all my energy into brainstorming.

As it happened, the perfect opportunity presented itself when Charlie Bingley followed me on Instagram, a notification that popped up on my phone during lunch the Wednesday before homecoming. I didn't usually check my Instagram, but I could only stare straight forward for so long, so I accepted without hesitation and scrolled through his profile, absentmindedly picking at my plate of pasta.

Fitz was in a couple of his most recent pictures, and I glanced at the half-smile on his face with a pang of envy, but it was the most recent post on his Stories that made me pause.

Wednesday night—Fall Colors Party at Alpha Chi! Orange and Red and Brown or NOTHING. Be there!

He'd placed the text over a picture of what I had to assume was the last party this frat had thrown. The picture caught my eye because *Fitz* was in it. Fitz. At a frat party. He wore a tie around his head like a bad college stereotype, which would have been enough to shock me, but more importantly?

Lizzie Bennet was in the picture, too.

Fitz, Lizzie, Charlie, and Jane grinned at me in a group shot, and Fitz stood just close enough to Lizzie that I could tell he was specifically thinking about the distance between them. Measuring it.

This was my shot. My next step. Sure, it was a Wednesday night, a school night, but surely this was more important to the plan than my chem homework, and I owed this to my brother. Someone needed to take the distance between those two and squish it down to nothing, and that someone was going to be me.

Besides, I'd been invited, technically, even if it was almost certainly a mass invite to every single one of Charlie's five thousand followers. And a properly accomplished Darcy *never* turned down an invitation.

Hey, I texted Avery. *How would you like to attend a frat party tonight?*

The message came back immediately, and I grinned.

This sounds like a terrible idea and I'm one thousand percent in. Is this, perhaps, related to Operation: Matchmaker?

Yep, I replied. *Cue the theme music.*

It was SO on.

cll

"I acknowledge that a fully brown ensemble is not the most interesting." Avery shrugged, looking me up and down as we got out of his car. We'd parked a safe enough distance from the frat house that, hopefully, no one would throw up on the hood of the car. I'd put on red pants and an orange shirt, an outfit that was a lot louder, comparatively, than Avery's. More important, though, his plain brown T-shirt was *way* more fitted than I'd anticipated. I kept glancing over at it, at the way the edges of the short sleeves cupped at his biceps. Not that that was the sort of thing you should notice about a friend, but all that conducting had clearly been working for him.

It was definitely working for me.

Wait, no.

"But you have to use what you've got. And what I've got, it turns out, is brown."

Avery was still talking, apparently, even as I was lost waxing rhapsodic about the way his arms flexed. I needed to pull it together. Maybe frat houses gave off pheromones or something. It would explain a lot. I popped my hand up to my head in a quick salute, only wincing a little at how childish it must have looked.

"Roger that."

"Do we have a plan here?" Avery seemed clueless to my mental breakdown, thank God. Or maybe he was just distracted by the way-below-freezing temperatures. It was, somehow, even colder up at Meryton than it was at Pemberley, and I could *see* Avery shivering, the hair on his arms raised to standing. We'd both abandoned our coats in the car, because I had watched enough movies about college to know that if you took off your coat at a frat house, you'd never get it back. "Or are you just going to lock your brother and his friend in the bathroom and hope for the best?"

"I'll have you know I've seen at least three Hallmark movies where that exact plot works out perfectly." I was freezing, too, and wrapped my arms around my chest to try and preserve any body heat I had left. Hopefully we wouldn't stick out as super high school when we got in. I didn't have any bodycon dresses in the colors dictated by Charlie's invite, and that seemed to be the major frat party uniform, but I'd at least gathered my T-shirt into a knot where the fabric met my pants to make it a little tighter. Avery kept glancing toward it. "Besides, I need to assess the full romance situation before I make any decisions."

"Spoken like a true spy."

"I never claimed to be fully trained for the FBI." Up ahead, a beaten-up white house with a porch that only looked half-attached had the most lights on of any house on the street. The blaring music and the people spilling out onto the sidewalk would have been enough indication that we were nearly at our destination, even without the wooden ALPHA CHI sign that had been nailed into the front yard. The poor grass. "They won't give you a badge until you're eighteen, anyway."

"Disappointing." Avery sighed as he stepped up onto the sidewalk beside me. "Here I was hoping we could use your credentials to sneak across the Canadian border."

"Right." I laughed, coming to a stop in front of the house. Everyone here looked a lot more . . . normal than I'd expected. They were older than us, obviously, but they weren't all in matching button-down shirts and super-tight dresses. The color scheme was sort of being adhered to, but the majority of people wore T-shirts and jeans, like us. I let out a sigh of relief. "But listen." I'd come up with at least one good idea on the drive over, something to make up for dragging Avery into school-night shenanigans. "Do you want me to drive us home? I can DD. You came all this way to help me."

"Really?" Avery eyed the red Solo cups that surrounded us with some skepticism. "I don't want to keep you from having fun. I knew what I was getting myself into, driving you here."

"Seriously." It wasn't like I wanted to drink. "Pemberley is a pressure cooker. Go party your problems away."

"All right." Avery shrugged, then grinned down at me. "But we're still sticking together. Who will explain to everyone here that we're in high school if I run off and leave you by yourself?"

"Shut up." I laughed, bumping my shoulder into his, and he bumped mine back, and as we pushed through the flimsy porch door—seriously, this house was one aggressive dance move away from being entirely condemned—the electric excitement that flooded through me felt like more than just a party.

I had been worried about avoiding Fitz once we got inside—just because I was here to matchmake him didn't mean I wanted him to *see* me—but it was packed enough that I felt way better about my chances the second we entered the living room.

Music roared through the cramped space, pulsed a beat so loud I felt it in the arches of my feet. A tightly packed dance floor took up the center of the small room, with hallways that branched off toward the rest of the house. It was dark enough that you could hardly make out anyone's face if they weren't right in front of you.

Even if Fitz *was* in there, I'd have no idea. *Sage Hall* ballroom, this was not.

But I kind of loved it. Loved feeling anonymous in a crowd, knowing that no one knew or cared who I was. I spotted a keg in the far corner of the room, and pointed it out to Avery. He nodded—it was way too loud to try to talk to each other in here—then grabbed me by the hand to pull me through the crowd with him.

His touch was warm, reassuring. In a room of fleeting fancy, I had never been so sure of something being solidly *there*.

It was possible I was picking up some secondhand weed smoke, with a ridiculous thought like that. But I'd been feeling weirdly better since we'd watched *Sage Hall* together. More like myself. I'd barely checked my email for Wickham notes, and seeing Braden in the halls didn't freak me out like it had before. I'd even smiled at Emily once, across a hall, and been rewarded with a nod of acknowledgment, though that definitely could have been an accident.

Maybe I'd just needed to hit rock bottom to see that I could pull myself up. Or, in this case, pull my brother into a separate pit and throw the girl he had a total crush on in there with him. Same difference.

Avery dropped my hand when we made it to the keg, and I clenched and released my fist, feeling the weight of its absence, as he tried to figure out how to work the nozzle. Since movies didn't have detailed keg instructions included in them, I was just as clueless as he was, and we spent about a minute spraying foam everywhere before someone finally came up behind us.

"Here." A deep, reassuring voice hit my ear as a pair of hands reached for the nozzle. It was a little less aggressively loud over here, at least. "Let me get it. What, have you guys never seen a keg before—Georgie!"

I turned to see the source of the voice and discovered that it was, naturally, Charlie Bingley. Shit. I hadn't wanted *him* to see me, either, in case he told Fitz or got super mad at me for crashing his party, but he certainly didn't seem mad. In fact, he seemed exuberant.

"It's you, right? Georgie Darcy?" Strong, muscled arms wrapped around me and pulled me into a huge bear hug that lifted me off the ground. Charlie Bingley, it turned out, was absolutely *ripped*. This had not been apparent from his Insta pics, which were mostly selfies, or from the times he'd wandered by in the background of Fitz's FaceTime. "Fitzy's sister?"

"Fitz . . . y?" As I was finally released from the hug, I was able to take a step back and process the sheer amount of Charlie Bingley in front of me. Not *just* because he was a big guy—for real, though, he was gigantic, and also nearly shirtless with the exception of some strategically placed autumn leaves—but because of the energy he brought into the room. I wasn't the only person who was watching him.

"Well, you know." My God, he was like a dream frat boy from a CW show. I'd never seen anyone look sheepishly handsome before, but he managed it. I wasn't like, suddenly in love with Charlie or anything, because he was my brother's roommate, and that would be gross, but I was amazed by his sheer existence. Every Darcy since the dawn of time had been taught to fade into the background and avoid making a fuss. Charlie Bingley was the opposite of all that our family stood for.

No wonder my brother liked him.

"Are you another lucky recipient of my mass invites?" he continued, oblivious to my gaping stare. He probably got that a lot. "Fitzy always says I have to stop doing that. Or at least filter them down. Is this your friend, or did a second, individual high schooler make his way into my party?"

"Right, sorry." I shook my head to clear the fog created by his muscles, then held my hand out toward Avery, who accepted the beer Charlie had poured for him while staring at his muscles just as much as I had. "This is Avery. He drove me here."

"Then give me back that beer—"

"I'm driving us back," I interrupted, before Charlie could grab the beer out of Avery's hands. "Sorry. Should have clarified."

"Yeah, well, I shouldn't be serving beer to sixteen-year-olds, but life is full of surprises." He shrugged, and I couldn't help but smile, couldn't help but get caught up in all that was Charlie. "Have you seen Fitzy yet?"

"No!" I shouted over the music. The "Fitzy" thing was hard to wrap my head around. Our mother never even liked that he went by Fitz instead of Fitzwilliam. "He can't know I'm here. Okay? I'm just here to . . . um . . ."

"We're trying to get her brother to fall in love with the girl he hates so that he'll finally find happiness and fulfillment."

I turned toward Avery, who grinned over at me with a beer-foam mustache, half his drink already gone.

"What? That's what we're here for. Charlie seems cool."

"You're talking about Lizzie?" Charlie asked, full of enthusiasm, before I could swat at Avery for blowing our cover.

"Yes!" I let myself relax a little as Charlie pumped his fist into the air. "You see it, too, right?"

"That's perfect!" Charlie shouted. "Oh my God, are you two teen guardian angels sent from heaven to save me? Are we going to form a band after this? Because this is *exactly* what I need to—"

"What?" I called back, as the last of his words were lost to the music. Someone had pumped up the volume way louder than human ears could handle. "I can't—"

"Come on." Charlie cocked his head behind him, then started

to move through the crowd. I followed him, Avery trailing behind me as he swallowed the last of his beer. We pushed through autumnal-colored partiers until we emerged in a dingy but well-lit kitchen, where it was, thankfully, quieter. "Okay. Better. Punch?"

He grabbed a plastic cup from the counter that looked passably clean and dumped it into the large metal trough behind him, filling it with a bright red liquid before he handed it to Avery.

Avery sniffed it, then took a gulp and grinned. "Sweet."

"Hey, if we're keeping secrets from Fitzy anyway, may as well go all out. Drink water when you get home. So." He pushed aside a couple of cups and hopped up on the counter. I winced at the sheer amount of *sticky* he must currently be experiencing. "What were you saying?"

"What were *you* saying?" I countered, crossing my arms over my chest and trying not to touch anything. "About . . . teen guardian angels?"

"Oh, right. Sorry." That adorably sheepish smile again. I was pretty sure I could hear girls swoon in a three-mile radius of the house. "I've been watching a lot of Netflix with this girl, Jane. She's Lizzie's sister."

"The one you're in love at first sight with?"

"Yes!" Charlie's emphatic pointing sloshed his drink over the edge of his cup, but it missed my shoes, thankfully. "She's—God, she's perfect. She's just so *nice*, you know?"

Charlie Bingley looked at me with a level of sincerity I did not know existed in the modern human.

"I can imagine," I managed. Next to him, Avery caught my eye and winked over the top of his cup.

"But Fitzy's weird about it." Charlie shook his head. "Jane, I mean. Keeps saying she's a distraction. And frankly, I think a solid trip to Bonetown is exactly what he needs."

Next to Charlie, a passing frat boy who seemed to exist only for this purpose high-fived him, while I did my best not to melt into the actual ground. Seeing my expression, Charlie's eyes widened.

"Not that—I don't mean that, of course. Fuck—I mean, shit, I mean—"

"It's fine." I held up my hand to stop Charlie from naming every curse word he knew. "Let's just skip over that part of the narrative, okay?" I could see Avery's shoulders shaking with laughter as he filled his cup with more punch.

"You got it, boss." Charlie saluted, and he looked so much like Captain America that I almost had to lie down. "As I was saying. I think if your brother fell deeply and respectfully in love with Lizzie, in a purely emotional sense, where they never touched and just took lots of long romantic walks, he might get off my back about Jane, and Lizzie would get off *her* back about *me*." He leaned in close. "Lizzie's cool and all, cooler than your brother, but they definitely share a love of being a buzzkill."

No wonder they were perfect for each other.

"So what's the plan?" He took another sip of his drink, taking a moment to fill up a second plastic cup of water and hand it to Avery. "Here. Alternate sips, bro."

"Not sure." I leaned back against the fridge as Avery accepted the water, which was at least marginally less gross than any other surface. "I mean, we've done some stuff. I've been sending Lizzie flowers—"

"That was you!" Charlie pointed with enthusiasm. He seemed to do everything with enthusiasm. "Kiddo. Those flower arrangements are huge. It's an allergy hazard for the entire campus."

"They are?" I winced, caught Avery's eye as he shrugged. Admittedly, I'd selected the most expensive option, but hadn't thought further than that in terms of like, practicality.

God, this was exactly what Wickham was talking about. I tried too hard, I pushed too far, I didn't know what regular human limits were—

I looked up and saw Avery, who was still looking at me, head tipped to the side. *You okay?* he mouthed, and I took a deep breath, then another.

It was fine. I was trying. Trying was okay.

"Sorry." I released my breath, tried to calm my heart, which was beating weirdly fast. Probably from the Wickham intrusion, and definitely not from Avery's reassuring smile. "I'll scale it back."

"Maybe switch it to food or something." Charlie stretched his arms above his head, and I couldn't help but be completely and utterly transfixed by his torso. Damn. His abs had abs. "I can give you her and Jane's address, if you want. Secret admirer pizza deliveries might be more up her alley."

"I can do that." I nodded. I'd just have to remember to cancel the flowers. "But I feel like we need something else. Grand gesture style, you know?"

"Grand gesture?" Avery cut in. "What do you mean?"

"Like in a rom-com or whatever," I explained. "The huge elaborate setup that proves their feelings for each other."

"Yeah, the fact that your brother doesn't drink really gets in the way of the whole 'get them super drunk and hope they declare their love' plan." Charlie grabbed his own cup of punch, took a long pull as he considered. "Honestly, they need to go somewhere else. Somewhere off campus, where they can see each other outside of classes and study groups and academics."

I thought hard as Avery refilled his drink. There had to be something . . .

"Got it!" I shouted, suddenly enough that Charlie splashed his punch onto himself, which would have been a bigger problem if he had been wearing a shirt. Without one he was just kind of . . . damp, which most of the girls back in the main part of the party probably wouldn't complain about. "Fitz is coming down to Pemberley on Friday night for the homecoming game. There's like, a big fancy alumni box for high-tier donors where he'll hang out. If you convince Fitz to bring you, I can get Jane and Lizzie on the list, too. If he asks, you can just say you invited them, and they can see each other in a more chill environment. Once they're in there, we can engineer something completely *Sage Hall* Christmas Special levels of romantic."

"A high-tier donor alumni box is a *more chill environment?*" Avery pushed his way up onto the counter beside Charlie, grabbing more punch as he went. He needed to slow down, gauging by the slur in his voice and the unsteadiness on his feet, but Charlie just filled up his cup and scooted over to make room.

"Well, it's different," I allowed. "Charlie? What do you think?"

"I'm incredibly in." He raised his cup to toast me, and I grinned. "Anything to get Fitzy out of my ass." And to move past what a huge disappointment I am, I thought, but didn't add out loud. Charlie didn't need to know about that part. "Send me the deets, and we'll get it all squared away. Hang out for a bit, all right? Have fun. Nice, safe fun. And I'll see you Friday."

As he left the kitchen and headed back toward the party, hands over his head with a celebratory "Wooo!" that was echoed by all the other guests, I was left with the distinct impression that I'd just met some sort of Dionysus party god, and not an actual person.

But hey, if he wanted to help, I'd take it.

"That was a lot." Avery shifted over so he was leaning against the fridge with me, our elbows just barely touching. Even with the alcohol on his breath, I still got that cinnamon Avery smell. "I don't have to be him when I grow up, do I? I don't think I could handle the pressure."

"No one else could." I shook my head. "That was a once-in-a-lifetime person right there, my friend."

Avery looked over at me, at that, and an unexpected feeling stirred inside of me. He opened his mouth to speak, but what I saw over his shoulder made me gasp.

"Down!" Sticky floors be damned. I grabbed onto Avery's arm, yanked him off the counter, and dropped so that we were crouching on the floor of the frat's kitchen, hidden behind one of the counters from the rest of the party, which was a terrible place to crouch. But I didn't have a choice, did I? Not when Lizzie Bennet was marching toward us, dragging a girl who looked close to my non-legal-drinking-age behind her.

"What?" Avery's eyes were wide, and he'd thrown his hand over the top of his drink to protect it when I pulled him to the floor. "Your brother?"

"Not quite that bad." I nodded toward the other side of the kitchen. "Lizzie."

"Oh shit." Avery paled. He also had to lean super close so that I could hear him without shouting, which was unexpectedly distracting. His breath tickled my ear. "But . . . would she recognize you?"

"There's definitely pictures of me in Fitz's apartment." I ignored the tingling from where our legs were pushed together, trying to concentrate on subterfuge. "Come on. I don't want her to see us." Avery shrugged and sank down farther onto the floor of the kitchen as I did my best to concentrate on what Lizzie was saying. Any intelligence would be helpful.

"What are you even doing here?" I heard Lizzie hiss. "It's a school night."

"Um, pretty sure it's a school night for you, too." That must have been the other girl, the one who *had* managed to find a body-con dress in fall colors. From what I could see of her as I peeked ever so cautiously around the side of the counter, she looked . . . a lot like Lizzie, actually, if way more made up. She was staggering a little on her kitten heels, and wasn't even wearing tights. Maybe she needed the alcohol to warm up. "Or do the rules not apply to perfect sisters?"

"They apply to underage sisters, Lydia." Lydia. This must have been one of the five million sisters Fitz had described to me. "How did you even get here? You better not have driven yourself."

"Lydia. There you are."

My blood went cold, and I pulled myself back behind the counter as fast as I could as another voice joined the two of them. A voice I knew. From the way Avery looked at me, even though his eyes had lost their focus a little, he recognized the voice, too.

"Wickham!" Lydia squealed.

What was he even doing here? Was this part of his new scam, somehow? Was he following me? Following Fitz? I was going to die. I was going to pass out here on the floor of this frat party and—

Avery's hand came over mine, cool and firm. I stared up at him in shock, and as our eyes met, he squeezed.

Behind us, I could hear Lydia giggle, heard Wickham chuckle. Lizzie, to her credit, didn't seem to be enjoying the conversation. But everything they were saying seemed like background noise as I stared down at Avery's hand.

I just barely heard Wickham as he spoke.

"I've gotta head out anyway, kid." The nickname landed like lead, but Avery's grip softened the blow. "You want a ride home, now's the time."

"I'll drive her," Lizzie cut in, in clipped tones.

"But Lizzie—"

"*Now*, Lydia."

I could hear Lydia whining as her sister presumably pulled her away, and heavy footsteps indicated that Wickham had followed them out. After a second, I remembered to breathe. Avery released my hand, and I found myself disappointed.

"You want me to go kill him for you?" Avery's question took me by surprise, and when I looked over toward him, his face didn't exactly say "joke." "I think I've got enough punch in me that I could do it."

"Nah." I shook my head. "I'm . . . I'm weirdly more okay than I would have expected." And I was, actually. It had been a shock, a close call, but I didn't want to run out after him or anything.

"Well, if you change your mind." Avery shrugged as we both pulled ourselves to our feet. A couple of passing partygoers pretended not to notice us emerging from the ground. "I really do hate that guy."

I smiled.

This had been, so far, a surprisingly good night.

"What now?" I asked, changing the subject, as Avery took a slower sip of his drink. I could smell the sugar in it from here. "Want to head back?"

"Or we could dance." He swayed from side to side, though whether that was from the music creeping in from the main room or the alcohol I couldn't tell.

"You sure? It's late."

"A little bit longer?" Avery stuck his bottom lip out into a pout that transformed his whole face and instantly made me appreciate the lean-nerd look over Charlie's brawny muscles. Which was . . . a weird thought, and one that I quickly banished to the back of my mind. "Please?"

Worries about Fitz or even Wickham could have stopped me. But for once in my life, they didn't.

"Fine." I grinned as Avery whooped and hopped off the counter, grabbing my hand to pull me back into the living room. "Clearly, I'm a terrible influence." This was a stupid idea, the whole thing was undoubtedly ridiculous, but the feeling of his hand in mine . . . I didn't hate it, that was all.

"You're just the influence I need, George Darcy." Avery squeezed my hand, and I flushed, though that could have been the heat. Could have been a lot of things.

And this time, when we reached the center of the floor, when Avery twirled me under his arm and I let myself laugh, I was glad that I hadn't let go.

cll

"My car is so loud."

"I guess." I glanced over at Avery in the passenger seat, his head pressed against the window. We'd gone half an hour into our drive home without Avery speaking, and I'd kind of assumed he'd fallen asleep. "You feeling okay?"

"I feel great." He shifted in his seat to half-face toward me, and even though his words were slurred around the edges, they weren't as bad as they had been before. Good. I didn't need the extra difficulty in terms of sneaking back onto campus. "I feel better than I ever have, you know? Because I'm not living out the perfect Avery life. I had fun tonight. I went out with a girl and had fun."

"Um . . . cool?" My voice caught around the edges, though Avery was definitely still too drunk to notice. Still, I flushed. The way he'd said that—went out with a girl—set off something in my chest, something that I did my best to tamp way back down, because it was just the alcohol talking, and I wasn't about to say anything back to Avery that we'd both regret. "Hopefully you still feel that way when we have to park in the visitor lot behind the north gate, because we have way broken curfew."

Obviously, there was more stuff that I thought about saying. Like that I'd had a great time, too, not being perfect. Like that being anywhere with him was quickly turning into my favorite place. But you couldn't just *say* stuff like that to your friends. Not without them thinking you cared about them in weird different ways than you did. When you definitely didn't.

I wouldn't go down that road again, even if I did like Avery that way. Wickham's face plastered itself across my mind. I just wouldn't. It wasn't safe, not for someone like me.

"It was worth it." He'd closed his eyes again, I saw when I glanced over for just a second, cognizant of the dark and winding roads. "It's always worth it to hang out with you, George."

"Oh . . . thanks." It was cold in here, that was all. That was why I had goose bumps. "You too, Aves."

"Good." His voice got quieter as he settled into sleep, and I smiled as we came around another bend. "I'm glad."

"Yeah," I echoed, as I heard his breathing slow. "I'm glad, too."

CHAPTER SIXTEEN

t was weird. Most days since school started, I'd had to drag myself out of bed, constantly reminding myself that if I didn't get up, I would fail my classes, and then I wouldn't graduate, and I could only loaf around at home for so many years before Fitz cut me off and I'd have to wait until I was twenty-one for my trust fund to open up and what was I going to do in the meantime with exactly zero skills, anyway?

It was an involved pep talk.

But the morning after Charlie's party, the day before the homecoming game, I woke up an hour before my "seriously your brother will kill you" emergency alarm. I'd had plenty of restless nights since The Incident, but this time I didn't feel exhausted and sleep-battered. I felt . . . okay.

I wanted to write, actually. I had that tingling in my hands that called to the keyboard, the pitter-patter in my chest that said, "Let's make a story."

I sat up as quietly as I could, pulled my laptop off the floor next to me so that Sydney wouldn't wake up and ruin my mood. It was just a few minutes before I had my Word document open, staring down at Jocelyn and Henry's grand romance.

My mind wandered to the party last night. We'd made it back to campus without incident, and before Avery stepped through the back door to his dorm, he'd leaned against it and watched me. Just stood there and looked at me.

I'd wondered, in that moment, if I was going down a road that I should avoid.

But that was stupid, right? My keyboard clacked gently beneath me as I typed, knocking out a quick scene of banter between Henry and his brothers. It was ridiculous. Avery and I were just friends. Wickham and I had never *been* friends.

What was the point of everything I'd been through, after all, if I didn't know better now?

Satisfied, I moved onto the next scene, but before I could throw together some truly epic carriage montages, I saw the email notification pop up.

It made sense, really, because I was having a good morning, that an email would finally arrive from Wickham.

I didn't see past the subject line, which was characteristically uninformative. He knew I'd have to open it to see what he was talking about. I waited for the palm sweat, the heart palpitations, all the usual stuff that came with an email from Wickham—

But they didn't come.

I mean, I still felt shitty. But I didn't feel like I was on the verge of an anxiety attack or anything. Just regular bad. That kind of felt like a victory.

And then, hey, I was on a roll anyway, right? May as well see if I could make this good feeling last.

I toggled over to my in-box and, without reading it, deleted the email.

Wow.

Deleting Wickham's email felt . . . it was hard to describe. Good, I guessed. Kind of really good. And I didn't feel like I was doing it because Fitz had told me to. It felt like I'd managed to do something for me, for once.

That may not have seemed like a wild concept to the average person. But Darcys didn't do things that felt *good*. They did things because they were right. Or economically sound.

It was kind of like how I'd felt last night, when Avery and I had stayed at the party even though our initial goal was accomplished. Like I was discovering Georgie. Like maybe she could make some okay decisions.

Maybe.

I closed my laptop, satisfied. Maybe I'd get down to the band room early, try to snag one of the practice rooms to work on my part for the show. Avery and I were supposed to meet there later this afternoon, but extra practice never hurt. Doing something I liked, it turned out, didn't hurt.

I slipped out of bed, avoiding any wrath from Sydney for the still-early hour, and went out to meet the day with a lot less fear and trepidation than usual.

cll

Once classes had finished, I leaned back against the cold metal of my chair in the empty band room, trombone on my lap, and scrolled through my phone. *Sage Hall* Twitterverse notifications waited for me, but I didn't check them, just opened my conversation with Avery and read through the last few messages.

There was nothing substantial in them. A few confirmations of times we were going to meet. Some Reddit links. A surreptitious picture of Mrs. T yawning wide enough during rehearsal it looked like her face would split open. Nothing that said, "I know it's sudden, but I'm your best friend now, and I like it, too, a whole lot, and maybe we can go down this road a little farther and see where it takes us?"

Not unless I was misreading those Reddit links, anyway.

I jerked my head up from my phone as the doors to the band room burst open and Avery ran in, panting and looking a little green around the edges.

"Sorry!" He skidded to a stop at the front of the room, his tie so crooked that it was more of a shoulder accessory than anything else. "Sorry. Van Fleming wanted to talk to me after class. And then I figured I could run here and barely be late at all, but I forgot to account for the fact that my insides are currently trying to become outsides." Avery collapsed into the metal chair beside me, propped his feet up on the chair in front of him.

Okay, he was definitely hungover AF, but that was only a little bit his fault and a whole lot Charlie's.

I grinned. "If I ask you how you're feeling, can you answer without vomiting?"

He cocked his head to the side, considered. "Barely." The ever-present Avery smile spread across his face, undeterred by nausea. "Would it be okay with you if I murdered your brother's roommate? Because he didn't tell me his punch was made of *poison*."

"Dude." I shook my head as Avery dropped his feet back to the floor and slunk down even lower in his chair, rubbed his hand over his forehead. His khaki slacks pressed up against the side of my uniform skirt, which I did my best to ignore. "It was punch at a frat party. Every CW show in the world could have told you to avoid that."

"Fair," he allowed with a long exhale, then glanced over at me from behind his hand. Outside the band room, I could just barely make out the chatter of other students, but in here it was just him and me, our voices echoing in the space. "Sorry if I acted like an idiot last night, though. I obviously didn't plan on getting that wasted."

"No way, it's chill." I shrugged, still ignoring the slightly wrinkled fabric of his pants as it brushed against my skirt's pleats. "You were mostly sleepy."

"That does sound like me." His laugh barked out, though from the way his skin blanched afterward, he regretted it. "I've only done that once before, over the summer with some of the other lifeguards. I fell asleep next to the pool in like, an hour. I'm just glad no one drew on my face."

"That would have been a tragedy," I agreed. Avery's face was just fine the way it was. Better than fine.

Yikes. Maybe I was dehydrated or something, because I sounded ridiculous, even if only to myself. Avery had a fine face. A regular, normal, fine face. The face of a friend. Etc.

We both fell into silence for a second, my hands reaching up to tuck a loose curl behind my ear. Avery tracked the movement with his eyes, then shook his head and smiled at me.

"Um." He cleared his throat, then looked like he regretted it. "I think that playing is out of the question for me altogether, today. I'll be feeling fine, and then boom, cue Ben Wyatt 'I threw up in the shower,' you know?" His voice sped up, his words running together as he rambled. "I miss it, though. Playing. Didn't think I would. But again, today I would definitely vomit and it would get all in the mouthpiece and the slides and—"

"Maybe you shouldn't talk about that if you're not feeling well," I interrupted, as cute (Friend cute! Friend cute!) as his rambling was. I shifted my trombone off of my lap and onto the chair on my right, then turned left, just a little, to face him. He matched my movement, the metal legs of his chair scooting across the scratchy carpeting. "We can just hang out or whatever."

"Right." Avery nodded, fast. "For sure."

"You're sure you're okay, Aves?" Honestly, he looked worse than he had when he'd come in. Full-on white as a sheet now, barely making eye contact. "Do you need to go to the nurse or something?"

"Doyouwanttogotohomecomingwithme?"

The words came out so fast that I could barely understand them.

Well, I could. But I didn't.

For all of my self-actualization epiphanies or whatever, I hadn't expected that.

"What?" I stared at Avery as I leaned back in my chair. I couldn't tell if the buzzing that filled me was good or bad. "What did you say?"

"Do you . . ." Avery took a deep breath as pink tinged his ears. "Do you want to go to, you know, the homecoming dance? With me," he added, fast, and honestly my whole chest felt like such a mess of emotions I couldn't sort them out. "I don't know. It could be fun. And I'd, um, I'd kind of like to get a second chance at dancing with you? Because we barely got to, last night. And I was pretty drunk."

I should say no. I was just barely making moves toward the positive. I'd managed to delete a single email from Wickham, and suddenly I thought I was America's Next Top Model Teenager Who Had Her Life Together and Was Also Super Dateable? Avery deserved better than me. This was something I knew.

But also, I thought suddenly, screw that. Maybe what I deserved was to be happy.

God, his grin was impossible to resist.

"Um. Sure. Why not?" I tried to sound casual, though I felt anything but. "It's Saturday, right?"

"Yeah, George." He cocked his head to the side, and his grin spread. "Have you not been paying attention to Mrs. T's announcements for the last month? She's going to be insulted."

"Shut up." I grabbed my forgotten sheet music off the stand in front of me, cursing my trembling fingers as I tucked the pages into my backpack. "I'm an excellent listener."

"Tell me exactly what I said at the beginning of practice yesterday, word for word." Avery moved the music stand out of the way as I put my trombone up, then stood to meet him, moved with him through the back doors of the band room that led out toward our dorms.

"I'm assuming it had something to do with me being the greatest trombone player in the history of Pemberley?" I braced myself for the freezing wind as we opened the doors to the outside world, but it didn't sting as much as I'd expected. "And my impeccable friendship skills?" I wanted to text my brother, I realized, but I wouldn't. He had his own thing going on. He didn't want to hear about me.

"Wow, you *were* listening." Avery applauded as we headed out into the cold, and I curtsied my way down the stairs. "George Darcy, you truly are amazing."

And he was probably joking. He usually was.

But even though it was probably a joke, my heart leapt all the same.

cll

I had just parted ways with Avery, halfway down the quad, prepared to go back to my dorm and pour all my feelings into fic, when I felt someone tap me on my shoulder and jumped about a mile into the air.

"Whoa there." I whirled around to see Emily, hair pulled into two braids, as she backed away from me, hands held wide. "Calm down. Not trying to attack you or anything."

"Um." Had my jaw dropped down to the ground entirely? I hoped not. "What's up?"

"Just saying hi." Emily shrugged, as if that weren't an earth-shattering sentence where I was involved. Not that Emily had Braden levels of hatred toward me or anything, but she'd definitely avoided conversation. "You were hanging out with Avery, right?"

"Yeah?" Maybe she was going to tell me to stay away from him for the good of the band. Maybe I'd fight her for him. "Is that a problem?"

"Down, girl." Emily raised an eyebrow at me, and I heard how my words sounded, how sharp I'd gotten. "I'm only asking."

"Right." What was wrong with me, anyway? Were my emotions not properly calibrated with normal society? Admittedly, if you went by the evidence of my family, that would make sense. "Sorry."

Emily nodded, then looked down at her shoes, clicked her heels together. "Anyway." She shrugged, then looked back up at me. "I really was just saying hi. So." She raised her hand, waved. "See you later, I guess."

She turned to leave, and it would have been easy to let her go, to head back to my room and keep my circle small, keep it safe. That's what a Darcy would do. I trusted Avery, but everyone else . . .

For whatever reason, though, I wanted to keep reaching out. Wanted to see if I could win back more than just Avery.

If you're gonna leap, leap, right?

"Are you decorating your locker Friday?" The words came out a lot squeakier than I would have liked, but at least they came out. Either the question or the timbre of my voice seemed to catch Emily's attention, as she dropped her hand, stared at me.

It was a dumb homecoming tradition, locker decorating. You'd sneak into the building early, before the janitors unlocked everything, and make your locker as school-spirited as possible. I'd done it my first two years here, followed the trombones through the halls as we snuck in before the sun even rose, covered our lockers with cheap streamers and balloons. Our section leader last year, Alyssa, was way more into that sort of thing than Braden. He probably thought that having the whole section get up early would mess with our REM cycles, which would make us miss steps in our marching or something.

Or maybe he had planned a whole excursion, and I just wasn't invited. That seemed just as likely.

"No one organized it this year." She shrugged, pulled on her hair as she began to rebraid it.

Silence filled the space between us as I realized, from the way Emily watched me with curiosity, that I was facing some kind of test. She'd stopped me first, after all. This part was up to me.

Well, what the hell?

"Why don't we organize it?" If I made it through this whole conversation and didn't throw up or pass out, I'd have to buy myself a medal. "The freshmen deserve to go out, right? It's tradition. We could take them tomorrow morning."

Emily moved on to the other side of her head, unbraiding and rebraiding again as she considered my offer. Then, by some miracle of miracles, she nodded.

"I'll text everyone." She pulled out her phone. "Braden won't want to come."

"Oh, no." The sarcasm slipped out before I could stop myself, and the faintest hint of a grin appeared on Emily's face, so fast I may have imagined it.

"And Jackson is fundamentally opposed to getting up early, so it'll probably just be us and the freshies." She dropped her phone back into the pocket of her skirt, then looked back at me. "Sound good?"

"You told the freshmen I'd be there, right?" I brushed a curl out of my face as I nodded toward her phone. "Since they seem constantly horrified that I'm going to hold them down and shove cocaine up their noses."

"Are you?"

"What do you think?" The words had bite to them, but at least this time I felt like I'd earned it. The wind nipped at my ears, threatening frostbite.

"Well, there you go." Emily shrugged, like the matter was settled. "We'll meet on the front steps at four thirty tomorrow morning. Can you bring decorations?"

"As long as you're not going to *Carrie* me." This time, it was Emily's turn to look confused. "Like the . . . like the movie, *Carrie*," I explained. "With the pig's blood. And the prom."

Emily considered it. "I feel like if we were going to do that, homecoming itself would be a better place for it."

". . . Right."

"And we're not," she added, though not as quickly as I would have liked, twisting her hair tie around the end of her braid. "Besides, then *we* would have invited *you*. You always this trusting?" She dropped her hands down to her sides, pushed them into the pockets of her skirt.

That was me all right. Trusting.

"Can you blame me?"

To my surprise, she grinned. "Not in the least."

"Okay, then." I held out my hand, and Emily shook it without hesitating. A nice change of pace. "We've got ourselves a decorating party."

CHAPTER SEVENTEEN

ack in my dorm that night, right before curfew—which meant that I was only minutes away from Sydney scuttling in—I was hit with the distinct realization that I had neither any decorations for the band's lockers nor a dress to wear to homecoming. I also had no means of obtaining either of those things.

Which . . . shit.

I pulled my hair into a bun at the top of my head, then flopped down on my bed to stare at the *Sage Hall* poster and think. This was the first trombone-based friendship overture I'd managed since The Incident. I didn't want to blow it, but I wasn't sure I'd have a choice. Maybe I could cut up all of Sydney's clothes and pretend that they were fabric ribbons I'd bought? Though with my luck, she'd come into the room halfway through, wrestle the scissors out of my hands, and stab me through the heart with them. If I were home, I'd just have one of the staff go out and pick me up something, but that obviously wasn't going to fly here.

Last year I'd have texted Wickham, and he'd be here in an hour, the smell of cigarette smoke lingering in his car, his smile curved up rakishly as he teased me about school spirit. But also, if this were last year, I wouldn't have done something like this at all, because I'd be sitting by the phone waiting for him to text me, waiting for him to call me, waiting and waiting and waiting.

This year I didn't *wait*. I just . . . did.

Even if that "did" meant that I "did" panic.

Somewhere in the midst of that deep existential crisis, my phone lit up with a dumb picture of Fitz I'd taken a few Christmases ago, his face half-submerged behind a turkey carcass, rearing up to pounce on it like a raptor. Even though I didn't feel like talking to anyone, I picked up the phone. He might not miss me but, I realized, I missed him. Call it weakness.

"Hey." Fitz sounded sleepy, distant. "Just wanted to check in, Beanpole."

"Cool." My voice sounded way higher than it usually did, even to me. There went my plan of acting even a little bit chill. "Cool. Everything's great here. Super great."

"Georgie?" Ah, yes, there was the alert, parental Fitz we all knew and loved so well. For once, though, I didn't mind the concern in his tone, as I twisted my comforter into knots beneath my hand. "You okay?"

"It's just . . ." I paused, gripped the fabric in my fist. I didn't need to unload all of this on Fitz. Wasn't the whole purpose of my matchmaking plan to give him something else to concentrate on besides me? He should be out with Lizzie, where she'd casually mention that she appreciated the pizza (that I sent her) and scoot closer to him on a bench or something. He should be happy.

I thought about hanging up, tossing my phone out my window so I wouldn't hear when he called back, but Fitz spoke before I got the chance.

"Hey." Even over the phone, I could picture him, sitting up straighter now, all alert, trying to portray caring big brother while also calculating the distance to the nearest hospital. I glanced down at the old Caltech shirt I had on. A few threads had come loose at the bottom from the aggressiveness of the campus laundry. I needed to be more careful with it. Fitz had brought me this shirt the first time he'd gone out there to interview, and he'd looked so happy. Happier than he'd ever looked around me. "You can tell me, Georgie."

I should have kept it all to myself, but it spilled out.

". . . and I'm supposed to decorate lockers in like, six hours, and I don't have anything, let alone a dress." I exhaled, loudly, after a solid five-minute monologue. Silence. I had to hope Fitz wasn't going to lecture me on the importance of staying in my room after curfew. With Fitz, a lecture was always in the cards.

His next words, though, managed to catch me by surprise.

"If I can get there in a few hours, will that be soon enough?"

"What?"

"I've got to finish up this paper." Fitz didn't seem to realize the magnitude of what he was offering me. "But then I can head down your way. I'm sure Charlie knows of some twenty-four-hour big-box stores around you that sell decorations. He has an odd knack for that sort of thing. I can pick you up, and you can come with me and find what you need. And then I can take you shopping for a dress after your classes let out tomorrow. You'll have time before the game?"

"I . . . yes?" I squeezed the comforter tight again, released it. This was a total step backward in my independence plan. "Fitz. You don't have to do this."

"I know." Through the phone, it almost sounded like he was smiling, but since it was my big brother and he was going out of his way to do me a huge solid, I'd probably just imagined it. "I'll call you when I get to campus, all right?"

"It's after curfew."

"Irrelevant." Fitz sounded more awake already, alert with the promise of a plan. "I'll call the school on the way over, give you permission to come out with me for a bit. They'll be fine with it."

"Right." I felt a wave of disappointment I hadn't earned. It made sense that this would all be done legally and properly. It was still my brother, after all. I should just be grateful he was willing to help. "Of course."

"Would it make you feel better if you dressed in all-black and I didn't fully stop the car to pick you up?"

I laughed.

"Yes, please." Tears welled up in my eyes, though I couldn't have said why. "Thanks. Just call me when I should come outside."

"You got it, Beanpole."

I rolled over on my side and blinked the moisture back. I had, in some cases, a fairly excellent big brother. One who didn't deserve how miserable I made him.

Maybe I shouldn't be trying to push him away, I thought. Pushing Wickham away was the right choice, for sure. But I was actively trying to distance myself from Fitz this year, too, unburden him of my problems. For just a split second, I wondered if that was a mistake.

No, I decided, still clutching at my comforter. Pushing away Wickham was for my sake—pushing away Fitz was for his.

Fitz didn't need me. Even tonight was all for me, just another way I made his life harder. That was the whole reason I hadn't gotten him involved in this year's Wickham shit, right? Because

I made his life difficult. I'd take this one last favor, and then I'd keep doing everything I could to push him toward Lizzie, where he'd be happy. Away from me.

cll

When Fitz pulled up to the building several hours later, I was waiting in the driveway with my hoodie pulled over my head for both subterfuge and warmth. I'd finished an overdue essay just before midnight, but I'd barely been able to sleep in the time between, adrenaline coursing through my system. Fitz cut his lights before he pulled into the driveway, even though the front desk monitor had waved merrily at me as I left the building, telling me to say hi to my brother. He turned off the ignition and stepped out of the car as I crossed over to meet him.

"You said you weren't going to stop the car," I mentioned as I reached the passenger side. "This car is like, fully stopped."

"Unfortunately, my precision driving license hasn't come through yet." Fitz climbed back into the car and got it started again as I pulled open the door to take my place in the passenger seat.

"Maybe next year." I leaned my head back against the seat as we backed away from Pemberley, headed out into the night. "Where are we going, exactly?"

"There's a twenty-four-hour Target not far from here, apparently."

"Charlie looked it up for you?"

"Um, no." To my absolute shock and delight, Fitz went slightly red at the ears. "That girl from my study group, Lizzie. Some of her sisters work there? She said they can help us find what we need." Wow. Now *this* was a development. I resisted the urge to pull out my phone and immediately text Avery—he'd just be asleep and anyway, I wanted the reward of getting to tell him in person. He was going to *flip*.

I tried to play it cool.

"I mean, it's just a store, right?" I looked out the window as I spoke, so that Fitz wouldn't see me wigging out with excitement. "How complicated can it be?"

cll

Holy mother of *Sage Hall*.

This was a *store*?

The building that emerged from the darkness in front of us was like nothing I'd ever seen.

Several stories tall, it was endlessly long, with shopping carts that wrapped around the bright white structure like a snake. Even as we turned off the highway, the huge neon red sign announcing that this was a mecca of purchasing basically blinded me. I gulped, and beside me, Fitz paled.

"At least it shouldn't be crowded," I managed as Fitz pulled into a parking spot inexplicably far from the entrance to the store. "We won't be run down by hungry shoppers."

"I honestly thought they made this sort of thing up for movies." Fitz spoke in a whisper, as if the church of capitalism in front of us required some level of reverence. "Who *needs* this?"

I had no answer for him. Instead, we both stayed quiet as we got out of the car and bundled up in our coats, walking briskly to the glowing entrance of the store. However I'd expected to spend my evening before I got Fitz's call, this sure as hell wasn't it.

Inside, the store was no less overwhelming. Rows upon rows of everything I could have imagined spilled out in front of us in garish red and white. If there was an organizational system, I couldn't parse it. An aisle that *may* have had party supplies seemed promising, but luckily before I could go full Elsa into the unknown, a chipper voice spoke up from behind us.

"Hi! You must be Fitz and Georgie Darcy?"

Unfortunately, I recognized that voice.

I turned around, slowly, to see Lydia Bennet, Lizzie's little sister and official Wickham Hanger-On. I mean, yes, there was definitely a chance that *this* would be the sister of Lizzie that Fitz had mentioned, but honestly, didn't she have a full baker's dozen of sisters? What were the chances I'd run into this one?

Luckily, she'd never seen me at the party, so all I had to do was keep myself together and I wouldn't have anything to worry about.

"Yes. Hello." Fitz stuck out his hand to shake Lydia's, and she stared down at it for a second before she took it in her own. She looked a lot younger than she had at the party—in retrospect, she was probably exactly my age, dressed in a red tank top that was entirely inappropriate for the weather and tight, artistically ripped jeans. Even though it was simple, it was the sort of very carefully cultivated look that I never knew how to pull off.

And she was involved with Wickham, somehow.

"Hi," I forced out after Fitz gave me a very pointed look. "Nice to meet you."

"You, too!" Lydia seemed to come with a permanent exclamation point. "We're looking for decorations, right? Lizzie said this was a total clandestine mish." She glanced over my outfit, an eyebrow raised. "Is that why we've gone all *Spy Kid* at a funeral over here?"

"Decorating supplies, yes." Fitz stepped in, the full Darcy authority turned on before I could respond. Probably for the best. "Ribbons, streamers, that sort of thing."

"Kind of a weird emergency, but sure." Lydia shrugged, then skipped off ahead of us, auburn hair just a couple of shades darker than Lizzie's flowing behind her like a shampoo commercial. "Let's go!"

Lydia led us down aisle after aisle, throwing things in a cart she'd assigned to Fitz. We followed behind her, obedient servants to the self-proclaimed "total goddess of Target," as the cart filled with more decorations than I knew existed.

By the time she declared us finished, Fitz had a stunned look in his eyes that I assumed matched mine.

"Okay, come on." Lydia waggled her fingers at a couple of cashiers as we passed them, headed toward an empty register. "I'll check you out." She pulled our cart up and began to scan as we unloaded onto the conveyer belt. Next to me, I saw Fitz eye the in-store Starbucks (amazing) with interest.

"Why don't you get something?" I tilted my head toward the store. "You've still got a lot of driving ahead of you."

Fitz hesitated briefly, then nodded. "Anything for either of you?"

"Caramel macchiato? Half-caf? Here." Lydia pulled a red ID card out of her back pocket, handed it over to Fitz. "Use my discount. Rita totally won't care."

"Oh, no." Fitz looked horrified, probably both at the idea of not purchasing Lizzie's sister a fully caffeinated beverage and also at cheating the Target Employee Discount System. "My treat."

"Cool." Lydia shrugged as she returned the card to her pocket. "Thanks!"

"Nothing for me," I said. "Gotta conserve those cup holders."

Fitz shook his head before he headed toward the coffee counter, leaving me . . . alone with Lydia.

As soon as Fitz was gone, Lydia leaned in conspiratorially. "Dude. Your brother? Total hottie."

"Ack." That was apparently the only sound my body could produce as my brain misfired on every cylinder.

"Not for me, obviously," Lydia continued as she scanned a package of washable window markers, oblivious to my horror. "But I get why my sister is so into him. She'll never admit it, obvs. But they're totally doing it. Or going to."

Why? Why in the world did everyone I interacted with about this insist on bringing up my brother's sex life? She must have seen my blush, because she giggled.

"Sorry. Maybe they're not, anyway." She leaned in conspiratorially. "*Nerds*, you know?"

I did not know. I had the feeling there was a lot that Lydia Bennet experienced that I did not know about.

"Anyway, you go to Pemberley, right?" As she rang me up, I deeply regretted the number of items we had purchased. Each new item she exclaimed over left more time available to hear further sex-ed theories about my brother. "One of my friends used to go there. Do you know Wickham Foster?"

It had to come up eventually.

"No," I managed, my mind racing. Evade, evade, evade, and most important, move this conversation along before Fitz got back. Any reminder of Wickham would only freak him out, and with the homecoming game tomorrow—attached to my big fancy matchmaking extravaganza—I needed him to stay in a good mood. "I don't think so."

"I don't think you'd be in the same crowd, anyway." Lydia wrinkled her nose a little as she looked me over, for just long enough that I knew she'd wanted me to see. "But hey, if you ever need anything in the research paper department, or a lab report or something . . ." She giggled again. "Let's just say he's really good at recycling."

What?

Before I could say anything else, *ask* anything else, Fitz returned, a small black coffee in one hand and an enormous whipped cream concoction in the other. He looked strained, like he'd officially reached his limit for how long he could spend inside a chain store, as he handed Lydia her drink and inserted his credit card into the requisite slot.

"Yay!" she squealed, taking a sip. "Awesome. You guys are all set. Do you need help carrying anything out?"

"No," Fitz said, fast, even though we had a ton of stuff and a third pair of hands would have been extremely useful. "Thank you."

"Okay." She shrugged, then settled back against the register, sipping at her drink. "Nice to meet you both, I guess."

"You, too." I waved, as Fitz was already out the door, pushing the shopping cart back into the parking lot with the speed of a man on a mission. I had to run to catch up.

"She was . . . fun," I managed when we reached the car, passing bags to Fitz, who loaded everything into a canvas duffel bag he'd provided for the occasion. "Is she a lot like her sister?" I had a solid guess at the answer, but Fitz's look of absolute horror told me everything I needed to know.

"Lizzie," he spoke carefully, closing the trunk and heading toward the driver's seat as I slid into the passenger, "is absolutely nothing like her sisters."

"Oh." I hid my smile as he started the car, backed us out of the space—even though there were no other cars in the lot, and he definitely could have driven through the empty spaces—and pulled back onto the highway. "Good."

cll

"You are lucky I'm the world's best big brother, you know." The bags under Fitz's eyes looked like they should have their own zip code, and I ignored the fresh shot of guilt as we pulled back up to the gates of Pemberley. It was after three in the morning at this point, and it didn't seem like the coffee was doing as much work to keep Fitz awake as it should. I hopped out of the car and grabbed the duffel bag from the trunk as he stepped out on his side. "We bought the entire store out, I think. But I suppose it's better to have too much than not enough."

That could have been the Darcy family motto. I could see it now, embossed on a decorative plate. How much had we spent on this? I didn't even look. Too much. Tacos all over again. Not that there was anything I could do about it now.

"Thanks, Fitz." I grabbed the bag and held it in both arms to redistribute the weight. "You're the best. Seriously." I was feeling guilty again, guilty for dragging him out of bed and all the way here. I wouldn't need him again after this, I reminded myself. Once my grand matchmaking plan came together at homecoming tonight, I'd be out of his mind and I wouldn't have to worry about slipping and needing him to rescue me. Just one more day, and then the idea of needing my brother wouldn't even be a possibility.

And as I gripped the bag tightly, I made a decision—that I wasn't going to involve Fitz in any of my Wickham dealings. There would be no admitting that I was the perfect Darcy. I didn't know how I'd get rid of Wickham otherwise, how I'd stop him from just turning around and telling Fitz we'd been talking, but I was going to figure it out.

I had to. But that could wait until later.

"You're welcome, Georgie." Fitz stepped back, opened the door to his car, and climbed in. "Text me a picture of your locker when you're finished, all right? And I'll see you later today."

"See you." I waved as Fitz backed out, though he could probably barely see it in the dark, zipped my hoodie up the rest of the way, and headed out to make mischief or friendship or whatever it was that was in store for me.

CHAPTER EIGHTEEN

I sat on the front steps of the classroom building, legs pulled up against my chest to keep in the warmth even as the cold of the concrete steps seeped through my jeans. It hadn't taken long to walk over, and I still had ten minutes, at least, before any other trombones showed up, if they showed up at all. I still wasn't feeling entirely certain on that front. Either way, it left me plenty of time to get lost in my thoughts.

For example, what had Lydia been talking about? Wickham and . . . essays? That made no sense. What was he, like, writing papers for people? That didn't seem up his alley. Way too much work for not enough reward.

She'd said something about recycling, though. Recycling like . . . papers. Old papers, like from other students?

Of course. The realization hit me as the night air whistled around me. *That* was the new business, the enterprise he'd wanted me to join. It was the perfect scam for him—low risk, since it wasn't like they could expel him again. High reward. Half the students at Pemberley were like me, legacies whose whole families had come through the school, who had older siblings with book reports and history papers that could easily be copied. He could be running a full plagiarism ring at Pemberley at this point, with his contacts in the school from last year.

And with that information . . . I could get rid of him, I realized. I could fulfill what I'd set out to do, and get rid of Wickham without involving my brother at all. Perfect Darcy, be damned. Wickham didn't need to have a hold on me anymore.

"Hey." I looked up from my revelation to see Emily, dressed in a black hoodie nearly identical to mine. "Have you seen the freshmen yet?"

"Not yet." I tried to keep it cool, to tuck away this intriguing new information to deal with later. The last thing I wanted to do was let Wickham ruin this, too. "They knew where to go, right?"

"That's what I thought—oh, there they are." From behind a tree at the edge of the quad emerged the two freshmen, scuttling along the edge of the sidewalk like crabs. Since I hadn't seen them come up, I suspected they'd been there for a while, and just didn't want to come over until they saw Emily. "Hey, Cole, Sam."

I had been super wrong about their names. Cole. Sam. Not even close. I was definitely going to write them down in my phone the next time they looked away.

"Okay." Emily gathered us all around her with a wave of her hand, the world's saddest football huddle. "We're going in the window by the science labs—the latch is loose. From there, we just have to hug the lockers in the hallways, because the security cameras are pretty much only focused on the center of the halls. As long as you don't turn your face up to the monitor, it'll be chill."

"Won't they know who we are when they see us decorating our own lockers?" Sam asked, her voice unsteady. The navy hoodie she had on was way too big for her, the sleeves hanging down over her shaking hands.

"No one gets in trouble for this, ever," Emily said dismissively. "We just take precautions in case someone does something stupid and we need to cover our bases. Like, five years ago, some kids released a bunch of mice in the halls, and that's obviously a no-go." Fitz had told me about that with the sort of horror and disgust most people reserved for encountering dog shit on their lawn. "Okay?" Sam nodded, eyes turned down. "Georgie, what'd you bring?"

I took a deep, albeit trembling, breath. Time to find out if this was *actually* Tacos 2.0 or not. I tried to keep my voice light and airy as I hoisted my bag up in the air as high as I could—which really wasn't that high; I definitely needed to add strength training to my post–football season exercise routine—to show off to the others. If I was going to do this thing, then I was going to fucking do this thing.

"If you can think of it, I have it." I stared the others down, a challenge to reject me again. "We can decorate half the lockers in the school."

"Damn." Emily poked through the bag, awe in her voice. "This is a lot of shit."

My heart sped up. Was it too late to throw half the supplies behind a tree like they didn't exist in the first place? But my anxiety eased as Emily nodded at me.

"Let's go, trombones."

That included me. For once, in a positive, non–Braden yelling way, that included me. I could almost picture Avery standing behind her with an encouraging thumbs-up.

Our entry into the building was smooth, probably because we were all so eager to get out of the cold that we worked as efficiently as possible. Emily and Cole boosted me up onto their hands to let me reach the top of the window, and Cole actually made eye contact with me before he did it, which was a cool change, since he usually treated me like a war criminal. I got the window open easily, and then Cole and Emily boosted up Sam, then came Cole, with the three of us finally pulling Emily up behind.

We hit the freshmen's lockers first, covering them in streamers and washable marker while we blew up balloons to attach to the locks. And we even had fun, maybe. Cole and Sam were still on the timid side of shy, but they no longer looked like they wanted to flee at the sight of me, and Emily kept the conversation moving, made sure to include me as we gossiped about classes, teachers, band—Sam even pulled out a hilarious imitation of one of Braden's lectures.

This was what band was supposed to be. This is what it had been, sitting on the bus with Avery and Emily, hiding in the back of the trombones but still one of them, before Wickham showed up. Before band was just another excuse to see him, it was this. It was fun and exciting and yeah, a little dorky. It was a place I could belong.

Wickham had called me an ice queen. And you know what, maybe he had been right. But I was here, fixing it. Proving to these guys that I was more than my family's name on a bunch of buildings, that I was more than my daddy's money and a bad reputation. That I could let them in, let them get close to me if they wanted to.

And I knew I shouldn't blame myself for always pushing people away—the therapist Fitz had managed to bring in for a single session over the summer, before she started to ask *him* too many questions and he'd sent her away in a huff, had told me that.

But I always did, anyway. So, as I looked around at the evidence that, somehow, my life was not completely and irrevocably fucked, I let it buoy my hope to the surface, where it floated alongside all the self-doubt and blame and guilt I usually carried. A welcome addition.

If Wickham could see me now—

No. If *Georgie*, if me last year, or the year before, could see me now.

"Damn, dude." Emily nodded in approval as Cole put his final touch on her locker, an elaborate braid of streamers that crisscrossed over the door. "You're super good at that."

"I've watched a lot of YouTube videos." He shrugged. "Braiding relaxes me."

"You're doing my braids before the game tomorrow," Emily declared, and I smiled at the way Cole's eyes widened. "It's decided. You're too good to have your talents squandered."

"Mine, too, please!" Sam squeaked as she raised her hand in the air like she was in class, and then Emily looked at me.

"Um. Me, too?" I offered. Cole managed to look me in the eye before he nodded.

"We're going to look awesome." Emily held her hand up for a high five, which Cole met with surprising enthusiasm. "The flutes are always bragging about their braiding skills, and it's both obnoxious and a super-weird flex."

"That's all of the lockers, right?" Sam asked, looking up and down the hallway. We'd worked our way through the entire trombone section over the last hour. Emily had even produced a sign out of her backpack that said #1 SECTION LEADER to stick on Braden's, and while that was a blatant falsehood, I was too happy to have writing on my own locker that didn't accuse me of being part of a drug cartel to say anything.

"Hey." The idea came to me so fast that it was a wonder I hadn't thought of it before. "We've got more stuff. Should we do Avery's?" He should have been here, with us. That was what was missing from this group, from my specks of hope. "He didn't come out tonight."

"You're sure?" I couldn't quite place the expression on Emily's face, her head cocked to the side as she watched me. It almost looked like a smirk. "One of the other sections might have invited him."

"No, he texted me before bed." And for a few hours before that, but I kept that part to myself. "Said he'd have to skip it this year because he's got a test today."

"Right." She had a harder time controlling her smirk, that time. "Lead the way."

His locker didn't take long to decorate. Cole did his fancy braids again, which Avery would be massively impressed by, and Sam and I shared the washable markers to draw tall hats and batons all over the door. Before we left, I snapped a picture to send his way, just to give him something to wake up to. He'd given me most of my grins over the last month. The least I could do was return the favor.

cll

"Strapless? Are you sure?" Fitz shifted uncomfortably in his chair, which was spindly and old and, frankly, did not look sturdy enough to support his weight. At the moment, though, he seemed preoccupied with a different kind of support. "Aren't you worried about your . . . you know?"

"My bosom overflowing?" I saw Fitz wince in the mirror behind me, and I grinned. Menstrual flow he could talk about, but once we'd gotten into more of the "Dress for Your Body Type!" part of growing up, he'd handed me over to the help. This dress wasn't even my style, but the second I'd seen it I knew I had to try it on, if only to give Fitz a coronary. Just because I was super grateful to him for taking me out today didn't mean I could neglect my sisterly torment duties.

Even running on like, two hours of sleep, I couldn't remember the last time I'd felt this happy. Avery had loved the locker—he'd texted me back a string of smiley face emojis, as well as a selfie of his excited face, head against his pillow, with his hair all mussed and his black-rimmed glasses on his face. I knew he wore contacts—I'd seen him switch them out for his glasses before, during late-night practices and on bus rides home from away games—but I'd never really noticed said glasses, the way they framed his face, made his cheekbones more pronounced.

Even my classes had been bearable. And when I saw my locker in the hall, decorated like all the others . . . I don't know. It felt nice to belong to something.

Fitz had picked me up right as classes ended, and in the last half hour of trying on dresses at the only little boutique in town (one big-box store had been enough for both of us), he'd managed to even act like he didn't hate it. He probably did, but I appreciated the effort.

"I just feel like you'll be able to dance more comfortably in one of the other selections," Fitz said, stiffly. "But if this is what you want . . ."

"I'm kidding, Fitz." I giggled as I crossed back into the dressing room and pulled the curtain closed behind me, unzipping the overly tight dress and letting it fall to the floor. It was a gorgeous dress for someone, but that someone wasn't me. "Don't have a heart attack."

"I'll have you know my heart is extremely healthy."

I shook my head as I pulled the next dress up around my waist. This one was a definite possibility. A deep blue with more personality than navy, the fabric had some sort of sparkle woven all through it that made me think of the night sky. With a V-neck deeper than I usually wore every day but not deep enough to kill my brother, it hit a good line between "I couldn't bother to try" and "I tried too hard." It felt like me. I released my dark curls from the clip that held them back, shook out my head to let them fall around my shoulders. This could work. The skirt hit me right around the knee, and when I spun around it twirled, just a little. It was the sort of dress you'd wear to cosplay as the TARDIS.

When I stepped out of the dressing room that time, pulled the curtain back with a dramatic flourish, Fitz nodded.

"That's the one." He stood up from his chair to come over beside me, then put one hand on my shoulder. "You look lovely."

"You think so?" I turned from side to side in front of the mirror, just to make sure it worked on all angles.

"I do. You didn't go to any dances last year, did you?"

"No." I was pretty sure I'd skipped homecoming last year because Wickham had thought it was lame. The year before, Fitz hadn't gone, so I hadn't, either.

"I'm glad you're going now." Fitz patted my shoulder, then sat back down in his chair. "Are you . . . are you going with friends?"

"Friend. Singular." I had a pair of silver high-tops that would look awesome with the dress. I just needed to dig them out of my closet.

"What's their name?"

"Avery." I resisted the urge to roll my eyes. There was Dad!Fitz again, coming out to interrogate me. But it was nice. Once I got him properly set up with Lizzie, he wouldn't be around to do this sort of thing anymore. I'd take it where I could. "He's the drum major. He was a trombone before that. He's cool."

"Ah." Fitz made some sort of strangled throat noise that I didn't want to examine. I was extremely ready to exit this conversation, which was clearly heading toward uncomfortable territory. "And you're . . . you're friends, you said? Just friends?"

"Fitz." This time, I did roll my eyes, then turned on my heel and headed back into the dressing room. Avery hadn't said we were going as anything *other* than friends, after all. I didn't want to make assumptions. Even if I did kind of want to make assumptions. "Don't be weird."

"I'm not weird." The sound of Fitz's lie drifted through the curtain as I pulled on my jeans and band shirt. "These are normal brother questions."

"These are normal dad questions," I rebutted as I emerged, the soft fabric of the dress over my arm. "You don't need to ask them."

It was sharper than I'd meant to be. I wished I wasn't always sharper than I meant to be. I saw a flash of hurt cross Fitz's face, but it was quickly replaced by his neutral seriousness, so fast I might have imagined it. My brother had pretending I hadn't hurt him down to a science.

"Then let's not worry about it. We should pay and get you back to school." Fitz took the dress from me as I grabbed my backpack from his feet, headed toward the cash register. He may have said not to worry about it, but I could see traces of worry on his face, worry my big brother didn't deserve. "We've got a game to get to."

And *that* was why I was pushing him away. It was for his own good, even if I wasn't as sure anymore that it was for mine.

CHAPTER NINETEEN

his was, easily, the coldest homecoming game we'd had in years.

It was all anyone could talk about, as we changed into our uniforms and prepared to march into the stands. It had the potential to drop into the twenties later, which was frankly unnecessary for this time of the year. I pulled on a sweater over my coverall pants, which would be super bulky under my jacket and go against Mrs. Tapper's normally strict uniform regulations, but she'd given us permission to stretch the dress code for our time in the bleachers. When it was time to get onto the field for halftime, the sweater would have to come off, but at least I had a better chance of surviving until then.

"There she is." I glanced behind me to see Avery, who had a fluffy knitted hat pulled down over his ears under his drum major helmet. I smiled. "Locker decorator extraordinaire."

"I think I may have finally found my future college major." I turned to face Avery fully, my hands supporting my weight on the chair behind me, elbows behind my ribs. "Locker decorating. I think Syracuse has a program."

"Well, you've got a real future in it." The hat pushed Avery's hair down over his eyebrows, giving him even more of a sheepdog appearance than usual. "Seriously. Thank you. I had resigned myself to a bare locker this year."

"You work hard." I shrugged, my eyes on the longer piece of hair that had escaped from his hat to curl around the side of his ear. "You deserve it."

"Thanks."

"You said that."

"I meant it the second time, too." Avery grinned again, and it felt like a jolt of electricity going through me, especially when he reached over to the chair I was leaning on and laid his hand over mine, just for a second.

"Avery!" Mrs. Tapper's voice cut through whatever it was we were doing, and Avery and I each took an immediate step back. I ran into a chair and he almost tripped over some rogue drumsticks. Smooth. "Do you think you can manage it in your busy schedule to warm the band up, please?"

"Sure," Avery answered her, but his eyes were still on me. "Yeah, Mrs. T, I think I can probably pull something together."

"Now, Avery."

"Yeah," he repeated, and as he finally pulled his gaze away, I wanted to follow him, to keep his eyes locked on mine. "Warm-ups." He looked back over his shoulder just once more before he headed toward the front of the room. I grabbed my trombone off the chair I'd almost collapsed on, and when I looked over at the other trombones, Emily was watching me with that same perplexing expression she'd had on early this morning, when I'd said I'd wanted to decorate Avery's locker.

He was just grateful, I reminded myself, as Avery led us in scales. Maybe I should convince Fitz to get me a cat or something. Just to maintain a base level of contact in my life, so that a single touch from just-friends Avery didn't send my heart spinning quite as much.

You're not asking Fitz for favors anymore, I reminded myself. Right. Well. I'd figure something out.

cll

The show went okay. The show actually went okay.

Was it the best marching performance we'd ever turned in? Hell no. But the trombones stayed in formation, and I didn't knock anyone over, so that seemed like a solid improvement. Braden, who hadn't said a word to me since our fight, continued to leave me alone, which honestly was better than talking, from him. Sam even mustered the courage to give me a high five once we'd gotten safely off the field.

"Hey," she asked, as we stood next to each other in our final pose, horns popped high in the sky. "Did you really deal as many drugs as everyone says you did?"

"Nope," I answered, more concentrated on the burn in my abs from the sustained thrust of the pose than my response, and she nodded and moved on.

Emily shared her popcorn with me after the first quarter, when her roommate snuck it down the row to us while Mrs. Tapper wasn't looking, and the braids Cole put in before the game started—some sort of twisting fishtail thing—looked dope as hell.

No one even threw anything at me. Maybe the band was ready to move on from Wickham, move on from hating me quite so much.

Now that the third quarter was about to start, we had some time off to hang before we had to report back to the stands at the start of the fourth. My anticipation grew as I headed up to the Darcy Box at the top of the stadium, hoping beyond all hope that Charlie had been successful in our plan, and that he, Lizzie, and Jane would all be up there. We'd been emailing back and forth, solidifying the details of my grand scheme, but I'd still feel better when I actually saw them.

It wasn't, of course, *technically* called the Darcy Box. Was that what everyone in my family called it? Yes. But it was, in actuality, a VIP box for school alumni and their guests who had made major donations to the school. In the Darcy family heyday, when my dad was a kid with a dozen aunts and uncles who'd all attended Pemberley and donated large sums every year, we tended to dominate the top of the donor charts and take up all the spots available. Hence, the Darcy Box. The only Darcy in it these days was my brother. We were a dying breed.

This had to go well, I told myself as I made the climb, passing classmate upon classmate whose stares and whispers didn't bother me as much as they used to. Positive thinking. Lizzie would be there, Fitz would be thrilled, they'd conclude their falling in love, and I'd do the "Y.M.C.A." with Charlie at their wedding. All they needed was one final push from me.

"There she is!" A familiar voice caught me as soon as I entered the dark-wood-paneled box, lined with plaques that bore my family's name. "My girl!" Charlie crossed over to me with so much enthusiasm that he practically ran, coming to an abrupt halt just in front of me like a puppy who had accidentally skidded across a tile floor. "Schemer of schemes and coordinator of Cupid's arrows. Can I hug you while you're in uniform? Is that okay?"

"Sure?" The word was barely out of my mouth before I was lifted off my feet in a tremendous hug. Weirdly, this did not inspire the same sort of electrified feeling as Avery's simple hand touch had, but I was probably just more tired now. "It's good to see you."

"You, too." Charlie placed me down on the ground and stepped back to get a good look at me. "Can you believe it? I talked to my guys, and everything's in place. We pulled it off."

"Almost," I said, but relief swept through me. Getting everyone here was definitely the hardest part. I managed to restrain myself from jumping up into the air, even though Charlie would probably encourage it and then join in. "You are truly a master. And how do you like homecoming so far?"

"Oh, this is absolutely nonsensical." Charlie waved his hand around at the rest of the box, where twenty or so VIPs gathered in cocktail attire, speaking in soft voices as they sipped at wine and nibbled on hors d'oeuvres. With his Pemberley football jersey (which I had no idea how he'd gotten, because they weren't like, available for sale) and enthusiastic attitude, he stood out like a sore thumb, but he didn't seem to care one bit. I kind of loved it. "I'm super into it. And your brother is around here somewhere . . . I lost him talking to Lizzie."

"Already?"

"She doesn't exactly know anyone else here." He shrugged, grabbing a canapé from the tray of a passing waiter. "Jane wandered off somewhere to go look at the school. She wanted to see the facilities."

"You didn't go with her?"

"Um, no." Charlie's face changed from enthusiasm to distraught in an instant, and as he stared down at the floor, I had the distinct impression of a child who had just lost their favorite toy. "She doesn't really want to—I didn't think I should—"

"Is everything okay?" I asked as a waiter passed by with a tray of bacon-covered dates, and even through Charlie's emotional distress, he managed to reach out and grab a handful.

"Thanks," he muttered toward the waiter, his mouth already full of bacon. I waited patiently as he swallowed, but it wasn't exactly easy. If he and Jane were out of the picture, how did that bode for Fitz? "It's fine. We're just . . . we're not right for each other. Fitz was right. I need to concentrate more on my studies, it turns out."

"Oh." Quite the change from the love at first sight Charlie was confessing to a few days ago, but maybe this was what college was like. If so, I wasn't looking forward to it. "Sorry."

Charlie shrugged, already looking for more appetizers.

"I'm going to go find them?" I felt kind of shitty abandoning Charlie here, but he'd been having a great time before I made the mistake of bringing up Jane. He'd bounce back. He looked like the sort of guy who could bounce back. "Lizzie and Fitz, I mean. Make sure they're well-positioned, get on with the plan."

"And I will continue to try and convince the bartender that my ID is totally real." Charlie bowed, even though he didn't sound particularly chipper, then turned and headed toward the disillusioned-looking bartender at the side of the room.

Well. Nothing I could do about *that*. I was, after all, just one matchmaker.

As I pushed my way through the crowd, avoiding elbows and cocktail shrimp and small talk, I finally saw Fitz. He leaned on the railing that marked the edge of the box, looking out through the thin sheet of glass that kept what would soon be a crowd full of wine-drunk VIPs from tumbling into the stands below, as he spoke in low tones to the girl next to him.

Lizzie.

She looked nice, in gray pants and a soft purple sweater. Maybe a touch more casual than some of the women here, but while they seemed stuffy, she looked comfortable. Her auburn hair was pulled into a loose bun at the back of her head, a few tendrils down around her face, and she stood closer to my brother than he usually let people stand.

All of a sudden, I got hit with a weird wave of dread. What was I even doing? Sure, Fitz might wonder why I never showed up, but he'd get over it. My work here was basically done. Fitz looked . . . happy. The chances that I would make everything worse only increased the longer I stayed here.

I started backing away, back into the crowd, but Fitz caught my eye before I got the chance.

"Georgie." There went my escape route. I walked over to him, caught onto his outstretched arm to pull me through the remains of the crowd. "I was wondering if you were going to grace us with your presence tonight."

"This box is super high in the air," I reminded him as I studied Lizzie, the closest I'd ever gotten to her. She had a spark of something in her expression, like she was watching me a lot more closely than I realized. "That's a lot of steps."

"Cardio is important." Fitz smiled—twice! In one night!— which almost made me fall down in shock. "Georgie, this is my friend, Lizzie. We have a class together."

"You mentioned." I spoke faster than I meant to as I stuck my hand out in front of me. "Hi. Fitz talks about you all the time." I saw my brother go crimson out of the corner of my eye, but Lizzie just laughed.

"Probably about how bad my presentations are, right?" She shook her head, causing the tendrils of hair to sway in a way I sensed Fitz watching. "No amount of his study group techniques can save me."

"Pretty sure he just talks about how smart you are, and how much he enjoys spending time with you—ow!" A sharp poke in my back cut me off in the midst of my totally legit matchmaking speech, and when I looked back at my brother, he had his eyes on Lizzie with a completely false innocent expression. From out of the corner of my eye, I saw one of the waiters cock his head toward me in question, and I nodded as surreptitiously as I could.

"Your brother is kinder than I deserve." Lizzie's gaze flipped from me to Fitz, and her eyes lit up like a chemical reaction. I wanted to cheer. "But thanks anyway. To Fitz for saying it, and to you, Georgie, for saying that he said it." As she winked, I almost blushed. Damn. No wonder my brother was in love with her.

"Strawberries?" The waiter appeared by my side, a tray of chocolate-covered strawberries in his hand.

"Sure." Lizzie smiled at Fitz, then reached out to take one off the tray. Before she could, the waiter shook his head, then placed the entire tray down between them.

"For you," he said, then backed away, perfectly following the script Charlie had slipped him earlier. *Success.*

"Odd." Fitz frowned at the waiter's back before he turned toward me again. "Do you want to take anything back with you, Georgie?" I shook my head, but I also understood the subtle undertone in my brother's voice—time for me to go.

Which was fine. What was coming next . . . I didn't need to be there for. The third quarter was about to end, anyway, and if the whole point of this was to let Fitz be happy without me . . . I had to let him be happy without me.

Something in my chest panged at that.

"No, thanks. I better go, anyway." I raised my hand to wave. "It was super nice to meet you, Lizzie." I gave her my best smile, if only to keep reminding her that Darcys were very pleasant people whom she'd love to spend time around. "I hope we can see each other again."

Lizzie laughed, just a little. "Me, too, Georgie."

After Fitz said goodbye, I let myself fade into the crowd, hesitating for a moment before I headed back toward the band. Lingering at the edge of the Darcy Box, unable to resist seeing the full fruition of my plan come into action.

And as the first burst of light erupted from just outside the perimeter of the field, to the shock and gasp of the crowd, I got my reward.

Fireworks, purple and white and glimmering gold, exploded overhead, but I was only watching Fitz and Lizzie. She burst out laughing, laughter that made her whole body shake, and as she shook her head she reached out and laid her hand on my brother's shoulder. He smiled, restrained but happy, reaching all the way to his eyes, and touched her hand gently with his.

That was my reward. That was my brother, happy. Content.

Good.

The show didn't last long—Charlie's frat brothers only had so many fireworks in their possession (though that number was still way higher than I would have expected). But it was the perfect endcap for the evening. I was practically humming to myself as I headed down the stairs, slipping back in among the other trombones just as the third quarter ended. I didn't pay a single bit of attention to the score, but between the way Lizzie and my brother had looked at each other, and the way Avery smiled at me now, happy to see me back in the stands . . .

I had won plenty, for tonight.

CHAPTER TWENTY

I was still buzzing as I got ready for the dance the next evening.

By five thirty I already had my dress on, hair and makeup ready, even though Avery wasn't going to meet me until seven. I paced back and forth in the five feet or so between Sydney's bed and mine, filled with a restless energy I couldn't place. I shouldn't have been so keyed up. This was just *Avery*. Avery.

And yet.

When my phone buzzed at six, I expected it to be a text from him, some meme or a selfie of him trying to slick his hair back. I grabbed for my phone so fast I almost dropped it.

When I saw the text, I did drop it.

Come outside, kid.

The message was from an unknown number, but only one person ever called me that.

Shit. When Wickham hadn't showed up for the game last night, I'd assumed his threat of appearing with flowers had been blessedly empty. Maybe he'd moved on, decided I wasn't worth the attention. But he was outside, and even though I wanted to put my head under the covers and pretend this wasn't happening, that wouldn't make the problem go away.

I'd already decided, after all, that I wasn't letting him get anywhere near my brother. So I'd face him, and I'd end this. Make it clear that he wasn't welcome in my life. Because when I searched inside myself, to see if any part of me was still happy to see Wickham, still wanted him . . . there was nothing. No need to prove myself. No need for him to want me.

Besides. I had information on him now, information I could use against him.

I shrugged my winter coat on over my dress and tried to keep my breathing regular as I headed out the door and down the steps outside. I hated that I knew where to find him—by the tree where we'd always met, where I'd watched him sneak in and out through the gate and treated him like he was my world—but maybe part of me would always have those connections to Wickham. That didn't mean I had to give in to them.

When I caught my first glimpse of him, leaning against the trunk of the tree the way he leaned against everything, hands tucked into the pockets of a tailored suit, with seemingly no mind for the cold, I did my best to steel myself. To brace for whatever he threw at me. I could take it. I was better than I had been a month ago.

I managed to speak first, by the skin of my teeth, beat him to the punch even as he opened his mouth.

"You really shouldn't be here." I kept my distance, arms crossed over my chest. "I could call security." Not that Rodney would actually get here in time to do anything, but maybe Wickham wouldn't remember that.

"Must we start all our interactions this way?" He sighed, pushed himself off the tree, then reached down behind the trunk to pull out a bouquet of grocery-store carnations. "Come on, kid. I promised I'd bring you flowers. You look good, by the way."

"I don't want them." They were aggressively red, those flowers. He held them out in front of him briefly before he dropped his hand down by his side and shrugged.

"Suit yourself," he said. "Maybe I just wanted to see you. Check in. It's my duty, you know? As one of your oldest friends. And you didn't seem so hot the last time we spoke. After you didn't answer my email . . ."

"Yeah, Wickham." His name was sour acid in my mouth, but I didn't stop. I wouldn't stop for Wickham, not again. "I didn't read it. Because I'm done, get it? Like, for real. Maybe I'll never be Miss Popularity around here or whatever, but it turns out I don't need you. I'm doing just fine on my own."

"Your brother must love that."

"My brother is happy." The wind whipped around me, sneaking in through my coat to press a chill against my chest. "And you can't ruin that, Wickham. Neither of us can."

As he watched me, I did my best to keep my posture tall, strong. I didn't belong to Wickham anymore. I'd spent so long trying to be perfect that I'd discovered I was okay with who I was. I didn't need him.

Wickham didn't seem to like that, if his expression was anything to go by. And I should have expected it, probably, knew what the look in his eyes meant, when he'd run out of words, when he turned to what had always been enough for me before, what had always been the answer to questions he didn't like, the way he best knew how to have power over me.

He pulled me toward him, rough, and kissed me.

Mouth against mine, hand snaking out to the small of my back, Wickham pressed me against him, and unlike every other time he'd kissed me, every other time he'd stood under this tree and told me I was everything, I didn't melt in his arms. Instead, I grabbed onto his shoulders and pushed, hard, so that he stumbled back from me.

No.

I didn't even know if I said it out loud, but he knew what I meant.

He looked down at me from a couple of feet away, licked his lips, and I did my best to control my breathing.

"I really am done, Wickham." My words came out more like gasps. "I swear. I really am done."

"You know you're not that special, right?" Wickham's eyes had more venom in them than ever. "There's a million girls who would die to be with me."

"Like Lydia Bennet?" If he was going to play dirty, I would, too. "Is she part of this new business enterprise of yours? Tell me, does she help you write the papers, or is she just there for moral support?"

The smirk slipped entirely from Wickham's face and when he spoke, his voice was rough. "What do you know about that?"

I'd never talked to Wickham like this. Never had the upper hand. It felt . . . *so* good.

"I know that I'm not one of your girls anymore." I didn't shout. I didn't need to. "I know that you're running some kind of new scam here, and I know that even if the school board can't stop you, one phone call to Daddy Foster will." I pulled my phone out of my pocket, held it up to show I was serious. "We still get a Christmas card from him, did you know that? And I'm sure he'd love to hear what you were up to. Love to keep financing your not-so-good habits."

"You wouldn't."

"Don't tell me what I wouldn't do." I pointed out toward the gates. "Just get out." Adrenaline pumped through me.

"I don't—you won't—" Wickham made as if he were going to step forward, then thought better of it. I was more proud of that, maybe, than I was of anything else. "You know what? Fine." He smirked. "See ya, kid."

And then he turned, and he left, he actually finally left, flicking the collar of his suit jacket up against the cold before he shoved his hands back into his pockets and I got to actually watch him recede into the distance for once in my goddamned life.

I'd done it. I'd actually *done it.*

Wickham was gone.

Once I couldn't see him anymore, I let out a deep breath, my shoulders sagging like my strings had been cut. The idea of a life where I actually managed to rid myself of Wickham had rarely occurred to me. I wasn't naïve enough to believe that I had freed myself of all his aftershocks, because I was going to deal with those for years, probably, but the worst of him was over.

I'd earned myself a dance.

CHAPTER TWENTY-ONE

When my phone vibrated again at 6:55, this time with a text from Avery to let me know he was in my lobby, I had never been so eager to slam my laptop closed and shut off what must have been the slowest episode of *Sage Hall* in human history.

I wasn't going to tell Avery about Wickham's visit, I decided. It would only make the mood weird, and I deserved to celebrate tonight, to be free of what had haunted me for a year. I could tell him later in the weekend, if I wanted. Tonight was my victory lap, my real proof of accomplishment.

I bolted out the door, grabbing my coat on the way out as I took the stairs two at a time. I turned the corner to the front lobby, and saw him, hands in his pockets as he waited for me.

Damn.

I guess I'd always known Avery was good-looking. I'd be lying if I didn't admit to noticing it all year, even if he was just *Avery*, with more defined muscles than the year before. Besides, when he wasn't in a uniform, he tended to dress like he'd just pulled on whatever smelled cleanest in his laundry basket that day, with no regard for colors or patterns. It wasn't a bad look, necessarily. It was just very him.

But he looked. Well. Hot, I guess, would be the word.

I may have temporarily forgotten how to breathe as I looked at him. He'd done something with his hair, maybe gelled it, so it was pushed off of his face and parted down the side. He'd paired a dark blue suit with a white dress shirt and a trombone-patterned tie that made me smile, all of it fitted enough to show off how much he'd filled out over the summer. Lifeguarding and conducting had been good to him.

Shit. I still wasn't breathing.

The best part was his smile. That part hadn't changed, but when he saw me, it spread across his face. I felt my own grin widen in return, and I just felt . . . I was just really, really happy to see him. The edges of the world that had become crumpled and wrinkled in my anxiety smoothed and refocused, so that what I saw was Avery, what I thought was Avery, what I wanted was Avery.

And the possibility of him was suddenly open to me in a way it had never been before.

"Hey." He crossed the lobby, then stood just in front of me, like he didn't know if he should hug me or shake my hand or what. He settled for a nod, which I managed to return as I remembered to breathe again. "I see you dressed up, too."

"I don't think they let you into the dance wearing BBC-branded sweatpants." My arms swung at my sides, completely unnatural. Was I sweating? I must have been sweating. I was pretty sure I had remembered to reapply deodorant, but not sure enough to be confident.

"You look nice."

"You, too," I said. Avery didn't usually stand this close to me, so I had to look up to talk to him, look up at his smile and his dark brown eyes and his smoothed-into-submission hair. I flicked my gaze back down toward the tie again. It was safe there. "Cool trombones."

"My mom got it for me." He definitely smelled better than usual, too, though he always smelled good. There was something spicy in the air around him tonight. It made the hair on the back of my neck stand up. "I figured it was appropriate. Also, it's my only non-uniform tie."

"That makes it the perfect choice." The carefree way I usually felt around Avery was gone, replaced with something very different. I didn't hate it. We were on the edge of something. "Want to head over?"

"Sure." Avery nodded as he shrugged back into his overcoat. "Let's go get our dance on."

I winced the second we stepped outside. Even though I wore tights under my dress, and had pulled on my puffy coat, the wind was intense, even more than it had been less than an hour ago when I was out here with Wickham. It whipped through the trees that lined my dorm's driveway, and the distance between my building and the dance—in the gym, which I could literally see from where I was standing—seemed impossibly far.

"Do you want my coat or anything?" Avery asked as we set out, both of our hoods up against the wind. "To layer up? You look cold."

"You look cold, too," I pointed out. "You don't need to pull out the chivalry for me. I'll be okay."

"If you're sure." Avery grinned down at me, which sent a spark of warmth through my chest I desperately needed. "This is going to be a rough winter."

"They're all rough up here," I said. "It's character building."

"Is that what they call it?" Luckily, even with the attempted wind murder, we were basically at the steps of the gym, and we hurried up the rest of the way with everyone else.

A blast of warm air hit me as soon as we made it through the door, and I breathed a sigh of relief. Around us, our classmates streamed in, but we both stood still for a second, like rocks in a river as the water flowed down.

"This must be how frontiersmen felt," Avery commented as he pulled off his coat. The sight of his suit again made my breath catch. "If they survived, anyway."

"And were rewarded with . . . half-hearted decorations!" I swept my hand grandly at the streamers that covered the gym's entrance, even as I received a stern glare from the girl running the ticket table. "Quick. Guess the theme."

"Oh, that's easy." Avery took a moment to study the black-and-gold streamers, the red balloons, the arch of paper flowers in front of a photo backdrop on our right. Inexplicably, there was a giant cardboard cutout of a blue whale that took up the entire far wall of the gym. "David Bowie fever dream."

"I'm so sorry." I shook my head as we stepped toward the ticketing table. "The correct answer was Elton John fever dream."

"Damn." Avery laughed. "I was so close." Even in the dim lighting of the gym, I saw the sparks in his eyes.

"Two tickets, please." We had reached the table, where the girl who had *not* appreciated my half-hearted decorations comment watched us with a sour expression.

"No, come on." Avery held out his hand over my credit card, which I'd pulled out of my wristlet. "I invited you."

"It's really nothing." I wanted to do this. To give Avery something. And besides, I wanted the scornful ticketing girl, who was now looking at me with growing recognition, to know that I was here with someone. That I was a normal girl with a normal date, and not just the narc from the second floor she'd almost certainly whispered about in the bathroom. "I can get it."

"It's not nothing." There was a hint of frustration at the edge of Avery's voice, which made me look up at him with surprise. "Come on, George. Let me. Please."

"Someone needs to pay for tickets." The girl's voice was dry and disinterested as she drummed her fingers on the table. "Pick one."

"Okay." I nodded at Avery, dropped my credit card back into my wristlet with a weird twinge in my chest. "Thanks."

"You're welcome." He pulled a carefully folded handful of bills out of his wallet, handed them over. The edge was gone from Avery's voice, a quick enough switch that I wondered if I'd imagined it the first time. Even if I hadn't, I had better things to do than worry about it. "Let's go." I followed him past the desk with the surly ticket taker and into the gym, which looked only marginally less sad than usual.

"Want to dance?" Avery had his eyes fixed on the center of the floor, where a bunch of our classmates were already full-on gyrating. Admittedly, most of what I'd seen of high school dances had been in teen movies from the early 2000s, but this mass of teenage hormones was still considerably more sexual than I'd expected. It may have been worse than the frat party. The chaperones around the edges of the floor didn't seem to care, either. Or maybe they did care, but just operated under the whole "better to do it here than in your dorm rooms" mindset.

And Avery wanted to go out there. Cool.

But it was fine. I was confident Georgie Darcy now. I could handle it.

Besides, I'd already promised myself a dance.

"Sure." I nodded, the music loud enough to not betray the crack in my voice, and after we laid our coats on the bleachers closest to us, Avery grabbed my hand—there went my heart again, beat-beat-beating in my chest like the cadence I'd marched to during halftime the night before—and pulled me onto the floor.

"Bets on how many songs we'll actually recognize?" Avery wasn't the world's best dancer, but he had rhythm, and most important, he made dancing look fun, like something I wanted to try, too, even though I'd never really danced. He also hadn't grabbed onto my waist and pulled me toward his crotch like so many of the guys around us, which was a definite plus. "I'll give you over/under on five."

"I might need to go under." I eyed the DJ, who had a metallic helmet on covered in LED lights. I would have made an additional bet that he was the cousin/stepson/nephew of someone on the faculty, if that bet wouldn't have been wildly unfair. "This is a lot of techno. I don't know if any of it has names."

"If only we spent all our time in the clubs." Avery had to lean in to be heard over the pounding beat, and I giggled as his breath tickled my ear. "We could have a real shot at a career."

"As song recognizers?" I twirled under Avery's outstretched arm as my skirt whirled around me. Other dancers had packed in around us on the floor, but I didn't look at anyone else except Avery, who had already loosened his tie. Someone bumped into me from behind, pushed me closer to him. "I don't know if that's a major the Pemberley guidance counselors generally want people to pursue."

"Because they're all trying to achieve notoriety there themselves, and there's only a small number of positions available in the world?"

"You got it." I turned in a circle again, close enough to Avery to hear his laugh.

I was lucky, I decided, as Avery danced and grinned just a few inches in front of me, to have found a friend like him. In what should have been a year of pure crappiness with no redeeming qualities, he had been there for all the good that happened to me. And I didn't think he'd caused it or anything. I wanted to give myself slightly more credit than that. But he was there for it, and I didn't want to share all of those good things with anyone else.

Also, the whole pressing up against his chest to dance thing suddenly seemed a lot more appealing.

"You okay?" Avery bent down toward me again as the song changed. Or maybe it was still just one long song. I literally had no way to tell. "You look kind of flushed."

"Do I?" My voice was definitely higher than it should have been. Maybe I was just catching the hormones of everyone around me. Or maybe it was Avery's smile. "Weird. I don't feel flushed."

"You definitely are." He cocked his head to the side, then placed his hand on my forehead. I managed not to gasp, because as much as I was starting to feel like a character in *Sage Hall*, I was *not* about to swoon just because a guy who happened to look surprisingly good in a novelty tie touched my face. I was a modern woman, damn it. I was better than this. "You feel okay. Do you want to get some air or something?"

"Maybe a soda." Even though I didn't want to leave the dance floor and my forced proximity to Avery, I was clearly losing it. That sweet, sweet potion of sugar and caffeine might help jog me back to reality. "If you want."

"Yeah," he said. That smile again. Always that smile. "Sounds good."

Avery took my hand, apparently completely unaware of the

effect it had on me and my ability to breathe like a regular person, and pulled me through the crowd. I told myself that he was just doing this so he didn't lose me. He'd been nice to me since the moment we'd met, when he'd seen an outcast freshman without a bus buddy, and he'd just kept being nice. This was a bus buddy extension. That was all.

But that feeling I'd had earlier, that feeling of being at the top of a roller coaster, the precipice of something inevitable, that I'd already set in place and couldn't undo if I tried . . . it stuck with me. Why couldn't I take a risk here? Why didn't I deserve to be happy, now that everything was falling into place for me? It was the same logic I'd applied to Fitz and Lizzie, after all.

Avery grabbed me a soda and I fought down the urge to brush away a piece of his hair that had fallen, laden with sweat, into his eyes, and I tried to remember that I'd just gotten rid of Wickham like, an hour ago. I needed time to heal. To figure out who I was on my own.

But I'd rather figure out who I was with Avery. That seemed easier, safer.

As we both cracked our soda cans and clinked them together, I couldn't help but wonder what would happen if I leaned forward, just a few inches forward, and tipped us over that edge.

CHAPTER TWENTY-TWO

Avery and I spent the next hour sitting on the bleachers, drinking sodas, and watching the dancers. We kept up a running commentary about all of them, and Avery's dog-show-announcer accent made me snort soda out of my nose. Which was exactly what you wanted to accomplish when you realized your best friend was hot and you were in love with them, right? To be disgusting?

I was saved from any more bodily-fluid outbursts by Emily, who stopped in front of us with a wave.

"Hey," I managed through my snort-induced laughter. May as well try to cultivate *two* friendships, while I was at it. "Having fun?"

"God, no." Emily wrinkled her nose. She looked awesome in a tailored purple suit, her black hair down and loose around her shoulders. "But, you know. My parents expect at least a dozen pictures of me 'having fun at a dance' so that they get off my back about not being social enough. Smile, you two." She pulled out her phone as she bent toward us for a selfie, and as Avery leaned in to me, I held my breath. The brush of his shoulder against mine was pure fire. "Great." She leaned back, her fingers flying over the screen. "Thank you both for your assistance. I'll tag you, so you can remember what a super-fun time we're currently all having."

"Are you here with anyone?" Avery asked, regrettably sitting up again. I needed to get it together. "You can hang with us, if you want." My heart sank at the thought. I mean, Emily was supercool. Redeveloping that friendship was something I looked forward to. Really. But I . . . I wanted to hang with Avery tonight. Just Avery.

Luckily, it didn't come to that.

"Oh . . . no." Emily looked back and forth between us, her eyebrows raised, whatever that meant. "You know Sabaa? She's a flute. We're kind of dating."

"Cool." Avery nodded, and I tried to remember how to smile like a normal person. Romance in fics was so much *easier* than IRL.

"Well, as fun as this has been." Emily caught my eye, but I looked away. She was clearly trying to communicate something in her gaze, but since it was probably "don't be an idiot, he'll never love you," I didn't want to deal with it. "I'll see you guys out there." With a half-smile and a wave, she vanished into the crowd of dancers.

From his pocket, Avery pulled out his phone.

"Check it out." He leaned over toward me, and his shoulder still felt like something way more powerful than a shoulder should ever feel. "It's a good picture, for once. I'm notoriously bad at them."

"Yeah, right." I didn't spend a lot of time on Snapchat or Instagram, because to use social networks you needed to be social, and we all knew how my track record with that was. I didn't take a lot of selfies, or try to document my life visually in any way, really.

But the three of us were smiling at the camera—well, Emily looked kind of put-out, but I was starting to suspect that was just her face. And Avery and I . . . we looked like something.

I was tilting, and headed down.

"Hey." My voice surprised even myself, as Avery looked up from his phone. "Do you want to dance again?"

"You think we can handle it?" He turned his gaze out onto the crowd, which had only gotten more writhing since we'd gotten here. "I don't want either of us to throw out our backs."

"Yeah." Confidence hovered at the edge of my voice. This time, I stood first, and I held my hand out toward him. He looked down at it, and this time he wasn't entirely grinning. A smile played at the edge of his mouth, like he was afraid to let himself give in to it. "Put me in, Coach. I'm ready."

"Cool." Avery reached out and took my hand, intertwined his fingers with mine as I pulled him to his feet. I could feel the beat of my heart all the way down through the pulsing of my wrist. "Let's go show those *Footloose* parents what they were missing."

"You're mixing your references." I pulled Avery toward the edge of the floor, because I wasn't sure we'd be able to penetrate the inner masses, when, naturally . . .

A slow song.

Maybe the gods of *Sage Hall* were on my side after all.

I didn't recognize it, but it didn't matter. Avery looked down at me, the question in his eyes, and I nodded before he placed his hands on my waist. I put mine on his shoulders with as much care as I could manage, because if he didn't really want this, I didn't want to be too forward. He'd asked me to the dance, but that could have been a friendship overture.

He glanced toward his shoulder, at my stiff hands, then looked down at me, and I saw the smile in his eyes before it even reached his lips.

"George." His voice was lower than usual. Throatier. "It's cool."

He gave the smallest tug on my waist, pulled me closer to him. My hands went around the back of his neck, our chests pressed together, and even though I couldn't see his face anymore, my head turned so my cheek pressed into the spot just below his collarbone, I knew, just knew, that he was smiling, and that it was 100 percent because of me.

Wickham had never held me like this. I hated that I even thought of him, in a moment with Avery, but it was so undeniably true I couldn't help it. I'd been held like I was *wanted* before. But not like I was cared for. Not like this.

The music kept playing, slow and crooning, and I couldn't see much in the dim lighting of the gym, but I didn't really need to see anything, except the lapels of Avery's jacket. That felt like enough.

"George." His voice cut through the music, cut straight through to me. I lifted my head off of his chest, leaned back a little so I could look up at him the best I could. His chocolate eyes crinkled around the edges as he looked down at me, and my breath hitched. I swayed closer, almost without realizing it, dancing to a new song that only we heard. Avery's grip tightened on my waist as his head dipped.

And then the music changed in an instant, back to the fast and pounding techno, and for the second time in as many days, we both jerked back from each other.

"I'm pretty sure that's a tactic they use in interrogations." I did my best to laugh, though it sounded super weird. "Change the tempo of music so fast that it freaks you out."

"How much club music do they play in interrogations?" Avery dropped his hands from my waist and shoved them deep in his pockets, like he didn't know what else to do with them. I knew the feeling. Stupid patriarchy that kept my own dress from having pockets. "I definitely assumed that cops had more of an easy-listening attitude."

"Regional differences." Other students who had ditched the dance floor when the slow song had come on, since they, apparently, weren't living in their own fanfics, flooded the floor as the beat sped up. "I, um, think I'm going to run to the bathroom. All that soda." Cool, perfect, nothing like having an almost-moment with the guy you'd realized you have "feelings" for and then immediately discussing your bladder needs. I was officially the smoothest. "So."

"For sure." Avery stepped back, giving me room to leave the floor. "I'm going to explore the snack situation. Meet you over there when you're done?"

"You betcha," I said, for whatever reason, while throwing finger guns Avery's way and backing off the floor. *Finger guns.* Acceptable only to actual sheriffs, I was certain, and yet here I was, tossing them out at the best-looking guy at the dance.

Your best friend, I reminded myself, as I exited the gym (finally) and headed down the much quieter halls to the nearest bathroom. Small pockets of people hovered in the hallway, but they didn't pay me any mind. They probably didn't even realize who I was. I looked a lot nicer than usual, and fallen girls weren't expected at school dances, anyway.

Once I made it to the bathroom, I splashed the world's smallest amount of water on my face, trying to be cognizant of my makeup. I was still red, I discovered, my hair a little mussed. But I didn't look bad. The flush brought some much-needed color to my skin, and this dress really did look amazing.

All thoughts of that flew out of my mind, though, when I pulled my phone out of my small wristlet to see half a dozen missed calls from my big brother.

CHAPTER TWENTY-THREE

S hit. I swiped my phone open with shaking fingers to call Fitz
back. Fear swept through me, threatened to overwhelm. If
something happened to him, if someone had found his phone in a
ditch next to the road and called the most recent number on it . . .

I couldn't lose Fitz, too.

The worst of my fears were assuaged when he picked up the
phone a moment later, but it didn't eliminate the dread.

"So, you decided to call me back." His voice was terse, biting.

I let out a whoosh of breath. "You're okay?" I leaned back
against the sink, clung to the edge of the counter for support. The
smell of industrial-strength cleaning fluids stung my nostrils.

"Oh, I'm just fine." Sarcasm wasn't a familiar tone from my
brother, but I recognized it here. "And you? Too busy out enjoying
your dance to check your Instagram, I guess?"

"What's that supposed to mean?" I didn't think I'd ever heard

Fitz *mention* Instagram before. I knew he had one, and that he followed me, but I'd assumed it was kind of a sibling formality. Had he seen the picture of me and Avery and Emily and flipped out, for some reason? "I'm at homecoming. I'm with my friends."

"Why don't you take a look at your tagged photos and tell me about the friends you're spending the evening with, Georgiana."

I lowered the phone from my ear, hands still shaking. Unless Avery or Emily were secretly enemies of the state, I didn't know what Fitz could possibly have to freak out about like this, but clearly *something* had happened, and it seemed like I was about to find out what.

I had a few notifications on my Instagram when I opened it. Some likes on the picture that Emily had posted. The notification that I'd been tagged in it in the first place. And below that . . . more likes, on another tagged photo. I didn't recognize the user-name of whoever posted it.

I definitely didn't expect to see a zoomed-in picture of me and Wickham from just a few hours before. Kissing.

Spotted at Pemberley Academy . . . The caption read. *Old habits, huh? Business really is booming.* I scrolled up, frantic, back to the user who'd posted it. I didn't recognize the username, and the profile pic was just an overly-artsy silhouette. But when I clicked through to the profile, I realized I knew the girl posing in front of a hundred colorful walls and floral backdrops. Lydia Bennet.

It was a good thing I had a grip on the counter, because my knees nearly buckled beneath me.

It was possible Wickham was smarter than I'd given him credit for.

"Fitz." I pulled the phone back up to my ear as soon as I could with my trembling hands. Wickham must have brought Lydia along; he must have fed her some crap story, snuck her onto campus first and had her take the picture and then sent it to Fitz. *Insurance.* That was what he called shit like this, when what he meant was *revenge*. I shouldn't have been surprised; this was, after all, what he had promised would happen. I'd just been stupid enough to think I'd beaten him. "You don't understand."

"Oh, I'm sorry." His voice was ice-cold steel, anger pulsing through a blade. "Is that *not* a picture of you kissing Wickham? Outside of your dorm room? In the dress we bought yesterday?"

"Yeah, but—"

"Then I understand *perfectly.*"

"I only saw him so I could tell him I was done with him," I babbled, tears running down my face as the dam burst. I clutched the counter, slippery with soap, and prayed that this was some sort of sick dream, that I'd wake up and this wouldn't be happening. "He kissed me, but I stopped it. I promise, Fitz."

"Even if that's true—and it sure as hell doesn't look like you're stopping him in that picture, Georgiana—then that heavily implies that you've been in contact with him. That you've seen him since the spring. Have you?"

I didn't answer, I couldn't answer, but Fitz knew what my silence meant.

"I can't believe you."

"I'm sorry." My throat felt like it was on the verge of closing off, like soon I'd stop breathing altogether. "I didn't mean to."

"What sort of answer is that?"

"It's what I've got." My words jumbled together as they mixed with my sobs. "He had my email still, and I didn't have anyone else, and I just—"

"It's excuses." I could *hear* my brother shaking his head. Hear whatever was left of our relationship evaporate into thin air. "It's childish, and it's selfish."

"I—I didn't tell you because I was trying to *not* be selfish, for once," I protested. "I just wanted to prove that I could take care of myself, and I tried to leave you alone, except for the stuff with Lizzie . . ."

"What 'stuff with Lizzie'?"

Thank God there was no one in this bathroom but me. I glanced up toward the mirror and saw what a mess I was, makeup streaked down my face, my hair coming out from its clip where I'd pulled at it in distress. I'd felt pretty when I started the night off. Proud. Now my outside did an even better job reflecting my inside.

I'd thought I was better. But I could never, ever win. I just couldn't.

"I kind of . . ." I pressed my hand over the waist of my dress, tried to grab at the clingy fabric. Stupid dress. "Tried to get you two together."

A beat of silence that was the longest one yet.

"Are you kidding me, Georgiana?"

"Fitz." My cheeks were soaked with my tears. "I'm sorry."

"Sorry doesn't cut it anymore." He'd never talked to me this way. For all that I suspected Fitz had started to hate me, after everything I'd done, I'd never heard it so clearly in his voice. "It hasn't cut it for six months, since you ruined your own life beyond recognition. It's honestly appalling to me that you thought you had any business meddling in my affairs when you so spectacularly destroyed yours."

Something stirred again inside of me. Something like anger, because I had *tried*. I'd tried so hard, and I'd almost succeeded, even—if it hadn't been for this one slipup, this single ruination that brought everything crashing to the ground. I'd failed, but I'd tried, and it didn't seem like too much to me to ask for a little acknowledgment of that.

Maybe Fitz did hate me. It certainly seemed like it, like the grand conclusion of everything that had happened this year and last was the irrevocable destruction of my relationship with my brother. Maybe he thought I was a worthless stain on the family name.

If that was true, I wasn't about to take it lying down. I might be a horrible Darcy, but pride still ran through my veins.

"Yeah, well." I pushed off from the counter, tried to wipe the worst of the tears from my face. I was just pushing around the mascara at this point, but I didn't care. "I am sorry, all right? Sorry I wanted to make you happy. I know I ruined everything for you, when you had to leave LA, but you've made yourself into some sort of martyr for me, and it's not necessary. Lizzie clearly likes you, and you like her, and if you had someone to be with, maybe you wouldn't blame it on me that you were so miserable all the time!"

It was too far, but I couldn't step back. I couldn't. I couldn't go back to groveling on my belly for forgiveness from the world.

Fitz, it turned out, still had one more arrow in his quiver, ready to strike.

"How extremely noble of you," he hissed. "But trust me, Georgiana. It wouldn't matter if I had someone to be with. I'd still be miserable because I'd still have to spend all of my time worrying about *you*."

And then he hung up.

Like I wasn't even worth saying goodbye to.

I slid down until I was crouched over the floor, wrecked.

It didn't matter what I did. What Fitz did. We were both going to be trapped in this cycle of misery for the rest of our lives, because he'd never learn to trust me again or even to like me and I was never going to live up to his expectations. Sure, maybe I should have told him about Wickham, but if it hadn't been

Wickham, it would have been Lizzie, and if it hadn't been Lizzie, it would have been something else.

The walls of the bathroom closed in around me, like Pemberley had finally decided to crush me under its weight, under the weight of my legacy, under the weight of my brother.

Wickham in the doorway, trying to block Fitz from entering, but Fitz shoved past him, shouting like I'd never heard my brother shout before. The pills in his hand, the look on his face, and I knew, with absolute certainty, that my brother would never, ever forgive me for what I'd done.

I had to get out of here.

I barreled out the door, ran down the hall as fast as I could—praise be for sneakers—even as other students stopped their conversations to stare at me. And why wouldn't they stare? That was all anyone at this school would ever do, stare and talk and whisper about how I didn't deserve anything, how I shouldn't be here, how I was an asshole and an ice queen and none of them would ever like me, anyway. I shouldn't have even tried. I was flunking most of my classes because I was trying to be something I'd never be. Why was I even here, in a stupid too-tight dress, imagining I had a chance with a boy, imagining I had friends who cared? Emily barely knew me and Avery just pitied me. That was all. If I let either of them get any closer, they'd just realize what a tremendous screwup I was, anyway.

That wasn't a real *life*. The closest I had to a real life was online, and in my fics, and that was the most pathetic thing I'd ever thought. Which made sense, considering that I was pathetic, but it didn't make it hurt any less.

Avery must have still been hanging out at the snack table, since our coats were unattended on the bleachers. I grabbed mine as I pushed through the crowds, grateful for the darkness that kept the rest of the world from seeing my absolute disaster of a face. I just needed to get outside, and then I could call a Lyft or something. Something that would take me far away from here without asking any questions.

Because that was the only option left to me, right? You have to go home and you can't stay here. Rochester was just a few hours' drive, if the car drove fast and didn't hit any late-night traffic. It wouldn't be forever—if I was actually running away from Fitz, that would be the first place he looked, once the school realized I was missing. But if I could make it there tonight, I could grab my passport and the cash I knew my parents used to stash around the house in case of emergency. With that, I could get anywhere. We had a dozen properties around the world I could hide out at. Friends, or at least business associates, in plenty of high places. Maybe I'd even go somewhere warm. Somewhere I'd finally stop shaking.

Coat in hand, I made straight for the door to the outside world, head down so I didn't have to make eye contact with anyone. I was almost out, almost gone as I burst through the doors into the cold air outside that hit me like a shock, and I was about to pull out my phone when I heard my name from behind me.

I shouldn't have stopped, or looked. But I recognized the voice, and I couldn't help myself.

"George?" Avery stood behind me, at the top of the stairs, looking down at me just past the sidewalk. He had his coat in his hands and a bewildered look on his face. "Are you . . . going somewhere?"

"We get Lyft up here, right?" Though the darkness hid the tears on my face, you could definitely hear it in my voice. Cool. "I don't need anything fancy. But there should be one person in this nowhere town who wanted to make a little extra money as a driver."

"George?" he said again, taking the steps two at a time down toward me. It wasn't worth trying to move, and when Avery reached me, I didn't bother to hide my tears. I'd done that for too long. "Hey. What's wrong?"

"The usual." I shrugged, tried to make my voice sound more nonchalant and less emotional breakdown. "Turns out you can't ever move past your mistakes. And I'm done trying." Tears overcame me, closed up my throat so I couldn't speak, and as Avery stepped forward to hug me, I backed away, tried to catch my breath. "It's fine. Really. But I need to go home."

"I can walk you back to your dorm." Avery looked lost, his arms still partially up like he was hugging me. "If that's what you want."

"I'm not going back there." I shook my head. The cold bit through my skin, even with my coat. I shivered. "I'm going home-home. Rochester."

"You are?"

"Just to start." I shouldn't be trying to explain this to Avery, because it didn't matter. "I'm not sure where I'll go from there. Maybe England. Live my best *Sage Hall* life."

He looked back down at me, studied my face, and I felt the precipice again. Then he sighed, reached into his coat pocket, and pulled out his car keys.

"Come on." He walked past me with brisk efficiency, in the direction of the student parking lot. "Let's go."

"What?"

"You really think I'm going to let you take a Lyft to Rochester in the middle of the night with some random driver when you're clearly upset?" Avery shook his head but didn't slow down, and I had to run to catch up. "No way. Come on."

"You don't have to do that, Aves." The nickname felt broken in my mouth, like I'd crunched on glass. "I can take care of myself."

"I know. You don't need anyone." Still a little bit behind him, I couldn't see his face, but it didn't sound like he was smiling. "Let's go to Rochester, Georgie." Not George. Georgie.

But we were going, I reminded myself as I hurried through the freezing night. I was getting out. This should have made me happy.

"Should have" being the operative phrase.

CHAPTER TWENTY-FOUR

The interstate unwound before us, curving and dipping through mountains only to disappear around bends.

"We'll be on this road for the next hundred miles." I shut down the maps app on my phone and dropped it by my feet. I didn't want to look at it right now, and with the way reception was out here, it was going to stop working in a minute anyway. We were twenty miles out from Pemberley, headed north toward Rochester, and we'd spent the last half hour communicating only in directions. "Watch out on the turns."

"I've driven through here before." Avery's eyes were locked on the road, refusing to stray toward me. "I've got it."

"Right." The fire of my despair had cooled slightly, turned into a dark lake I'd sunk into, down into the water, where even Avery was just a shape above me. I didn't know how to reach him anymore, how to get through to his blurred outline.

I'd tried the radio when we first got in the car, but reception was shitty and Avery's radio wasn't great even with a pristine signal. Instead, we both stared out into the night, and I wished it would swallow me up.

"Hey, can I ask you a question?" Avery's voice made me jump. I picked my head up off of the window and turned to look at him, but his eyes were still straight ahead. "What *do* you want to be when you grow up? Not the pit musician thing, from when you were a kid. But what do you want now?"

"What?" His question cut through all the fog in my head. "Why?"

"I don't know." He bit down on his bottom lip, dark eyes squinting just a little to see better in the dark. "You know what I want to do."

"I guess I just assumed I'd figure it out in college." I leaned back against my seat, the material scratchy against my bare back. "Take a bunch of different classes, see what I like."

"Yeah, but you must want to do something."

"I don't know." I shrugged. "I like writing." My current AP English grade didn't exactly reflect that, but whatever. "Music. But those aren't like . . . viable options."

"They're not?"

"That's not what a Darcy does." I felt gross even saying it. "I should be majoring in like . . . biochemical business engineering medicine or something. Living up to the family name." I laughed, though it wasn't particularly funny. "Though maybe this will put an end to all of those expectations. Finally."

"What's Fitz's major, again?"

"I don't want to talk about my brother." The sharpness in my voice surprised even me. Avery winced, and I did, too. "Sorry."

"It's okay." Avery eased the car to the left, around a tight bend, gripping the wheel so hard that his knuckles were white. "I just want to know you. That's all."

"You do know me." I ran my hand over the embroidery at the bottom of my skirt, the gold thread that stood out against the blue. "More than anyone does. Just because there are things I don't want to talk about doesn't mean I'm holding back from you. It just means I . . . don't want to talk about them."

"Right." Avery shrugged as darkness passed outside his window. "Sorry."

"Me, too," I said, though I didn't quite know what I was apologizing for. I sighed. "Fitz is perfect, Aves. He's got his life all together, he's everything a Darcy should be. You know my aunt Catherine, she sends out a family newsletter once a week? And for a while, she'd rank everyone we were related to on the basis of how successful they were."

"That's awful."

"That's Aunt Catherine." When I looked over toward him, his eyes were still on the road. "Fitz was always third or fourth, easy. He'd be higher, if Aunt Catherine didn't put herself and her daughter, my cousin Anne, in the top two every time. Fitz tended to switch off with this second cousin of ours who I'm pretty sure is like, the king's hand to the prime minister of Canada."

"And you?"

"Never even made the list." I laughed again, watched the stars blur by. "Wasn't even a good enough Darcy for that, no matter how hard I tried. This"—I held my hand out to gesture to the car, to the road, to the whole situation—"is probably going to get an entire newsletter issue itself."

"Sorry." Avery glanced over at me, quickly, before he turned his eyes back to the road. I began to speak again, to brush off his apologies, but Avery kept talking. "But like . . ." He shook his head and I watched some of his carefully gelled-back hair fall and lose its shape. "I'm not one of your terrible relatives trying to interrogate you. I'm here, aren't I?"

"Yeah." Warmth swept through me, a better feeling than the artificial blasts from the air vents. Maybe Avery did still see me, even with everything that had happened. Maybe I still had him. "You are."

"Good." He reached over, across the center console, across his cup holders, and patted my hand, just for a second. Then he put it back on the steering wheel and kept on driving, a small smile playing across his face. "Good."

cll

We'd been on the road for two hours, and the weather was taking an aggressive turn for the worse.

"Fuck," Avery swore, an unfamiliar sound from him, as he squinted through the fog that had overtaken the road entirely. "This is really bad. Can you see at all?"

"Not really." It had gotten bad as soon as we'd entered the Endless Mountains region—an actual geographic area, because the wilderness of New York was a nonsensical place—and showed no sign of dissipating. I grabbed my phone, tried to open my weather app. "I don't have any service."

"Here, check mine." Avery nodded toward the cup holder where his phone rested. I opened it with a quick swipe, and quickly confirmed what we both already suspected. "Nothing."

"Fuck," Avery repeated, which really betrayed how freaked out he must have been and made me freak out even more. "We can't drive in this."

"I think there's a truck pull-off up ahead." I could just barely make out the illuminated sign in the distance. "We can get off there. Wait for it to pass."

Avery nodded as he crawled the car forward. With his high beams and blinkers on, we could at least make out the vague shape of the road, but if there were other cars coming toward us that weren't going slow enough, we'd be in real trouble. My heart stayed in my throat until we reached the sign, veering off to the right and into the small parking lot at the side of the road.

I let out my breath.

"Now what?" I looked over at Avery, who hadn't released the steering wheel yet. "You can let go."

"Right." He lifted his fingers one at a time, peeled them back slowly. "Sorry."

"It's okay." I shrugged. "So, we just . . . wait out the fog?"

"It might be a while." Avery grimaced. If anything, the weather was just getting worse, the fog now so thick that I felt like we were trapped in a cloud. I shivered. Thank God we'd found the pull-off, or we'd be in even more trouble. Even as it was, the sinking feeling crept over me that we were in a distinctly Not Good situation. "But I don't think we have a choice." He shut the car off, and I whipped my head toward him.

"What are you doing? It's freezing outside."

"And I don't want to use up all of the gas." Avery sighed as he reached for his phone and flipped on the flashlight so that we weren't in complete eerie and foggy darkness. "Just head into the back seat."

"What?" All the blood rushed to my face.

"No, not . . ." Avery coughed. "It's a bench seat, and I've got a bunch of extra blankets and coats back there. We'll be a lot more comfortable."

"Oh." Obviously, he wasn't like . . . propositioning me. That would be absurd. Unfortunately, my logic hadn't caught up to my blush, though it was dark enough that I doubted Avery could see it. "Sure."

I unclicked my seat belt and crawled over the center console, careful not to completely flash Avery in my dress as I settled onto the worn-down fabric of the back seat. Thank God for an A-line skirt and tights. True to his word, the whole floor was covered in a mess of blankets and coats, and I pulled the first one I found over me with gratitude. A second later, Avery vaulted over the back of his seat, long legs splayed out, and settled next to me with a thunk. He reached for his own blanket, then hesitated.

"Here." I barely knew what I was saying, but I held out the edge of my blanket. Somehow, though, I knew I had to. Because Avery had reached for me the last time, and he wasn't going to do it again. "We should just share, and layer up. It'll keep us warmer."

"You sure?" I heard the hesitance in Avery's voice, did my best to push through it.

"Yeah." I put all the confidence and assurance I had in me into that one word. I mean, I had nothing else left. I may as well have this, right? "Come on."

I didn't know what tomorrow had in store for us, or the day after that. But I knew that if everything we had was going to end tomorrow, I didn't want to spend tonight curled up on opposite sides of this bench seat.

After just a second more of hesitation he scooted in my direction, pulled the edge of the blanket over him so that we were pushed together, side by side. He grabbed another blanket off the floor and pulled it over both of us, locking in our warmth.

"This okay?" I asked. I could feel him breathe, felt the blanket rise up and down with his breath.

"Yeah," Avery said. "It's okay."

Neither of us spoke, just sat there, still, with our feet on the floor and our gaze straight ahead, like we were going to get caught too close together in church. And then, finally, Avery laughed.

"Sorry," he said, and he turned his head down toward me. "I'm not trying to be super weird. I swear. This is just . . . a lot. I kind of can't believe it."

"The fog?" I shrugged, and tried to ignore the tingles that rushed through my shoulder when it hit his. "We should have expected this. I'm kind of cursed."

"No." He shook his head. "I can't believe I'm in the back seat of my car, at night, under a blanket with Georgie Darcy, and I'm too freaked out to make a move."

That time, I did forget how to breathe.

"Um." Oh, God. For the first time in my life, I had forgotten how to speak entirely. "Um."

"I don't have to." Ah, there was the panic in Avery's voice. I recognized it because I was currently filled with it myself. "Do you want me to just get out of the car? Would that be better? I can just sit outside. I'll freeze to death but that's fine."

I needed a word. *Any* word. Seriously, how did I not have a single syllable left in my body besides "um"? Sure, I was currently failing English, but I'd made it this far in school. I'd written thousands upon thousands of words of fanfic. And I couldn't say anything like, romantic or even affirmative here?

He was going to leave. I could feel him start to pull away from me, because Avery was a respectful guy who obviously wasn't going to do anything without my consent and so in my panic I reached down and put my hand on his thigh.

For clarity, I didn't do it in a smooth, romantic way. It was far from sexual. I just sort of reached over, under the blankets, and death gripped his thigh—luckily, I didn't miss in the dark, and grab anything else—and then looked at him in the flashlight-lit back seat, with as much meaning in my look as I could possibly convey. That was it. That was all I had. My big move.

Thank God Avery had always managed to speak my language.

He looked down at my hand, then back at me, and he grinned, and all the panic evaporated out of me like steam off of a hot sidewalk.

"If it wasn't clear. I would really love to kiss you now, George." Avery reached over and touched my curls, gently, then laid his hand on the back of my neck. "Is that okay?"

I still didn't have words, but I managed a nod, and that was enough.

Avery leaned down toward me, and I rose up to meet him, turned toward him so that our lips bumped and met at the halfway point. Even as we kissed, I felt him smile.

He tasted like Sprite and Tic Tacs. The blankets fell away as we shifted, as Avery pulled me closer in to him. My hand left his leg— thank God—and went up to his shoulders, felt the muscles there and used them as an anchor.

Most of the other times I had been kissed, I'd been filled with trepidation, with an undeniable fear that if I did something wrong, if I didn't show my best self, if I didn't manage to act sexy or attractive or whatever, I would screw everything up. But with Avery? He saw me. He knew me, and he liked me, he spoke my same weird language and he wanted to kiss me in spite of it. Maybe not even in spite of it. Because of it.

He pulled back and pressed his forehead against mine. His smile took up my whole field of vision, just as he took up my whole heart.

"Hi," he whispered, as if he didn't want to be overheard. I giggled. "You good?"

"Yeah." Screw fanfic. This was way better. "I'm good. You good?"

"I'm good," Avery said. He leaned back against the door, pulling me toward him so that I settled in the space between his chest and the back of the seat. I was kind of squished, but I wasn't mad. "I'm so good."

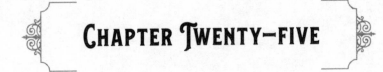

Chapter Twenty-Five

The light that streamed through the car windows woke me up first. It took me a moment of blinking to remember where I was, and who I was with, and what had happened last night.

Last night. Because we'd fallen asleep while we waited for the fog to clear up, and it was morning now. We'd been gone the whole night. Left the dance and then vanished into the darkness.

My plan of escaping without notice disappeared the same way the fog had. We were in *so* much trouble.

More trouble, I mean.

"Aves." I shook Avery awake next to me. We'd fallen asleep curled against each other, my shoulder tucked just below his and his head pinning my left arm against the door. It was all tingly now. "Wake up."

"What?" As Avery returned to consciousness, he shifted, and I winced as the blood started to flow back to my arm. His eyes widened for a second as he took in the car, me, and our proximity to each other. "Oh. Hi."

"Hey." I tried to divert my mouth away from him as I spoke. There had to be mints in the car somewhere. "It's morning."

"I see that." He grimaced as he shifted upward into a sitting position, rubbed at the back of his neck. "Guess the fog lasted longer than we thought it would."

"Good thing you had all these blankets." I glanced down at the floor of the car, where the huge pile we'd covered ourselves in to get through the night had fallen. "You're easily the most prepared non–Boy Scout I've ever met. Think we can turn the car on now, though?" I sat up the rest of the way, too, making sure my dress hadn't shifted out of place underneath my coat during the night. I was way ready to put on some real clothes. "We should . . ."

"Right! Right." Avery nodded with so much enthusiasm I half-expected his head to be thrown off of his shoulders. "We should go." He climbed up toward the front of the car again, so fast that I had to lean to the side to avoid a kick to the skull.

I followed him at a slightly slower pace as he turned the key in the ignition, and let out a sigh of relief as the first blast of warm air came out of the vents. I glanced toward Avery out of the corner of my eye, and when I caught him looking at me, he cut his gaze to stare straight ahead again, fiddled with the radio controls to try to get reception. I smiled to myself.

Still, even though last night had taken a brief foray into the excellent, I couldn't help but fear what waited for me in Rochester. The world had gone all soft and romantic last night, in the fog. Now, with the light of a cold fall morning pouring through the windows, where I could see the smudge of fingerprints, everything seemed . . . unsettled. Like we were surrounded by eggshells, and if I stepped the wrong way, I'd crush them into oblivion.

I glanced at the dashboard and did my best not to groan. It was eight a.m. Yeah, my whole running away plan was officially toast. The school would have noticed that I wasn't in my room at curfew and called Fitz, who must have panicked. If he wasn't already at the house in Rochester, he'd make sure someone was there on standby if I showed up. He'd probably put a tracker on my passport, so that he'd know if I tried to really run.

And, naturally, my phone was dead.

"Do you have a charger?" I asked Avery, who had finally given up on the radio dials that delivered nothing but static.

"Sorry." Avery shrugged. "This car is too old for that. It's not like there's service here, anyway."

"Right." I tossed my phone back down on the floor with a groan. "Let's go. I can just give you directions to my place."

"We're still headed to Rochester?"

"Obviously." Running away without a trace might no longer be a viable option, but I still wasn't going back to Pemberley. I'd just have to deal with Fitz when he caught up with me. I bet he'd ship me off anywhere, with how much he hated me now. "We're only an hour away."

Avery stared at me, opened his mouth as if he was going to say something. Then, after a minute, he looked forward, put the car into drive, and pulled back onto the highway, which looked a lot less threatening now than it had last night.

"Have you been to Rochester before?" I asked Avery after the longest ten minutes of my life, where he drove in silence and I pretended to be interested in the scenery.

"Nope." He hit the *p* with a strong plosive, let it linger in his mouth for a second before he continued. "No reason to."

"It's nice." There was so much false cheer in my voice that I felt like a mall-Santa. "You'll like it." Avery was probably just worried about the effect kissing would have on our friendship. And I was, too, don't get me wrong. That was a genuine concern. But I was convinced we could make it work. Avery was the only thing in my life that *did* work, the only proof that all the shit I'd put myself through this year was worth the trouble.

If he stayed in Rochester with me, just for a couple of days, he could help me deal with the fallout from my brother. I could always forge a doctor's note for him; I'd done it plenty of times last year when Wickham needed me for something. He'd stay, and we'd figure out my next steps.

I'd ask him when we got there, I decided. He was clearly stressed out about the whole situation, which I didn't blame him for. Hungry, too. He'd grin again once he got some food in his stomach. The house had a manager that checked in a few times a week when Fitz and I were away at school, and he made sure the house was stocked with basics. I could manage a cup of coffee and a bowl of cereal, at least.

I smiled to myself, head turned to the window as I watched the valleys weave below us, their trees red and orange with hints of grays. Even if the rest of my life was falling apart around me . . . this was going to work out, Avery and me. I hadn't gone through everything I'd gone through, I hadn't tried as hard as I'd tried this year, to still wind up with absolutely nothing. I'd make sure of it.

cll

"It's just about a mile down this road, on the left." I directed Avery past the final stoplight, my heart beating fast. "I'll give you a heads-up before we turn."

"You're sure there's not a gas station around here we can stop at first?" He eyed his fuel tank dubiously, where the needle was dangerously close to E.

"I know this place pretty well, Avery."

He nodded. Our conversation had been limited to directions since we started the drive home, no opportunities for me to slip in hints he should stay here or even gauge how he was feeling about last night. For once, Avery was a closed book, and it unsettled me. I kept trying to remind myself that he was exhausted, worried about his car. It didn't have anything to do with me.

Necessarily.

"Turn here." I pointed at the mailbox on the side of the road, the only indication that we were coming up on my childhood home. "The driveway is super long, so just keep on driving. I promise there's a house at the end of it."

"Did your family work for the CIA or something?" Avery had to lean forward over his steering wheel to watch the driveway as branches brushed against the top of his windshield, dangling down from the trees above. "Or like, actively work against the CIA? This is a supervillain driveway."

"My parents liked their privacy." I shrugged. It was weird—even though I'd lived in this house my whole life, the driveway was only passably familiar to me. We didn't leave the house much, growing up. My first few years of school were all taken care of by private tutors who lived in our carriage house, and the property was big enough that you didn't need to go anywhere else. Even when we did go into town for something, we always had a driver who took us around, the windows tinted dark enough that I never spent much time looking out of them.

One final curve of the driveway . . . and there it was. I smiled, small, as the house finally came into view. Set at the top of a rolling hill that Avery's car protested as it climbed, I realized I was glad to see the familiar green trim against crisp white paint, the wide wraparound porch, the tower room I'd insisted on turning into a practice space. The rest of the estate sprawled out behind it, and even though I couldn't see the carriage house, or the guest quarters, or the enclosed and heated pool, knowing they were there gave me comfort I hadn't found in weeks. *Home.* I might have felt suffocated here, over the summer, but this was still the last place where I'd been happy without consequences.

"This is your house?" Avery's voice broke the silence. I glanced over in his direction, expecting to see his wide smile, a nod of approval, maybe even some wide-eyed wonderment—but he looked more betrayed than anything. "You live here?"

"Yes?" This was not the reaction I'd been expecting. Then again, I'd never brought anyone here before. "I mean, unless it's a clone house. I hear that's a real problem in this part of the country."

Avery gave a strangled sound of assent as he pulled his car into the circular driveway. My anticipation froze in my veins, turning to something more ominous. Great. Loved that journey for me.

Avery switched off the car and we climbed out, stretched our stiff muscles. The air was brisk, and I shivered even inside of my coat, my dress tangled around my legs. The gravel of the driveway crunched beneath our feet as Avery came around to my side, leaning back against the car as he looked up at the house.

"Come on," I said after a minute, when it became clear he wasn't about to move or say anything. Dude definitely needed some protein. "It'll be warmer inside."

"Will it?" Avery eyed the porch as we came up the front steps. Our house manager had taken most of the furniture inside for the season, but a few rocking chairs remained. We could have breakfast out here, if we got some blankets. "A place this big must be freezing."

"We have a staff." I dismissed him with a wave of my hand. Of all the things I had to worry about, that was way low on my list. "It may not be toasty, but even when Fitz and I aren't home our house manager pops in a couple of times a week and makes sure everything is taken care of. For situations like this."

"Running away?"

"Unexpected arrivals." I enunciated the words carefully as I unlocked the front door, tested the syllables in my mouth. "Come on." I stepped through the front door into the foyer, Avery right behind me.

As I'd expected, our house manager, Mr. Germain, was waiting just inside, perched on a chair at the bottom of the stairs. He jumped up when he saw me, the wood of the chair creaking as much as his bones. He'd been with our family forever, and I was pretty sure he'd looked this old when I was a baby, so I had no idea what his age was now. Nevertheless, his face still managed to convey "Disappointed in Georgie" quite effectively.

"Miss Darcy." He nodded his head in a deep bow, which I waved away with my hand. "Your brother is worried sick."

"I'll bet he is." I pulled my coat off, since Mr. Germain had heated the house to near-boiling. Toasty, indeed. Next to me Avery stared, slack-jawed. "You can go and call him, if you need to."

"I was instructed to keep you in my sight at all times."

"Just use the phone in the security room." I handed the coat over, going through old familiar motions, and Mr. Germain took it instantly. "You can keep an eye on us or whatever. But I need a second to talk to my friend, please. I won't leave." He'd just try to run after me and break a hip. I didn't need that on my conscience.

"Fine," Mr. Germain agreed, straightening his suit jacket with just a glance at Avery. "I'll return shortly."

"Sure thing," I muttered as he turned on his heels and headed for the security room off of the kitchen, where he'd be able to watch us on the cameras that monitored the entire property.

As soon as he left, Avery managed to regain his ability to speak.

"Holy shit," he cursed. "Georgie. You can't seriously live here."

"What do you mean?" Okay, the foyer was a little over the top. Mom liked to make an impression, and she'd had the chandelier custom designed in Italy. She and Dad had gone over to Rome to supervise the creation themselves. "Of course I do."

"This isn't a house." Avery shook his head. "This is a museum. With a *butler*."

"It's not that bad." We didn't even have our most famous paintings in this part of the house. Mom thought *that* was gauche. "And he's a house manager. It's not . . ." I stumbled over the words, trying to let Avery know this was fine without seeming like Taco Table Darcy all over again. "Don't be weird."

"Weird?" Something snapped in Avery's tone, and I knew in an instant I'd said the wrong thing. I tried to take it back, to reverse the words into my mouth, but there was no turning back now. "Georgie, what's weird is that you live in the biggest mansion I've ever seen. Like, I knew you were rich, because it's Pemberley, and you can't pass the quad without hitting half of the Forbes list, but this is a whole different level."

"Aves." I wanted to cross toward him, but from the way he stood—backed up against the banister of our spiral staircase, arms crossed over his chest, eyes narrowed—I felt like he needed the space. "What are you mad about?"

"I'm not mad." He shook his head, sending his hair flying across his forehead, and I super didn't believe him. "I'm confused."

"You're probably just hungry." I made a move toward the kitchen. "Let's get some food, okay? Mr. Germain keeps the fridge stocked. And then we can settle in. You can pick out a guest room. They should all be open."

"I . . . what?" Avery cocked his head to the side, eyebrows raised. He didn't move from the banister, and I stood in the doorway that led down to the kitchen, unsure of my next step. "Guest room?"

"Well, yeah." My hands fluttered against the doorway's clean, white wood. Breathe in, breathe out. Control the things I could control. "Fitz has some spare clothes around here, too. You can change. We can even go swimming later, if you want. After breakfast."

"Georgie, I swear, I don't know what you're talking about." He kept calling me that. It unseated something deep in me.

"There's just no rush, right?" This wasn't how I had planned it out. I'd wanted to make breakfast, impress Avery with my meager domestic skills, and then fill him in. "For you to get back to Pemberley. You can stay here, for a bit. Help me."

I'd thought, beforehand, that that was the right thing to say.

As it turned out, it very much was not.

Avery's face turned to an expression I didn't recognize, his eyes tinged with anger as his arms fell from his chest. He ran his hands through his hair, then shoved them deep in his pockets before he turned on me.

"Are you kidding me?" His laughing, lighthearted tone was gone, replaced by something I recognized from other people, but never Avery. "Not only are you staying, you expect me to stay here, too?"

"Of course." I clung to the doorframe like it could protect me from this earthquake. Hadn't I won over Avery already, done the hard part, convinced him I was worth spending time with? Why was he fighting me now? "I told you. I'm not going back to Pemberley."

"Yeah, last night." He shook his head. "You were mad, you were upset, I got it. I figured a drive would get it out of your system."

"Really?" The dismissal was a punch in my gut. A familiar

punch. "What's the point of going back, Aves? Fitz is never going to trust me, no matter what I do there."

"And that's all that matters?" Fire flashed in his eyes. "Your brother gets mad, so you just give up?"

Above him, the chandelier glinted in the light that came through the stained-glass window over our front door. I watched it dance as I tried to pull together my thoughts.

"I'm not giving up because he's *mad*," I said. Avery looked foreign, suddenly, standing in our foyer, this boy I'd never imagined here. I'd thought he understood me. "I'm leaving because trying to live up to his legacy is making both of us miserable. You think I *want* to ruin my brother's life? Because I don't."

"And what does that make me?" Avery looked around the foyer, at the halls that led off into a dozen other rooms. "I didn't realize I was part of this grand plan to make your brother proud. Or was this about Wickham again, just to prove you could slum it with someone else to get him off your back?"

"What?" The punch to my gut turned into a stab. "Aves."

"You don't even get it, do you?" His hand went through his hair again, and I shivered, even though it was way warmer in here than it had been outside. "You don't get how lucky you are, and how you're about to throw it all away."

"Lucky?" I braced against the doorframe again. "Are you serious? I don't have anyone; I don't have a family . . ."

"Yeah, Georgie, you're a real Dickensian orphan." His eyes narrowed, his hands back in his pockets. "You're still like, filthy rich. You go to one of the best high schools in the country, and I bet your estate doesn't even notice the tuition costs. Hell, you didn't get expelled last year, when anyone else would have."

"Aves."

"And you're just going to give that up?" He closed the distance

between us as I blinked back unbelieving tears. "For real? You're
going to just . . . Some of us don't have the privilege of giving up.
This isn't *Sage Hall*. I'm not your carriage boy who can save you
from the monotony of riches."

"That's not what I said."

"Yes, it is." He was so close to me, but there was none of the
affection, the electricity that had been there last night. "That's
why you want me to stay. You got me tangled up in whatever this
is, your whole big expensive life, and I let myself get sucked in
because I *missed* you last year and I thought with Wickham gone,
things would be better. But he came back, right? He came back
and you think my purpose is to rescue you or something. Because
you think my whole life revolves around you."

"God, Avery, don't treat me like some asshole rich girl who
jerked you around for her own purposes." The words flew out of
me before I could help myself. How dare he accuse me of *giving
up*? He had no idea what I'd gone through. I'd thought things had
changed, thought that I'd found someone in the last few months to
care about me, but it turned out I hadn't and so fine, it was Georgie
on her own again, but I'd be damned if I went down without a
fight. "You want to feel all high and mighty about this? Go ahead.
But what would you have done this year without me? Try to find
some other sad and broken soul who needed your stupid jokes?"

Avery took a step back, away from me, and it felt like he'd
never step forward again.

Good.

I couldn't back down. Not now. Because Avery saw me the
same way everyone else did—another rich girl who got what she
deserved. And if that was how they were going to see me? If that
was how even Avery, who I dared to let in, actually saw me? If all
the worst parts of my family legacy were the only ones I'd managed

to accomplish, then they were going to feel the full Darcy rage rain down on them. I'd lock myself in my tower with everything I needed and I'd be exactly what they all expected me to be, and maybe I'd be a broken creature made of pure pride but I'd be *safe*.

This would not be another Wickham situation, where I was jerked around by a guy who thought he knew me. He was going to attack me, fine, but I would put up all the walls in the world, strengthen my defenses, and keep him the hell out because I had known, hadn't I, what happened when you let people in? They destroyed you. Every time.

Well. Let them fucking try.

"You don't get to tell me how this year was *supposed* to go." I forced the words out. "You don't get to say the way that I react is right or wrong when I was busy having my life ruined."

"Yeah, Georgie." Avery shook his head. I saw the anger in his eyes—it probably matched mine—and there was something else in there, too, but it didn't look like affection or caring and I didn't need it. "This sure looks like ruination."

I thought I'd fixed some things this year, but it seemed that I was right back where I'd started. And this time, I was through trying.

"You get out." My voice stayed strong. I suspected it would be my final triumph in that department. "Go back to Pemberley, and . . . and martyr yourself for somebody else."

"Fine." Avery barely spared me a second glance before he turned on his heels and went out the front door, slamming it behind him. I heard his footsteps run down the stairs, the rumble of his car starting, and the crunch of the gravel as he drove away. If Mr. Germain saw it, he had the decency not to come out and talk to me about it.

It was a miracle, honestly, that I'd made it that long, before I slumped down to the floor and began to cry.

CHAPTER TWENTY-SIX

 had gone full Jocelyn.

Maybe the comparison just seemed particularly apt because I'd fled the foyer and immediately put Season 2 of *Sage Hall* into the Blu-ray player, the season where Jocelyn pines over everything that she'd lost. Locked in my huge, fancy estate, away from everyone who thought they understood me but really had no idea what I was going through. I shoved dry cereal in my mouth as I watched her go completely Gothic, finally understanding her reasoning. Crumbs scattered over my homecoming dress, and I didn't bother to brush them away, ready to embrace my towered-princess destiny.

If I'd known Avery was going to act like such an ass, I'd never have bothered hanging out with him again in the first place. But I didn't need him, right? I had all my *stuff* that I was so *lucky* to have.

Something in my chest squeezed as I considered my living room.

Okay, fine. The plush leather couches, the huge television, the professionally framed family portraits no one had thought to take down. It screamed wealth and power from every angle. I'd left the window shades drawn so the light didn't interfere with my show, but if I pulled them up it would give me a glimpse of the grounds behind our estate, the lawn that led to the pool house that led to the gardens.

I was lucky in the sense that I didn't have to worry about this stuff, sure. Material goods had never been an issue. I never went hungry or worried about how I would pay for school or if my trombone lessons would be too much of a strain for the family.

But just because I had money didn't mean my life was perfect, no matter what Avery said. He didn't know everything.

I remembered Wickham, under the bleachers, laughing at me for throwing my money around. But being home wasn't the same as unnecessary catering, was it? This was just . . . this was different.

I wished I'd told Avery about Wickham. That I'd pushed him away, sent him packing, finally. That for a moment I'd found something strong enough inside myself to actually manage it.

It was possible he wouldn't believe me, now.

I kicked off the cashmere blanket I'd pulled over my feet, which suddenly itched more than it ever had. May as well check on the rest of the house.

My room was the same as I had left it, though it had been straightened out, dusted, and vacuumed, a noticeable contrast to my sloppy appearance. My spare phone charger was curled up on my desk, tucked neatly next to a stack of signed *Sage Hall* scripts Fitz had gotten me for Christmas last year. I plugged my phone in, but turned it over so I didn't have to see the notifications I'd undoubtedly missed. Fitz was on his way, anyway. I didn't need to read all the ways I'd disappointed him before he came here and told me himself. And it wasn't like anyone else would have texted me. I caught a glimpse of myself in my vanity mirror as I left the room—mascara streaked down my face, hair fallen out of its careful arrangement, dress still coated with crumbs. I considered changing, but honestly, it didn't seem worth the effort.

The halls of my bedroom's wing stretched out endlessly before me, and as I went, I couldn't help but remember when this house didn't seem so dead inside. When my dad was alive, there were always people here. We didn't have like, big *Nutcracker*-style parties or anything, but we had a decent sized staff, and Dad always let them bring their families with them to work, if they needed to watch their kids or whatever. You'd turn a corner and find the gardener's triplets playing hide-and-seek in the guest wing, or my tutor's old and super-senile cat hissing at you from the top of a bookshelf.

They weren't my family. Mom made that very clear. I never hung out with any of the kids, even the ones close to my age. The only kid either Fitz or I spent any time with was Wickham, and Mom still looked at him sideways when he and Fitz would spend hours in the pool house or watching movies in the theater downstairs.

Avery, I thought, would think I was a snob for not trying harder to reach out to the other kids. For not fighting against my mother's rules and expectations. I shook my head, tried to clear out the anger I still heard in his voice as it echoed around.

We did throw a big Christmas party a couple of times, I remembered, as I made it down the stairs and reached the formal dining room. The furniture was still covered—Fitz and I never ate in here anymore. I ran my hand over the sheet that covered the dining room table, remembering the dark oak underneath, how fancy it always looked when it was set for its full sixteen. Mom and Dad would have regular, boring dinner parties in here for Dad's business associates, formally dressed men and women who commented on how well-behaved I was before Fitz and I were sent up to our rooms for the evening. Snippets of conversation would float up the stairs, where Fitz and I would peer through the banisters and imagine what it would be like when we were let into that world.

The Christmas parties were different, though, the few times we had them. Fitz would always invite Wickham, and the two of them would let me tag along for the night. They'd abandon their suit jackets as soon as they could, ties loosened the moment Mom got distracted by guests, but I'd always liked dressing up. Putting on a green dress with a wide skirt, tying my hair up with ribbons braided through it. We'd snatch appetizers off of passing trays and take them out to the pool house, where we could see the glitter of the party, see Mom and Dad dazzle and charm their guests, pop back in for the main meal, where Dad would carve a turkey—the only time I ever saw anyone in our house besides the cook touch food—as Mom made a toast.

This dining room hadn't seen life like that in years. The last Christmas party had been when I was ten, a couple of years before Dad got sick. I'd heard my parents argue into the night after the last guest left, about how hard these parties were on the house and weren't worth the hassle. Dad had posited, and I'd silently agreed, from my hidden spot in the hall outside their bedroom, that a house like this was meant to be used. But Mom had won, in the end, and we hadn't had another Christmas party.

A few years later, the dinner parties stopped, too. It didn't take long after that for my family to stop altogether.

I didn't like, hold a ton of resentment against my mom for leaving. She'd never been that interested in having a family, something I'd realized earlier than a kid should. It was clear that my dad was the one who'd wanted kids, who'd wanted family experiences. With him gone, it made sense that my mom wouldn't want to stick around. It did. She sent me a card on my birthday every year, thin paper that smelled like her perfume. I didn't need her. I had Fitz. I had the house.

But this room felt more and more like a tomb the longer I stood in it, the longer I thought about the way things had been and how they'd never be that way again. How, for all that Fitz tried, he wasn't my dad, and he never would be. How we were barely a family, a family held together with scolding and anger and broken promises. How the two of us could never fill this house the way we were supposed to.

We never would, now.

Closing my eyes didn't stop me from hearing Wickham.

I told you it would all fall apart, you know.

"Shut up," I implored the room at large. "I'm done."

Are you sure? I imagined his smirk. *That's the last option, isn't it? You can come find me again. I'm not hard to track down.*

No, he wasn't. That was the problem. Wickham preyed on the parts of me everyone hated, circled in like a shark on everything that kept others away.

But it didn't matter. No matter what happened here, no matter what I did or where I went, I was never going down that road again. Whatever hold Wickham had over me was broken. I'd accomplished that this year, if nothing else.

I left the dining room behind, wound my way down to the home theater. May as well mix up the rooms that I binged television in. It was important to prevent a sense of monotony, after all.

I'd need to get my stuff sent over from Pemberley, my laptop, my trombone. They'd be able to ship them, I was sure. I couldn't have been the first person to flee Pemberley in the middle of the night. It would mean staying here a few more days while I waited for all of it, but I could manage a few more days before I ran.

Though maybe I should just cut my losses, get a new laptop so I didn't have to look at my stupid fic ever again. It still stung, the way that Avery had thrown *Sage Hall* in my face like that. He had no idea. I didn't know why our money differences had to matter.

Well, whatever. He was nothing to me now. Obviously.

Even as I told myself that Avery's opinions of this place were garbage, I felt like I couldn't sit still, suddenly antsy. I could go to the pool house, maybe. Something else that Avery would have judged me for having. I pushed myself out of my seat, headed back up the stairs toward the back of the house.

Unfortunately, I didn't make it past the foyer.

Seeing Fitz in the entranceway wasn't that much of a surprise, even if the expression of sheer disappointment mixed with worry on his face knocked the wind out of me. Something else fluttered around his edges, something that looked like anger, but I didn't spend a long time examining it, because my gaze went immediately to the girl standing behind my brother, holding a backpack down by the ground and watching Fitz watch me.

What was Lizzie Bennet doing in my house?

hat?" That was the only word I could manage as I stared at Lizzie, who waited just behind my brother, leaning against the door with her arms crossed over her chest. "What are you doing here?"

"You really think you have the grounds to *ask* questions right now?" Fitz looked, objectively, terrible. His dark curls stood straight up from his head, like he'd run his fingers through them again and again over the course of the night. Although I'd gotten used to seeing him with bags under his eyes, it looked like he hadn't slept at all, eyes bloodshot and his face drawn and gray. Instead of his usual button-down and slacks, he had on jeans—*jeans*—and an Alpha Chi T-shirt that had to have been Charlie's. Even after Dad died, even after Mom left, my brother had never looked like this.

Another wave of guilt rushed over me, but I pushed it back

down. I'd spent the last six months feeling guilty. Now I had a solution for him, a way for both of us to absolve ourselves.

"Get in the car." Fitz pointed over his shoulder, back toward the door, even as I shook my head. "We're going back to Pemberley, where we'll grovel in front of the administration once again to try and get them to forgive your midnight flight from campus."

"I'm not going back."

"Like hell you're not." He was breathing hard, chest rising and falling with the effort of all his anger. "I don't know what sort of messed-up rebellion this is, but I don't have time to deal with it. Get in the car. You can *attempt* to explain yourself to me there."

"No, Fitz." I took a step back, bumped up against the banister of the stairs. Lizzie just watched both of us. I didn't want to do this in front of her, to air out our dirty laundry in front of a virtual stranger, but if Fitz was going to do it then so was I. "I'm not *rebelling*. I'm done. I'm done trying to live up to impossible standards, to whatever it is you expect of me. I tried, but I still can't help but screw up, right? So let me go. You can give up on the idea that you're a replacement for Dad and write me off as just another loss."

"Where do you think you'll go?" His hands went to his hair again, pushed it up even higher. "You have nothing."

"We have plenty." *Ignore the thought of Avery, shaking his head at me. Ignore it.*

"This *family* has plenty." Fitz actually sneered. "You seriously think I'll keep your bank accounts open if you try to leave? That I won't freeze your cards the second you go out that door? I'll change the locks in London, in Paris, everywhere we've got properties you think you can hide in. You want to be a Darcy; you have to follow Darcy rules."

Fear gripped me, unexpectedly. That was my whole plan, my

only option. But I didn't let Fitz see me shake. Money wasn't the only part of the family legacy. Stiff, frigid behavior had a well-loved place in the annals of our family, too.

"Maybe I don't want to be a Darcy anymore." I tossed the glove down, expecting a scoff, not the panic that flashed across my brother's face.

"You have to be."

"Why?" It didn't disappear, the way his expressions often did, folded back into a stiff upper lip, but instead it spread all over his face, his body, and oh no, I realized immediately, I had done something really, really wrong.

"You have to be, because if you're gone, what am I supposed to do?" The shift in Fitz's voice was sudden, like the light had been sucked out of him, his angry bravado gone as I saw more vulnerability in my brother than I ever had before. It felt like getting the wind knocked out of me, to see him like this. To see the raw pain on his face, exposed for the first time.

"Fitz." I didn't know what I wanted to say.

"I told Dad I'd take care of you, Georgie." His yell had shriveled away to nothing, his voice small. "I told him, I promised him that I'd look after you, and I guess I messed up pretty bad, huh?"

And then Fitz slid down, back against the door, until he crouched on the floor, head in his hands. I stood shock-still, unable to move at the sight of my brother's collapse. Lizzie dropped to her knees beside him.

"I can't do this, Liz." His words were barely audible through his hands, obviously not intended for me. "I can't do it anymore."

It turned out I didn't know what gutted felt like, before he said that.

"Go." She helped him to his feet, then pushed him gently in

the direction of the hallway behind me. "It's fine. It's okay. Go get some air."

My brother, my big brother whom I'd never seen like this before, not even at our absolute rock bottom, nodded and let himself be pushed. He hurried past me without looking at me, through the hall behind me toward the grounds, so that it was just Lizzie and me in the foyer.

As she stood back up, she studied me, like I was a science experiment. I squirmed. Maybe I should have left then, shoved my way past this stranger and out the door—Fitz's car was almost certainly in the driveway— to make my escape. That had been the plan. To leave.

But I wasn't so sure, this time, if leaving would help my brother in the long run.

I wouldn't fall apart. I couldn't. Not while Lizzie was still here, this stranger, even if I'd built her up in my head like I knew her. This girl standing in front of me in dark jeans and a North Face jacket was not my salvation.

"Your brother can be kind of intense, huh?" She tilted her head in the direction Fitz had gone, all while keeping an eye on me. "Though I'm thinking it might run in the family."

"I guess." I shrugged. If I spoke more than a couple of words at a time, there was no guarantee that all my feelings wouldn't come spilling out of me.

"He did, however, mention something about there being food in the house, on the way up here." Her gaze never left me, curiously intense. "What are the chances you know anything about that?"

I wanted more than ever to make a break for it, to run past Lizzie and up the stairs to my room, to lock the door and never come out again. But I'd manipulated her as much as Fitz, and from the look on her face, she knew about it. I owed her lunch. Besides, I was shaken after seeing my brother's collapse. I didn't have it in me to run right now.

"Yeah." I turned, then looked back over my shoulder toward the girl. "Come on."

She didn't try to speak as we weaved through the halls of the house. It had been built before open-layouts took over HGTV, so even though my mom would have been happy to gut the place and make it into a living Pinterest board, there were too many support beams hidden in its many walls to make it happen. It made the whole house kind of a maze until you knew your way around.

Our kitchen, though, was pure modernity, sleek chrome and polished countertops. Lizzie dropped her backpack beneath our granite-topped island, then leaned forward onto the counter's surface as I opened the fridge.

Mr. Germain had done his job well, I thought, as I grabbed a prepared charcuterie platter out from underneath a glass dome on the middle shelf. I'd never wondered before what happened to this food, when Fitz and I were hardly ever home and yet the fridge was constantly stocked. Maybe Mr. Germain ate it, brought a feast home for his family every Friday night before he restocked the fridge with a fresh preparation on Saturday. He had a few grandkids, I was pretty sure. Maybe they were super into charcuterie.

Avery would have wondered. I never had before.

"This is good." Lizzie interrupted my inner monologue, speaking around a piece of prosciutto. "This is just here, whenever?"

"The house manager has to make sure everything's ready if we come home unexpectedly." If I stuck to just facts, simple, basic facts, I'd keep my emotions in check.

"Wow." Lizzie whistled, luckily after she'd swallowed the meat. "That's wild."

"I don't know." I shrugged. "It's always been normal." But maybe it wasn't. I mean, I knew it wasn't. But Lizzie looked at this place the same way Avery did. Maybe I was the outlier, not them.

"Yeah?" Lizzie looked at me again, curiously. "I get the impression that what you and your brother think of as normal is a little different than the rest of us."

I shouldn't have been surprised that she'd mentioned Fitz, but it caught me off guard anyway, and I felt a lump form in the back of my throat.

"Oh, whoa, hey." Lizzie reached across the countertop and laid her hand over mine, a move that took me by surprise more than—well, not more than anything else that day. It had been an exceptionally eventful few hours. "Sorry. I didn't mean—do you want to talk about it?"

"What is there to talk about?" I stared down at the wedge of Brie I'd cut off for myself, my appetite completely gone. I didn't deserve cheese. "He hates me, and I broke him. For real this time."

"I don't think that's true."

"Do you even know what happened?" I laughed as I grabbed a bunch of grapes and a knife, began to slice them in half on the counter in front of me. If I was going to spill out all my emotions, I was going to be a good host at the same time, damn it, and prevent our guest from choking on grapes. It was how my mother had always insisted they be served, ice cold from the fridge and sliced into perfect halves. I couldn't escape her, and her legacy, no matter what I did. Couldn't escape her desire to run away when things got hard, to hide behind decorum. "This isn't exactly the first time I've proven I'm a worthless sister."

"If you're talking about the stuff with Wickham Foster last year, yeah." I glanced up in surprise, luckily remembering to stop the knife. "Your brother told me about that. But I also know that dude is a dick who doesn't deserve the satisfaction of ruining any-one's life."

"You know him." It wasn't much of a question. I'd seen them together at Charlie's party, after all. I placed the knife back on the counter, careful of the blade.

"A little." Lizzie shrugged, her gaze temporarily averted from me. "He and my sister—she doesn't always make great choices, Lydia. They were hanging out for a while. But I thought he'd left town entirely until that Instagram post." Her mouth flicked up, a half-smile. "When Fitz saw it, I seriously thought he was going to hunt him down and kill him."

"Please," I scoffed, pushing the platter of fruit toward her. "Fitz wouldn't do that."

"You don't think?" Lizzie raised an eyebrow as she reached across and grabbed a grape half to pop into her mouth. "I've never seen anyone hate someone more than Fitz hates Wickham. That's why he flipped out so much over that picture, you know. Oh, damn." Her eyes widened as she ate. "This is a super-good grape."

"They're locally grown, I think." I shook my head. "But you're wrong. The person Fitz hates most in the world is me."

"No, he doesn't."

"Yes, he does." I didn't know why I was even arguing about this, arguing with this stranger sitting in my kitchen and eating my grapes, but it wasn't like I was flush with options. "You heard him. Between last year, and now this, he's probably looking up boot camps to send me to because I can't be trusted anywhere else. He only goes to Meryton because of me, did you know that? And I couldn't even last at Pemberley until Thanksgiving."

I leaned back against the stainless-steel fridge, completely devoid of magnets or mementos of any kind, and pressed the heels of my hands against my eyes.

"I wish I could make you realize that he doesn't hate you." Lizzie's voice was way closer all of a sudden, and I pulled my hands from my eyes just long enough to see that she'd come around to my side of the counter. She didn't try to hug me or anything, which I appreciated, but she stood close enough that I could hear her even as she lowered her voice. "The way your brother feels about you . . . it doesn't look like hatred. It looks like someone who loves you so much that it hurts him. His love for you is so sharp it makes him bleed, sometimes."

"I don't want that." I must have been dehydrated from all the tears today. I needed to grab a Gatorade or something, to replenish my electrolytes. "All I've done is make things worse for him. I thought . . ." This was going to be so, so embarrassing, but I was already crying, already giving up the Darcy spine, so whatever. "When Wickham came back around, I wanted to take care of it myself. To prove to him that I could take care of it myself. And then when Fitz started talking about you, I thought if I could push you two together, then I could do something good for him, for once."

"Right." Lizzie's voice didn't betray anything. "Charlie told me about that. I have to admit, it did seem weird, for him to invite us to some high school homecoming for a school he didn't go to. But it did explain the flowers."

"It seemed like a good idea at the time."

"I showed up, didn't I?" To her credit, she didn't laugh. "I get it. I don't love that you did it, and we're going to talk about it at some point in the future, but I get it."

"Are Charlie and Jane . . ." My voice trailed off, and she smirked at the look on my face.

"Wow, you really have a lot of matchmaking plates in the air, don't you?" She grabbed another grape, her expression briefly blissful as she ate it. "They're fine. Your brother, to no one's surprise, was being an ass. But we got it sorted out." I almost laughed, and she smiled at me.

"Still. I thought getting Fitz together with someone would make him happy, and it didn't." I drummed my fingers across the counter. "Like, you two can do whatever, I don't need to know any details, but it won't matter. He'll still have me, and I'll still ruin his life."

"Georgie, listen to me." Lizzie leaned on the counter, her eyes serious. "Think about what happened back there. Did that look like someone who would be happier without you in his life? If you just ran off forever?"

I didn't respond.

"Besides." She shrugged. "I'll admit I don't know the whole story, and I'll also admit, from what I know, that I think you should have told Fitz the second Wickham showed up again. But are you still seeing him?"

"No." I shook my head, hard. "I wasn't lying. I'm done. The Instagram thing was just his way of trying to throw the final punch."

"So, you did take care of it." She broke eye contact only to eat another grape, a small groan escaping her mouth as she ate. If my appetite ever came back, those grapes would be the first thing I tried. "I don't think it's easy for Fitz to admit there are some things you can handle on your own. He's spent his whole life, basically, taking care of you. What do you think he'd do if you didn't need him at all?"

"Be happy?"

Lizzie just shook her head.

"Talk to your brother." She clasped her hands in front of her on the counter. "Okay? If you two talk, and you explain *why* you did all of this, and how you're feeling . . . he might be more understanding than you expect." I mean, sure, I had definitely tried and he'd yelled at me before breaking down in a way I didn't think my brother could. It had been like . . . like if you saw Big Ben fall over suddenly. You didn't think something like that was possible.

And okay, maybe I had gotten kind of defensive and yelled at him, too. Maybe this whole learning and growth thing meant I had to give him a second chance.

The image of him on the floor, head in his hands, stuck in my brain. I didn't know if I'd ever get it out.

"Fine," I agreed, and Lizzie smiled, which I took as an in to jump on the question I couldn't help but ask. "Also, why are you here? I'm not mad about it, but this didn't seem like the sort of thing Fitz would bring someone to."

"Oh." Lizzie flushed before she turned her attention back toward the charcuterie, which honestly might have been answer enough, but she kept going. "We were working in the library together when he got the call from your school that you hadn't checked back into your room last night. He freaked out, obviously, and I didn't want to leave him alone, and well . . ." She shrugged, and I was rewarded with an even darker shade of flush. "I thought he could use the company for the drive. I didn't have a lot of homework this weekend, anyway."

"Right." I picked up one of the grapes, my hunger slightly returning. "Sure you didn't."

Lizzie rolled her eyes.

"Go find your brother," she said, picking up the whole tray of meats and cheeses. "Me and my new boyfriend, this charcuterie platter, are going to find somewhere we can be alone." She waved with her free hand before she headed back out of the kitchen, and I decided that, if I could add to the meager list of things this semester I didn't regret doing, it was forcing Lizzie into our lives.

Which meant I needed to tell her one more thing.

"Hey." I caught her before she left the room, and she glanced back toward me. "You said your sister Lydia, she *was* hanging out with Wickham? Like, past tense?"

"Yeah," she answered, her head tilted to the side. "Why?"

"I just think . . ." I took a deep breath. This time it *was* total narc-behavior, and Lydia hadn't exactly been my favorite person when I met her, but if I could protect anyone from Wickham Foster . . . "I don't think it's as past tense as you think it is."

"What do you mean?"

"The Instagram post from last night came from her account."

Understanding passed over Lizzie's face, and she nodded, before speaking, inexplicably, to her tray of meats and cheeses.

"Sorry, charcuterie." She placed it back gingerly on the counter, then straightened up. "I'll be back for you soon, I promise. But I think I have to make a couple of phone calls."

She gave me a thumbs-up as I headed out of the kitchen and I felt confident, for once, that this situation was going to be extremely well-handled. Lizzie Bennet just had that air about her.

CHAPTER TWENTY-EIGHT

 found Fitz in the pool house.

It wasn't a surprise. It was, in fact, the first place I'd looked for him. This was where he always came when he wanted to be alone, at least when it was too cold out to wander the grounds properly. The pool house was heated year-round, ready for action as steam rose off of the surface of the water in the hot tub. That was where Fitz sat. Not all the way in the hot tub, obviously, because that required a level of lounging that Fitz had never enjoyed, but at the edge of it, shoes and socks off, pants rolled up to his knees, and feet dangling in the water, his hands clutched at the edge of the concrete.

He didn't look up as I came in, even when I sat down next to him, kicked off my house slippers, and pulled up the skirt of my dress slightly so that I could drop my feet into the water, too. I followed his gaze and saw the memorial tree we'd planted for our dad, just outside of the pool house. It was getting bigger, more a testament to our gardeners and how long he'd been dead than to any upkeep Fitz or I had put in.

"Do you ever think we should have put up a tree for Mom?" I didn't expect Fitz to break the silence, but there he was, even if he didn't look at me. "Not a memorial tree like Dad's, obviously. But done something?"

"No way." I shook my head. "She left. Life got too hard and she bailed. She doesn't deserve a tree."

"Sometimes people have to leave, though." I didn't think Fitz was talking about Mom anymore. "They don't realize what they're doing is so bad."

I didn't answer, just kicked my feet in the water, cutting through the steam.

"He'd have liked to see you march." Fitz kept talking, his gaze still on the tree. "Dad. He'd get a real kick out of it."

"You think?"

"I do." Fitz sighed. "He loved how musical you were, and how competitive you got about things like band. It was different than the sort of things I got competitive about. Different than what we were raised to be competitive about. It would have tickled him."

"Doesn't matter." I shrugged, kicked my feet in the water, careful not to splash any of it onto my brother. "He wasn't here to see any of it."

"I'm here." Fitz's voice caught, an unfamiliar sound. "I'm here, and I care about that sort of thing, too."

"You are *now*." I might as well be honest. I had no lies left. "But you left, too, Fitz."

"College is different."

"I mean, it is." Fuck. The words were sand in my mouth. "But it's also not, because I didn't know how to do Pemberley without you. You went out to California and you were so happy, and all I did was fall apart." I ran my fingers over the surface of the water. "And I can't even blame you for going away, because it turns out I'm a nightmare. You should just let me do the leaving, this time. It'll be easier on both of us."

Fitz didn't answer for a while, just stared out at Dad's memorial tree. Then he sighed.

"Georgie, if you honestly think that you running away would make me stop worrying about you, you're not nearly as smart as all those psychologists said you were."

Oh good. Now he had jokes.

"I know you'd still worry for a while." I shrugged. "But you'd learn."

"I don't want to." He shook his head, his gaze still outward. "This is part of being family. Maybe I don't miss Dad as actively as I did, when he first died. But I'd still give anything to have him back."

"That's different."

"Perhaps," Fitz said. "But you're it for me, Georgie. The whole world I have left. And I know I'm hard on you. I'm sorry if I ever made you feel like I didn't want you around. I'm sorry if it felt like I was abandoning you, when I went to California. But my whole world is built on you, little sister. It would collapse around me with you gone."

I sniffed as I watched the tree, watched the wind take its leaves the same way it took our dad.

"But that's the problem," I managed eventually. "All of this happened because our worlds are built on each other. We're like a broken bone, Fitz, that healed wrong, so we got stuck together but it still hurts. I want . . . there has to be an in-between of those two things, between leaving someone and smothering them. A clean break, this time. Where I can handle things on my own, and you could have Lizzie. And she could help make you happy, so your happiness wasn't entirely dependent on my accomplishments or lack thereof."

"And how would I make sure you were doing okay, with a distraction like that?" He shook his head, and I sighed with frustration.

"It's not your job, Fitz."

"Yes, it is."

"No." Damn, I just wanted to make him understand. "It's not. I know you're my guardian, and I know you're in charge or whatever, but I need you to be my brother, not my dad. I'm sixteen. The same age you were when you got put in this position in the first place."

It was a coward's move, probably, how we both kept looking out toward the tree. But I didn't think I had the strength to look my brother in the eyes as I talked about this. We'd never talked about this. We'd just cried in separate rooms, pretending our grief wasn't interconnected, locked together like magician's rings. Pretended we could heal without the other.

But as much as I needed him to lean on, he needed to lean on me, too. We needed to separate, sure, to fix our jagged edges, but then we needed to come back together.

"I didn't tell you Wickham was back because I still needed him, at first." The words came out before I could help myself. Still, if I wanted to move past cowardly moves, I may as well start now. "I mean, I told myself that it was because I didn't want to be a burden to you or whatever, but it wasn't just that. He was still the only one who paid attention to me. It was sophomore year all over again, you know? I had no one, and he was there, and he wanted me."

"Georgie—"

"But I fixed it." I plowed over his interruption, because if I stopped, I wouldn't start again. I wasn't that brave, even as I stared only at the tree. "I really did, Fitz. He's gone. He'd been trying to get me involved in some new scheme, selling papers and stuff to students, and I threatened to call his dad if he didn't get out for good. That's what was happening in the Instagram photo. Honest."

I glanced over at Fitz, just out of the corner of my eye, a small enough movement that I didn't think he'd be able to track it. He had his eyes closed as he sighed.

"I still wish I could have stopped it sooner." He ran his hand over his hair, and he looked so much like Dad for a second that I almost laughed. "You get that, right? Why I wish I could have been there to stop it, even if I'm proud that you managed it on your own?"

"Yeah," I said, though I didn't entirely. But I could glimpse the edge of it. "Isn't there a line that connects those things, though? Where you want to protect and help me and all that but also trust me? Something where we could have an actual relationship that wasn't built on . . . whatever this all is."

"Well, last I heard you only shoved me together with Lizzie because you didn't want me around anymore."

"I'm not saying I *don't* want you around." I finally managed to turn and look at him, properly look at him, not just peek at him with my peripheral vision like a coward. His eyes were rimmed with red. "But I want my brother back. My friend back. And I want you to be happy, Fitz."

Fitz nodded.

I let out a deep breath, deeper than I thought I needed to. Good. That was . . . that was good.

Then, in an uncharacteristic move for a Darcy, Fitz opened up his arm so I could lean against him. I pressed myself into his side, and even though it had been years since I'd hugged him like that, it felt like home.

He pressed his head on top of mine and we stayed there for a while before he chuckled and leaned away, wiping at his face.

"I suppose dignity doesn't matter as much when it's just us."

"I promise not to tell anyone," I said, wiping at my own eyes. "Can we be good? Please?"

"As long as you don't involve Charlie in any more matchmaking schemes. He keeps leaving Valentines under my door that are signed 'a secret admirer.' It's getting embarrassing."

"Still." I grinned up at him, feeling more settled than I had in weeks. "It kind of worked, right?"

"Shut up," my big brother said, then reached down and splashed me with some of the water from the pool. As I shrieked and leaned away, I felt like an unbearable weight had floated away from me. Floated out of the pool house and past the trees, where it might, just possibly, disappear.

cll

We found Lizzie in the home theater, sprawled across three seats with a rom-com on the giant screen. She leapt to her feet as soon as she saw us, pausing the movie.

"Sorry!" She flushed a deep crimson. "I just, you said to make yourself at home, and I found this, and . . ."

"It's okay." Fitz crossed to her faster than I'd thought he could move, a hand on her elbow immediately. I raised an eyebrow, though neither of them seemed to notice, both way too caught up in each other. "This is what I meant by 'make yourself at home.' I'm glad you found the theater."

"Well." Her eyes flickered over toward me, and Fitz dropped her elbow like it was on fire. Not suspicious at all. "I'm glad you two found each other. Everything okay?"

"It will be." I smiled at Fitz, and he returned it. "'Family comes first,' and other inspirational stuff you might cross-stitch on a pillow."

"Well said." Fitz shook his head, but he smiled at the same time.

"Did you get everything . . ." I gestured toward Lizzie's phone, and she nodded.

"Taken care of." Her smile was wide and confident. "Thanks to you."

"Something happen while I was gone?" Fitz glanced between the two of us. "This isn't some sort of surprise birthday party scheme, I hope."

"Just taking care of some family business," Lizzie said, putting away her phone. "You've got a very good sister there, you know."

"She's all right," Fitz said, and I shoved my arm against his as he smiled. "Why don't you change, Georgie, and we'll go up to the kitchen, get some real food started, and figure out what we're going to do next."

Fitz, I discovered after I'd switched out my wrinkled dress for jeans and an old Pemberley T-shirt, had learned to cook, living in his off-campus apartment with Charlie with no cook or dining hall to make his meals for him. After he dismissed Mr. Germain, who had kept himself tactfully scarce during our whole family breakdown, he threw on an apron, washed his hands with care, and started cracking eggs with one hand, chopping peppers with precision, and doing all sorts of things I expected to see on a You-Tube channel. Not so much as performed by my brother.

"This is super good, Fitz," I said later, around a mouthful of omelet. "And here I thought you'd be living on takeout sushi."

"Charlie thought the amount of money I spent on delivery was, to quote, 'shameful and un-American.'" Fitz shrugged as he untied his apron strings. "I tried to tell him that actually, Americans spend more on takeout than any other country in the world, but he wouldn't hear it. He made me go to a couples' cooking workshop with him on the weekends."

"Adorable." Lizzie shook her head as she ate, though she, unlike me, managed to swallow her food before speaking. We were all gathered around the granite countertop in the kitchen, not bothering with stools. There was an energy in the room I hadn't felt in this house in . . . forever. And the way that Lizzie and Fitz kept glancing at each other? *Totally* fic-worthy.

"Now that that's taken care of," Fitz said, pushing his plate away from him, "let's plan our next steps."

"I can go." Lizzie straightened up before she dropped her plate in the sink. "Watch more TV, or—"

"Stay." My brother and I spoke in unison. Lizzie grinned.

"If you're sure." She pulled one of the stools out from under the counter, climbing on top of it to lean her forearms on the surface. "I'm always down to brainstorm life plans."

"I've spent a long time telling you what you needed to do, Georgie." Fitz turned his attention toward me, his eyes serious. "Let's start with a question. What do you *want* to do?"

It wasn't like I hadn't been thinking about this since the pool house, since Fitz told me that my sheer existence didn't ruin his life, but it still felt hard to say. Felt hard to give in to the tickle at the back of my mind that said I needed to leave my tower.

"I think . . . ." I took a deep, hard breath. "I think I want to try again. At Pemberley."

Both Fitz's and Lizzie's eyebrows shot way up.

"You're sure?" He paused with a fork of egg halfway to his mouth. "We can arrange for tutors here."

I smiled. I appreciated that, after our heart-to-heart, hiding away here was still a possibility, but it wasn't one I wanted any longer. Because even as I watched Fitz, content with the knowledge that I hadn't actually ruined our relationship, my mind kept flashing back to the other relationships in my life. Avery's face swam in my line of vision, but so did Emily's. Mrs. Tapper's.

It was possible that I owed them something, too.

"Yeah, but I've never been there without the shadows of you or Wickham hanging over me." I pushed my food around, restless. "It's not your fault. But I feel like I need to see if I exist there as me. Not just as the alleged narc or one more part of the Darcy family legacy."

"You'll always be part of the Darcy legacy," Fitz pointed out. Lizzie remained tactfully silent. "It's part of who you are."

"I know." I nodded. That scared me, honestly. Something I didn't know how to deal with yet. But being scared of something didn't mean hiding. "I need to see if I can make that legacy into something to be proud of. And I'm not ready to give up just yet."

Even though I'd been extremely ready to give up just a couple of hours ago, I knew what had changed my mind. Because I'd never forget the way that Fitz's face had crumpled when I told him I was done. How he'd let Lizzie see that. How we'd sat in the pool house and he let himself be vulnerable. How he wanted to do his best to fix us, where two hundred years of Darcy ancestry would have scoffed and abandoned the relationship for dust.

That was the moment that I knew. I didn't want to be the perfect Darcy.

I just wanted to be brave, like my brother.

"What about your grades?" Fitz asked, and I winced. There was that. "They've been, to be frank, atrocious this semester. You can't go back just to fail out."

"It's possible . . ." I wavered, but it was time to come clean. "It's possible I switched all my classes to AP at the beginning of the semester to impress you?"

"You did *what?*" Fitz looked, reasonably, horrified, but then seemed to remember himself and pulled it together. "That's—I mean—that's very flattering."

"I may have overextended myself," I allowed, playing with my eggs.

"Possibly," Fitz said, a hint of a smile playing at his lips, and I rolled my eyes as Lizzie smirked. "We can switch back whatever you want, probably. We're not too late into the semester. You think you can do better?"

"Yeah," I said. I had to try. "I do."

A moment, and then Fitz nodded.

"Then this is your responsibility." He carried his plate over to the sink, rinsing it off as he spoke. "You can handle it."

"Thanks," I said. If I wanted to actually do this, if I was taking responsibility for myself . . . it wasn't going to be easy. I wouldn't be able to blame failure on Fitz, or Wickham, or the world hating me.

I thought of what Avery had said, let those memories surface again even though they hurt. I did, in fact, have just about every privilege in the world at my fingertips. Sure, a lot of shitty things had happened to me . . . but I had the tools to move forward, tools most people never got. I wouldn't be able to forgive myself, down the road, if I threw all those chances away because I was scared of the consequences.

"You can leave the dishes for me," I offered. Responsibility started with chores. "I can get them later."

"I will not." Fitz shook his head as he started to clean up the kitchen, since fifteen minutes was clearly too long for him to leave dirty dishes. He was, after all, still my brother. "But thank you for the offer."

Progress.

CHAPTER TWENTY-NINE

Fitz drove me back to Pemberley the next day.

I sat in the back seat, happy to withstand mild levels of motion sickness for the view of my brother and his "friend" doing their best not to hold hands the whole way back. I was scared, nervous, as we drove through the mountains I'd last seen with Avery, but being scared was different from giving up. Being scared was natural. It didn't mean I'd stop trying.

Later that night, it was just my brother and me, sitting in my dorm room, which Sydney was clearly still avoiding, presumably just out of habit at this point. Fitz had sent Lizzie back in a town car he'd hired, so I didn't get to keep watching them stare at each other, but having my brother to myself wasn't half-bad, either.

"I like the poster." Fitz nodded to the *Sage Hall* print over my bed. Honestly, I kind of wanted a new one. I could get one of

Jocelyn's character posters, her standing solo. Strong. "Maybe I should give the show a real try."

"Yes! We can watch together!"

"I'd like that." Fitz smiled at me from across the room, though it slipped a little lower on his face when he saw me check my phone. "He still hasn't texted?"

"No." I sighed. "He hasn't."

"He will." Fitz examined a stain on my desk chair, which had been there long before I'd moved in and would probably be there long after. I'd filled him in on my whole Avery situation—leaving out the part where we made out in the car—during our drive. At his and Lizzie's encouragement, I'd texted him on our way here, to let him know that I was coming back and wanted to apologize, but I still hadn't heard anything.

"Hey, question." The thought had nagged at me since Lizzie saw our house, since she looked at our kitchen like it was unexpected. If I was being honest with myself, it had nagged at me before then, too. "Is it . . . do you think it's bad? That we're rich?"

I seemed to have caught my brother by surprise.

"And don't do that thing where you say 'we're comfortable,'" I added, as Fitz opened his mouth. He closed it just as fast, then sat in my desk chair, ignoring the stain. "It's just us. We can say we're rich. But is it a bad thing?"

"That's a complicated question, Georgie."

"It's a complicated situation," I countered. "And I keep having to deal with it. But it's not like we made our money in super-corrupt ways, right? Mom and Dad and their families—they just worked hard."

Fitz considered that for a moment, drummed his fingers against his khakis.

"It's not a bad thing to have money," he finally answered. "But to think our family just worked hard . . . that invalidates everyone who wasn't able to get where we are, doesn't it? Do you think that people who don't have money don't work hard?"

"No."

"Well, then." He shrugged. "It's a lot of luck. It's a lot of privilege, and if you want, I can pull out a three-hour lecture for you on the intersection of race and wealth, and how having money in the first place enabled us to make more, particularly because we're white, and how our family money was almost certainly made on the backs of the downtrodden. But that's not really what you're asking, is it?"

"Avery just said . . ." I sighed, stared down at the blank screen of my phone. Wickham had said it, too, but there was no way I was going to bring that up. "I don't know. I don't want him to have any extra reasons to hate me."

"I'm certain he doesn't hate you, first." Fitz ran his hand through his curls. "But it is something you have to be cognizant of, Georgie. The fact that you come from money and privilege does mean that most things in life will come easier for you. It doesn't negate the bad things that happen to you, but it means there are certain things you'll never have to worry about."

"Like getting expelled."

"Yes." Fitz nodded. "In this case. Like getting expelled."

I sighed again, lying back against my pillow. Jocelyn never had to talk about stuff like this.

Maybe she should have, though.

"But you can try and spread that privilege around." Fitz switched from the chair to my bed, sitting next me. "Be generous, and be conscious that other people don't have the same set of circumstances as you. Make space at the table for those without your privilege. Give them your space, sometimes. Learn without making people teach you. It doesn't solve everything, but it helps."

"And what if Avery still doesn't forgive me?" This level of vulnerability felt uncomfortable around my brother, but it was one I needed to get used to. "What do I do then?"

"You keep going." Fitz shrugged. "You keep going, and you do better next time."

"Yeah." I sighed. Tried to shake off the melancholy at the idea of a world without Avery in it. But it was okay. I would be okay. "Thanks, Fitz."

"Anytime, Georgie." He hugged me, and even though the feel of it was still unfamiliar, I welcomed it. "You got this."

cll

An hour later, after Fitz had left with a promise to text me as soon as he got back to Meryton, Sydney came into the room.

"Oh," she said, stopping in her tracks upon entering. "It's you. I thought you dropped out."

"Nope." I smiled at her over my laptop. "I'm not going anywhere."

Sydney seemed to consider that, then nodded and flopped onto her own bed. Neither of us ran away from each other, for once. I doubted that she and I would ever be friends, but it would be nice to not treat my room like an active war zone.

I turned my attention back to my computer, where a Word doc was waiting for me.

Ah, right. My fic. I had been closing in on an ending before homecoming, but obviously the events of the last few days had pushed it out of my mind. I scrolled down the page, gave it a quick reread. Maybe I'd throw some words down on it fast, get some fun writing out of the way before I got to work on the English essay I absolutely had to rewrite if I wanted to stay in that class. Balance. It was important.

It wasn't the world's longest fic—closer to a novella than anything too aggressive. Which meant that I reread it quickly enough to make the realization within the hour.

Henry may have started out as an OC love interest for Jocelyn, but how had I not realized that he'd taken on more and more Avery as the fic went on?

I scrolled back up, reread a few key scenes. One hundred percent him. He'd full-on seeped into my story.

Part of me wanted to bolt out of the room and run to find Avery, to grab him by the shoulders and point him toward the fic, convince him that I *did* care about him. I pulled out my phone, opened our messages. That's what I would do if I were a character in one of my stories, after all. If I were in *Sage Hall*. Grand gesture the hell out of him until he had no choice but to accept my apology.

But if I did that . . . that didn't prove anything. That was what Fitz had talked about. Because that had been half my problem, right? That I'd tried to grand gesture and strong-arm and throw the Darcy influence around to fix the circumstances I was in without fixing myself.

Maybe Avery would forgive me. Maybe he wouldn't. But the point of *my* story wasn't whether or not he did. The point of my story was that I was able to grow past my mistakes, to keep trying and learning and not giving up.

I owed it to myself to see what I could do without him. And I, frankly, needed to get my own house in order before I got involved with anyone else.

I closed out of our messages, then opened a new text. This time, to Emily.

Hey, I typed before I could lose my nerve. Sent the one word by itself so I'd be forced to finish the message, so that I couldn't backspace over my scary new gesture, grand only in its significance to me. *You're good at calc, right? Do you want to meet up and help me study?* I'd switched out of the AP class and into honors, but I could still desperately use some assistance.

I closed out of the fic while I waited, pulled up the latest problem set I was totally lost on. A second later, my phone dinged.

I only set a record for most perfect scores on pop quizzes
You can come over to my room whenever, I'm in Dalton

I grinned. I definitely wasn't headed to perfect score territory, but with Emily's help, I might pull off a passing grade.

Avery was probably done with me. But I was going to be okay.

CHAPTER THIRTY

The letter practically shone in bright red ink on the top of my paper.

B+.

I almost screamed with excitement as I clutched at my calc test. B+! That was, officially, the highest grade I had ever gotten in calc. Turned out that studying and attempting to understand the information instead of just outright ignoring it *did* impact my grades. I grabbed my backpack and followed my classmates out of the room, desperate to show this milestone off. Luckily, I had just the person in mind.

Outside of my classroom door, Emily waited for me, her hands twisting around her uniform tie, dark eyes watching anxiously. She'd put almost as many hours into this as I had over the last few weeks. And as soon as I held my test high in the air, her eyes lit up.

"Yes!" She reached out and high-fived me, then shimmied

her shoulders back and forth in excitement. "Georgie!" Emily wasn't big on enthusiasm, so knowing that my test score was good enough to get her to actually like, show some emotion in a super-positive way felt awesome. Almost as awesome as the score itself, to be honest.

We headed toward the band room together, our feet falling into step as we discussed my triumph. Braden had put Emily in charge of after-school sectionals, claiming that "delegating was an important aspect of leadership." So, I'd whispered to Emily, was being able to distinguish sharps and flats, but I'd learned to mostly keep those sorts of comments to myself. They were what my telehealth therapist called "counterproductive."

I'd been unsure what to expect when I'd reached out to Emily for help, but it turned out I'd landed myself a genuinely excellent friend. She helped me pull up my math and history grades, and in return I proofread all of her essays, which had a tendency to lean heavily on semicolons. We'd talked out what happened last year, over several long dining hall dinners where no one threw food at my head. She'd even convinced me to come jogging with her on the school track a couple of times, which was the absolute worst thing I'd ever experienced but was probably worth it for the friend-ship. We were both happy to move forward with a clean slate—me, forgiving her for shutting me out after The Incident, her forgiving me for being an ice queen in the first place.

It felt good, to have a friend I was on equal footing with.

She'd also offered to help me talk to Mrs. Tapper, but I'd needed to do that on my own. The Monday after I got back from Rochester, I went straight to her office before school started, ready to beg her (again) to let me stay in the band, even though I faced a boatload of demerits and an in-school suspension for disappearing from campus over the weekend. Fitz, too, had offered to talk to the headmaster, to reduce my sentence, but I wouldn't let him. Step one of minimizing my privilege was dealing with my own mistakes.

As I'd pled my case in front of Mrs. Tapper in the band room, her face hadn't betrayed any emotion.

"I care about this band," I'd finally finished. I didn't think I'd remembered to take a breath during my entire five-minute speech. "I care about what we do here." That room was always so echoey when there were no musicians in it, and my voice bounced back to me. "I know you've given me a million chances, and I also know I messed up. But I'm not going to mess up again."

"I'm sure you will." Her words had cut through me, but then she smiled. "But that's human nature. You know that I can't keep you here if your grades drop any further?"

"They won't." I'd leaned on her desk, scattered with sheet music. "I promise."

"Good." As she'd nodded, relief swept through me. "I believe you."

Now, Emily and I pushed our way through the band room doors, the other trombones raising their hands to wave at us. The freshmen were locked deep in a debate over *Game of Thrones*—which, let's move on, people, that show ended years ago, there were more interesting things to stream—but they stopped when Emily sat, pulled their trombones onto their laps, and sat at stiff attention. Jackson nodded toward me with a smile as I sat down next to him and unpacked my own instrument.

Braden still gave me a dirty look, of course, but some people were just assholes, and I was learning not to let that bother me.

"All right, kids." Emily lifted her trombone up, nodded at us to do the same. "Let's try it from measure ten."

The brassy sounds that filled the room (discordant in places as they were) brought me more comfort than I'd ever thought possible. A hint of the community I was building for myself.

An hour or so later, as we all stood up for a break and began the delightful process of emptying out our spit valves—I was pretty sure Cole and Sam were threatening to empty theirs on each other, but that was their own problem—Emily sidled up to me.

"Was measure thirty-five written by a masochist?" I asked. "Because trombones weren't meant to play notes like that. Right?"

"Avery wrote it, actually." She watched my reaction carefully.

Oh. Sure. Right. This.

I hadn't been avoiding Avery in the last few weeks or anything. We still had band together. We nodded at each other in the halls. Sometimes one of us would smile at the other, but it was more the sort of smile you did by accident, when you saw someone you weren't sure you recognized.

And no, we hadn't texted in three weeks. But that was fine. Honestly, it was. I was happy, believe it or not. My grades were improving, I had more friends than enemies, and Wickham had disappeared from my life. Jackson had told me a few days ago that he'd heard from his lab partner, who'd apparently used Wickham's services a hell of a lot, that Wickham had left town entirely. According to Fitz, he'd left Lydia alone, too, after Lizzie tracked him down and threatened to set the cops on him and his entire operation.

It was all good. Really.

But yeah, the loose thread of Avery still nagged at me.

"That tracks," I said, in response to Emily, trying to keep my voice light and airy. "Dude's kind of a masochist."

"You know . . ." Emily shook out her bell, making sure to dislodge any extra liquids that had gotten trapped in there. "You could always talk to him. I saw you say hi to *Braden* the other day. Comparatively, Avery should be a walk in the park." She kept her gaze on her trombone, like she didn't want to scare me away from an admittedly sensitive topic of conversation.

It seemed like we were going there, though. "Well." I shrugged. "There's no chance that me saying hi to Braden was going to be misconstrued as my trying to beg for him back, because the idea of being with Braden romantically is terrible."

"Obviously." Emily's smile, as always, was quick, gone in a second and replaced again with the inquisitive look she generally wore. "Just send him an email or something, Georgie. You can proofread it. But you're doing a lot better now than you were, as far as I can tell. I think it might be good to apologize and move on."

There was, I knew, something else I could send him besides just an email. But I didn't know if that was the right call.

You don't have to make every decision alone, I reminded myself. I suspected I'd spend the rest of my life walking the fine line between "I don't need anyone" and "people who love you can help you," but maybe that was a tightrope everyone had to walk. "Hey." I put down my trombone, picked up my phone. "Do you mind if I take an extra five?"

"Sure, but get me a snack from the vending machines." Emily grabbed a couple of crumpled ones out of her skirt pocket and shoved them into my hand. I resisted the urge to refuse them. Practice.

I pushed the money into my own pocket and headed out of the band room, waited until I was in the hallway halfway to the vending machines before I pulled my contacts up on my phone and pressed call.

"Georgie?" Lizzie Bennet's voice, warm as always, hit my ear.

"What's up?" I smiled. Lizzie and I had talked a few times since I'd started classes again, nothing too long, just some check-ins where she specifically refused to tell me if she and my brother have kissed yet.

"Just at band practice." I leaned back against a row of pristine lockers, one foot crossed over the other. I'd scratched the toe of one of my boots the other day, a noticeable enough imperfection that I normally would have sent them out for repairs, but I was kind of digging the scar. A few other kids passed me in the hall, on their way to whatever other after-school activities existed in this school besides band.

"You're not about to put me on speaker and play another love song, are you?" Her tone was dry, suspicious. *One* time. Emily and I had gotten a fit of the giggles after practice last week and Face-Timed Lizzie and Fitz to play an extremely poor rendition of an old Taylor Swift song while waggling our eyebrows at the camera.

"No, sadly, we haven't had time to learn anything new yet. It's just . . ." Yikes, it still felt so weird to just ask someone for advice, to assume that anyone would want to help me. But I knew Lizzie wouldn't mind. She'd reminded me over and over, just like Fitz had, that she didn't mind. I took a deep breath, drummed my fingers against the row of lockers. "Emily suggested I reach out to Avery again."

"Ah." Lizzie hummed. That was how she always filled pauses in conversation, I'd discovered. A little hum. Fitz had, to my delight, picked up the habit himself. "Georgie, remember what we talked about? About not needing boys to find happiness?" It had come with an accompanying PowerPoint, which was the moment I knew she and my brother were going to be together forever.

"I know. I'm happy." I didn't want Lizzie to think I'd completely lost my sense of self in pursuit of a guy but also, it was the truth. "This isn't for that. I just want to . . . I want to set the record straight, I guess. But I don't know if I should." I waited for her answer, the line filled with her hum.

"Go for it." She was smiling, I could tell. Lizzie had one of those voices where you could hear her smile. I felt some of the tension leave my shoulders; admittedly, a whole new patch of tension rushed in to meet it, because now I was going to have to do this thing. "I trust you to do it for the right reasons. If you want, you can send me the draft of what you're going to say to him. I can read it over for you."

Tempting, always tempting, but this was where I stepped onto the "I can do hard things" side of the line. I let out a deep breath. "Thanks, but I got it."

"Okay." It sounded like someone was calling for Lizzie in the distance, and that someone sounded just like my brother. "Let me know how it goes?"

"I will," I promised, then hung up. New confidence brimmed in me, despite the fear that pushed in. Fear didn't have to be bad.

There was a way I could tell Avery how I felt. How I had felt, at least. And it wasn't some big grand gesture, at least not to the rest of the world, but I thought he might know that for me, it was big. Or at least important.

And that would be that. I'd tie up the string, I'd delete the email from my sent folder, even, and I'd be okay.

Back on my phone, I pulled up the fanfic I'd written, the one that had accidentally been about Avery. I'd posted what I had so far on my favorite site earlier this week, to a solid reception. Copied the link, opened up a new email to him, pasted the link in, and hit send.

See? Not even as horrifying as it could have been. Less painful than being polite to Braden, honestly.

Well, anything would have been less painful than that.

cll

I stayed in the band room after our sectional ended, with a promise to meet Jackson in the library later to run history flash cards. I moved slowly, lazily, my homework for the night finished in study hall earlier that day, nowhere in particular to be except for a call with Fitz that wasn't for a couple of hours. I ran through my scales, flipped through the music until I got to my problem sections.

I was halfway through the Measures from Hell when the door to the band room opened and I almost dropped my trombone.

Avery.

He slipped over the threshold and stood just past the doorway, a brown paper bag in one hand while the other fidgeted with the bottom of his shirt. He had his glasses on, and the tie of his uniform was as crooked as ever.

Shit. For whatever reason, the idea that Avery would come looking for me after he got my email hadn't even crossed my mind.

"I can go." I jumped up from my chair, grabbed my case from next to me, and began to pack up my trombone as fast as possible. "I was just practicing." Maybe he wasn't even here for me. Maybe he'd come in here to be alone.

"I figured." His expression took me by surprise, for a second, until I realized it was because he was grinning. Not the hesitant half-smile I'd gotten in the halls these last few weeks. A real, full-on Avery smile, ear to ear, like the sun. "I got your email."

Oh, God. I mean, that made sense. I'd sent the email. Email

was notoriously instantaneous in its arrival. But damn, I hadn't expected to be confronted with the reality of that quite so quickly.

Before I could say anything else, he crossed the band room toward me, stopped in front of my music stand. I was grateful for the shield.

"I brought you a burrito." He spoke fast, and I'd think he was nervous if I wasn't the last person Avery should be nervous around. "Which is kind of a dumb joke, I acknowledge. Because of when you brought Mexican food? I mean, that stuff was like, authentic. This is from Moe's. But I thought you might appreciate the power of the small gesture."

"Avery." Even as I said his name, it didn't stop him from speaking. Hope warmed in my chest.

"I read your fic." His hands now unencumbered, he ran one through his hair, messed it up even more. I was pretty sure I could feel the pounding of my own pulse by this point. "You're really freaking good, you know that? Like, really good."

"It's possible I've won some web-based awards." Now both of us were fidgeting, overrun with nervous energy. I didn't want to run, but I couldn't stand still.

"Is it about us?" Oh. He was a fast reader, too. "The fic, I mean."

It was the longest he paused, after he said that, looking up at me, his eyes even lovelier than I remembered. Lovelier than I'd let myself remember, these past few weeks.

I'd accepted that Avery was a loss I'd deal with, someone I could move past and be stronger than ever without, and it was true that I could, that I didn't *need* Avery, but the longer we stood close together, just that music stand between us (which was starting to feel less like a shield and more like a barrier), the more I was reminded of how much I wanted him.

And that was the difference, wasn't it? Between him and

Wickham. That it *wasn't* a need, that Avery didn't pull me off the axis of my own rotation and throw me into his gravitational pull. He just let me be, and he liked me for it. For who I was.

He had, anyway.

Though I'd started to suspect, from you know, all of this . . . that maybe he still did.

"Not on purpose." I spoke almost as fast as Avery when I finally got it together enough to speak. To catch the breath that felt a little harder to catch than normal. "But you just kind of slipped in there. I'm sorry, Avery." It was the first time I'd said it out loud to him, properly. "I fucked up. I'm not going to say I didn't realize how much you meant to me, because I did. And it scared me. Whenever I need someone, I tend to . . . cling to them aggressively, because I've been left by a lot of people I love." My voice cracked, and Avery glanced downward, at both of our shoes. "That's my own baggage, though. It's not your fault. And I was a total dick about my privilege. So. Sorry." I paused, briefly. "Henry's not . . . he's not the carriage boy."

"No." Avery's voice was quiet. "He's not."

That was that, then. The loose string tied up.

Except the tension shimmering through the air didn't feel tied up, as Avery kept grinning down at me.

"You didn't finish it." It wasn't a question, which was good because I doubted I'd be able to answer anything, as he reached forward and, carefully, moved the music stand that stood between us to the side. Oh, good. My armor. But with Avery, I felt like I didn't need it anymore. "The fic. I was curious how it would end."

I managed a deep, shaky breath.

"So was I."

I didn't quite know who reached out first, whose hand stretched toward the other to grab in the middle. In a second our fingers had twined together in the small space that separated us, and then there was no space that separated us as he leaned down, and then I was *definitely* the one who closed the final inch of distance to kiss him.

He felt just as good as he had before, in the car, but this time there was no hesitation, no moments of disbelief, no wondering if this was right, or good, or anything except perfect. He pulled us closer together, his hand running up my arm as my left hand went into his shaggy hair and I felt him smile against my lips. I was pretty sure that, together, neither one of us was ever going to stop smiling.

After a minute, purely for breathing purposes and not because I wanted to stop, I tilted my head back.

"Is this a privilege of being drum major that Mrs. T keeps on the DL?" I asked. Avery's eyes twinkled. "Getting to make out in the band room?"

"Didn't you know?" Avery ran his hands over my hair, careful not to tangle much in the curls. "I'm a very important person to Pemberley Academy. They might just name a wing of the library in my honor."

"They should," I murmured, as Avery leaned in again. "You're very important to me."

By the time we got to the burrito, it was stone-cold. But in that moment, it was still the best I'd ever tasted.

EPILOGUE

SIX MONTHS LATER

Getting the band to perform the *Sage Hall* theme song for our spring break exhibition wasn't my *biggest* triumph of the year, but it came pretty damn close.

"I can't believe you did this," Emily said as we stood on the sidelines of the field, waiting to get in formation. "Did you blackmail Mrs. Tapper or something? Or does being a *Sage Hall* superfan just give you power over everyone?"

"I prefer the term fandom-based semi-celebrity, and you know that." I shoved my shoulder into hers, and we both grinned. We were in Sarasota, Florida, and I turned my face up to the sun, not even mad that I was going to get hot fast in my uniform once we started marching. Fitz had taken me surfing over winter break, and I was pretty sure that was the last time I'd been properly warm. "Don't make me sic my readers on you."

"I quiver." Emily shook her head. Avery, it turned out, wasn't the only one who'd liked my fic. After a YouTuber famous for her *Sage Hall* recaps tweeted out a link to it, my readership had swelled to viral status. I'd even gotten my English teacher to throw a little extra credit my way, once I'd showed her the hit counter on my page. "Your boy nervous?"

"I think he drank too much coffee to be considered nervous. More like clinically jittery." I hadn't seen Avery yet today. Fitz and Lizzie had picked me up from the hotel to grab breakfast before they drove me to the host school, insisting that they needed to celebrate a premature victory in our competition. "He's going to do great, though."

"He better." Cole popped up beside me, in a way that I still hadn't gotten used to. "We have to win."

"Calm down, short stuff." Emily rolled her eyes. "We've got a better chance if you've got your uniform zipped up properly."

"Is it not?" Cole looked down at his jacket in horror. Emily snickered, but I was too distracted by the sight of Avery, pale but determined, coming toward us. I cleared my throat, nudging Emily, and when she caught sight of him, she sprang into action.

"Let's go look at those palm trees." She grabbed Cole by the collar and pulled, which was a little aggressive, but I wasn't going to complain as Avery reached me.

"You clean up all right." I reached up to adjust his epaulets. His furry white hat, two and a half feet tall, was kind of ridiculous, but hey, he made it work. Besides, mine was only a little shorter. He passed his baton back and forth between his hands. "You okay?"

"Just wanted to see you." His eyes darted around the field for a second, but when they settled back on me, he smiled. "You ready?"

"Ready to high-step to victory."

"Don't jinx us," he warned. "The other schools are really good this year."

"They're not us." I stood on my tiptoes and kissed him, then held my fist out to his. He bumped it before we kissed again. "We're going to absolutely kill it."

"One more for luck." Hands around my waist, he reached down and dipped me before he kissed me, that time, and I was pretty sure I could *hear* Braden roll his eyes behind us, but I didn't care one bit. "See you out there."

He ran off just as Pemberley was announced over the loudspeaker. The crowds cheered, and even though I couldn't pick out Fitz and Lizzie specifically, I had to assume that their cheers were the loudest ones of them all. Charlie would be there, too, face painted in the school colors, Jane holding his hand in a WE ♥ PEMBERLEY BUT ESPECIALLY TROMBONES shirt he'd made for each of them.

I took my place at the end of the line with a freshman beside me, and beamed, just managing to resist a cheer as Avery ran out onto the field first, threw his baton up into the air, and caught it with perfect form. The swells of the *Sage Hall* theme rose up as we marched forward, and I ran my slide up and down as we sidestepped and pinwheeled all over the field. And I *knew,* just knew, that we had it.

The sun glinted off my trombone, and I caught my boyfriend's eye as he conducted with speed and passion. I struck my final pose, shoulders back, eyes lit up with pride. Not just Darcy pride, or Pemberley pride.

Georgie pride.

ACKNOWLEDGMENTS

We did it, everyone! We made it to the acknowledgments! I cried a non-zero amount of times while writing these, and the fact of the matter is that my gratitude for my community goes far beyond what I could ever express on the page. Nevertheless, I'm going to do my best to demonstrate a small fraction of the love I feel for all of you, starting with a reminder from the always-wise Leslie Knope—"no one achieves anything alone."

First off, a million thanks to Moe Ferrara, agent extraordinaire, certified musical theater nerd, and my co-president in the Official Christian Borle Fan Club. You and the entire Bookends team make me a better writer every day, even if we disagree about how often I should use adverbs.

A writer is nothing without a good editor, and I have the best in Sarah Grill. From our very first phone call, I knew you were the perfect person to bring Georgie and the gang to new heights.

Thank you for appreciating and sharing my emotional attachment to both the Jonas Brothers and my cat—Lydia and her kitten heels are for you.

Ever since I first read a book published by Wednesday Books, they've been my dream imprint, and it's still extremely surreal that I get to publish here. To everyone at Wednesday who has helped make this dream a reality—Rivka Holler, Sarah Schoof, Elizabeth Curione, Meryl Gross, Janna Dokos, NaNá Stoelzle, and Devan Norman—thank you, thank you, thank you! And of course, this book would be nothing without its absolutely stupendous cover (I may have cried in a Wawa when I first saw the mockup). Kerri Resnick and Amelia Flower, thank you for bringing my characters to life. I have honestly never been so happy about a piece of iconography as I am about those lilac trombones.

Writing can be a tremendously solitary pursuit, and I'm lucky not to have to go at it alone. To Patricia Riley, Kelly Dwyer, and Rebecca Speas—thank you for being Georgie's earliest supporters, and for laughing at all of my ridiculous puns. To Ann Fraistat, who offers that rare and beautiful combination of quick turnaround time and insightful comments—thank you for always replying quickly to my panicked texts, and for loving Georgie as much as I do.

A million thanks to Amie Kaufman—when the long road to publication got me down, I would think of you telling me that this *would* happen, and gain back my resolve. And to Meagan Spooner, the first author who ever listened to me pitch a book idea and tell me it was good—thank you. That boost of confidence was invaluable.

To Courtney Stevenson, whose feedback and encouragement have always meant the world: thank you for guiding me when I knew literally nothing about publishing.

I was lucky enough to have some of my absolute favorite authors offer their early thoughts on this book, and I'll always be grateful for their kind words. To Ashley Poston, Jennifer Dugan, Emily Wibberley, Austin Siegemund-Broka, Jennifer Iacopelli, Kristina Forest, Nina Moreno, Tiffany Schmidt, Erin Hahn, Jamie Pacton, and Stephanie Kate Strohm—thank you! You have my sword.

Thanks, as well, to everyone in the D.C. and Northern Virginia writing community who continually welcomed me with open arms. Additional thanks go out to Andrea Tang, whose powers of friendship are almost as strong as her power to make me fall over laughing while definitely kicking my butt in a fight.

The majority of this book was drafted in Café Kindred in Falls Church, Virginia. Thank you to the entire team there, and I hope that my nod to Townshend's Bar can be a small token of my gratitude for the endless refills of hot water in my tea mug.

To the standardized patient teams at the Uniformed Services University of the Health Sciences and Georgetown—I spent a *lot* of time writing and editing while I was on the clock (only on breaks, I promise) and the constant support I received from my trainers and fellow SPs was the absolute best ever. Special thanks to Renee Dorsey and her family for their endless enthusiasm.

There is no better place in the world than One More Page Books, partially because it's staffed by the world's best people. Eileen McGervey (#1 boss), Lelia Nebeker (my rock), Rebecca Speas (the Darcy to my Bingley), Anna Bright (my main source for all panicked author questions), Rosie Dauval (photographer to the stars), Eileen O'Connor, Neil O'Connor, Amber Taylor, Trish Brown, Sally McConnell, Jeremiah Ogle, and (honorarily) Lauren Wengrovitz—thank you. And to our customers, who rejoiced with me when I finally sold my book, who preordered and cheered and made me feel like a real author—thank you, too.

To Max Klefstad and Lindy Bathurst—thank you for always being my number-one fans. I love you guys more than I hate co-operative board games.

I wrote this book listening to the Jonas Brothers and Taylor Swift on a (very healthy) loop, so thank you to them for providing me with roller coasters and illicit affairs. A special thanks, as well, to the team behind *The Lizzie Bennet Diaries*, who first sparked my love of Jane Austen adaptations, and to Griffin McElroy for always reminding me of the power of storytelling.

Although it seems doubtful she'll ever read this, I would be remiss not to thank Jane Austen for everything her work has given me. Thank you for showing me that banter can change the world.

This book is a love letter to, among other things, my amazing time in marching band. From the eighth grade until my college graduation, marching band provided me with a home, with friends, with family. I owe a million thanks to the teachers who taught me, to the drum majors and section leaders who led me, and to my fellow bandmates who supported me. To my Ocean City High School bandies—I hope I was able to suitably capture on the page the love and devotion we all shared. This one goes out to our whole gang of absolute dorks who didn't need anyone else because we had each other. Thank you. To my fellow members of the Cornell Big Red Marching Band—to my flutes, to my saxes, to everyone else—how can I begin to thank you for what you've given me? Even now (insert undisclosed number here) years after graduation, I'm longing and yearning and always returning to all of you.

To Carly Britton, who has read every single one of my books, even the ones that were objectively very bad, and continues to hang out with me. That's either a special brand of masochism or a special brand of friendship, and I'm going to go with the latter. Thank you.

To my grandparents—Frank and Janet Wockenfuss, who taught me to love reading, and to Bill and Kay Quain, who taught me to love writing. Thank you for the life-changing gifts.

To my amazing extended family—thank you for everything you've given me. Not everyone gets to grow up surrounded by so many people who love them, and I am grateful every day to have cousins, aunts, and uncles who make up such crucial parts of my life. This is a book about the importance of family, which means that it's for you.

To my in-laws, Randy and Virginia Tiedemann. Thank you for your endless support and enthusiasm, and for always laughing at my jokes. To Ben and Erica Blaschke, thank you, for always cheering me on. I promise to show my gratitude by filling your house with more books than you could ever possibly need.

Thank you to my parents, Bill and Jeanne Quain, who have supported my dreams every step of the way, who showed me that being a writer was a real thing a person could do, and that pursuing your dream—no matter the obstacles—is always worth the work. Thanks to you, I'll always do whatever it takes. To Kathleen Quain, number-one sister—thank you for everything. I couldn't have written a book about siblings who love each other without a sister as great as you, and I promise to buy you your own copy of this book so that you don't have to fight with anyone over who reads it next.

Cats probably can't read, but just in case they can—Jenny, you're a star.

And finally, to Dustin Tiedemann. First, I know you always wanted me to write a book with a dragon in it, and since I couldn't get one in the story itself, I'll add one here—rawr! Second, this book literally would not have been possible without everything you've done for me. Thanks for sticking with band, for making me laugh every day, for Disney trips and climbing competitions and all the other small things that make up our wonderful life. You'll have to forgive me for repeating it from our wedding, but the sentiment still holds true—you're my greatest love story.